JAN TURK PETRIE
TOWARDS THE VANISHING POINT

To Richard
All best
wishes
Jan xx

REWIND

Central Assizes, Yorkshire, England. November 1957

She hits the keys to send the type bars flying into all their different formations to leave orderly impressions on the paper. A bell rings every time she reaches the end of a line. *Ding.*

Her hands are a busy blur. *Ding.*

She likes Court Three: the chair's got a decent back and the desk is big enough to get her feet comfortably underneath. Mindful of the threat of snow, most people have already left the building but she wants to get this transcript finished. She's good at her job, takes pride in her accuracy, though that sticking 'g' can sometimes rise up to spoil her perfect rows.

This afternoon she's made good progress; only the last few pages to go and she'll have made a truthful copy of every last word that was said in court.

Stop.

Stop those busy fingers with their polished-pink nails.

Stop her typewriter's black and red ribbon right there between the two spools. Her fingers begin to spring back from the keys, gathering speed as they deactivate all those tiny, inverted letters. The straight lines she's so proud of are disappearing, word after perfect word, as her fingers fly away from the typewriter.

1

When she looks up again, the left-hand spool has grown fat once more and every single sheet is blank.

On the stack of paper next to the stenograph she uses in court – where practice has taught her hands to fly like a musician's to capture every echoing word – the lines and squiggles she made during the trial are being sucked away from each sheet until each and every page is snowy white.

The sound of all those voices retreats from her ears and the solemnly bewigged men in their flowing gowns disappear face-forward through the grand courtroom doors. One by one, the people on public benches stand up to be drawn in a long and wavering line out into the wintery weather and back to their homes.

Though written innumerable times, those two seemingly inseparable words – Lily Bagshaw – have disappeared along with all the others; leaving no record of the events of the spring.

Outside the courthouse, the swaying Christmas lights disappear in one blink. Night follows day follows night follows day follows night, always accelerating until the streetlights are no longer lit. Cars and lorries run backwards to suck up ever-retreating men and women, many dressed in khaki and blue. Clouds of smoke and dust dissipate; emerging from towering flames, bricks fly together to rebuild houses and factories. Over and over the night sky rumbles with a sound that could almost be thunder until the last wailing siren falls silent.

Illuminated by the soft glow of gaslights, quarrelsome men are once more drawn out of public houses into homes and factories. Children dressed in forgotten colours are pulled in intermittent lines from crowded schoolyards back to the warmth of their beds.

CHAPTER ONE

July 1938

Lily

Her leg is being tied to the other girl's and the cord is cutting into her calf; Lily doesn't like the clammy feel of her skin. Miss Barratt has put them into pairs according to their height, and this is the first time she's been aware of anything she and Stella Marsden might have in common.

'Ow, that hurts – it's too damned tight.' Lily tries to pull away.

'Stop bein' a baby. It's got to be tight as you can get it, see, or it'll come undone and we'll be disqualified.' Outside of the classroom, Stella's a lot bossier than she'd suspected her of being. A sharp yank forces Lily's ankle back into the same bone-grinding position. 'You do want us to win, don't ya?' The girl's determined fingers are double-tying the knot that's binding them together.

Lily's not sure she cares a fig if they reach the finishing line before the others. She's irritated by the way Stella's fair hair is escaping the plaits hanging down her back. Her own hair is darker and cut in a neat bob though the sweat on her forehead has made her fringe wet and it's curling in that way she hates.

A bright green grasshopper has just appeared right next her hand. As she peers down at him, he rubs his legs, gives a single chirrup and disappears.

It's a baking hot day; her clothes are sticking to her and the threat of thunder hangs in the too-still air. Someone's mown the grass and there are dead daisies everywhere. The cuttings have left criss-crossing marks right up her legs; she brushes off the itchy blades of grass still clinging to her skin. Given a choice, Lily would much rather stay where she is and look for insects.

The other pairs around them are giggling and falling about like clowns. 'These are just the heats,' Miss Barratt says as she walks up and down to check they've done the leg tying bit properly. 'Gary and Dennis – you're facing the opposite way to each other you silly boys.'

Their teacher looks different today because she's wearing a red cardigan and a summer dress with poppies on; all that red makes her skin seem paler – like she's the ghost version of her usual classroom self. 'Only the wining pairs from these four heats will compete on sports day,' she tells them.

The two of them manage to stand upright after a fashion. Together they've become something with too many limbs jostling for position like them poor Siamese twins she's seen pictures of in her dad's newspaper.

Stella slips her arm around her waist at the back. To get her own arm out of the way, she has to hold the girl's bony body in the same way. This close, she smells of sweat and pencil sharpenings.

Lily looks over to where Miss Barratt is talking to Mr Graham, the starting whistle dangling loose against her chest. He's puffing on his pipe, leaning in to hear whatever it is she's saying. Neither of them seems in a hurry to begin the race. Some of the girls think Mr Graham is handsome but Lily's not so sure.

'Start with yer other leg,' Stella instructs her, stepping forward and then waiting for her to do the same. 'Now both middle ones together.'

They hobble around for a bit then stop. Stella sets her mouth hard. 'That were rubbish – we need to go faster like them two are doing it.'

Lily notices how the other girl's free hand is curled into a fist of concentration. Everyone knows Stella Marsden has been banned from playing football with the boys at playtime. Girls are supposed to keep to the top playground. The teachers might not have noticed her if she hadn't scored so many goals.

Around them the others are gigging or laughing out loud, but Stella's serious because she really does want to win this. Lily notices the way the more successful pairs are setting a steady rhythm together and that's what the two of them will have to do if they're to stand any chance at this.

A shrill whistle brings everyone into a shambling line. 'Right, class – get ready… steady… go!'

At first they lumber forward amongst the stragglers. Her ankle burns and a stray plait keeps getting in her eyes. But then something happens and their limbs begin to coordinate.

'One-two, one-two…' Stella is reciting over and over and she finds herself repeating it with her. They're improving with every step, running in time with each other. 'One-two, one-two…' Stella keeps pushing them forward – she can feel the pressure of the girl's arm on her back. Not wanting to fall, she has no option but to keep up with her.

Halfway to the line, they're beginning to close in on the frontrunners and Lily's head is up and she's staring straight at the rope because now she really wants to win this too. With each step they gain ground until they draw level.

The two boys throw themselves at the finish line taking the rope with them. They lie sprawled on the ground grinning in triumph.

'Well done, girls. Shame the boys just pipped you to the

post there,' Miss Barratt sings out in that la-di-da voice she puts on whenever Mr Graham is around.

The beetroot-faced boys are still groaning and rubbing at their ankles and Lily begins to hope one of them at least might have broken something.

Mr Graham comes across with his clipboard. 'For goodness' sake stop rolling around, you boys,' he says. 'We haven't got time for histrionics.'

Like some miracle of healing, the boys are on their feet, chests stuck out as they recite their names for his winners list.

Stella watches them red-faced and sullen. Leading Lily away by the cord still binding them, she slumps down onto the grass, grinding their anklebones together and almost catching her off balance. 'Them boys cheated,' the girl mutters as her fingers begin working away to untie the elaborate knot that's holding them together. 'It weren't fair.'

Lily rubs at her ankle and the bruises that are already staining her skin like ink blots. When she's finally free and that skinny arm is no longer around her waist, she stays where she is. 'We almost beat 'em,' she says, puzzled by how disappointed she feels considering she didn't care at all until the last few yards.

'Aye – but what's the good in that?' Stella looks like she's about to start grizzling.

Stooping to pick up a couple of daisies the mower missed, Lily bites a tiny hole in the stem of one and threads the other one through it. 'Maybe we can practice a bit together.' Shading her eyes with her hand, the girl looks up at her unconvinced. 'I reckon we could beat the whole lot of 'em next time,' Lily says.

The rain that's forced them inside is now beating in anger against the windowpanes. They decide to play cards for a bit, laying them down with care on the clinging chenille tablecloth.

It's midmorning but they've had to put on the overhead

light to see properly and Stella's tanned face looks yellow and sickly. She's gone quiet – too quiet. Though they live only a few streets apart, there's a world of difference between their families; Lily can see she's uncomfortable stuck inside a room that must seem far too tidy and noiseless.

Strip-Jack-naked soon gets boring because neither of them are any good at shuffling. It's Lily's idea to build a house of cards instead. Remembering her dad's instructions she says, 'You've got to lay cards down at the bottom or it won't stay steady.'

They're up to the third level when Stella's fidgety knees get wrapped in the end of the tablecloth and everything they've built up comes tumbling down. 'Now look what you've gone an' done,' she says, sounding more like her mam than she intended. Stella only shrugs.

The rain on the window is quieter now but it doesn't seem to be stopping. 'Won't be long,' her mam says, buttoning her mac up to the neck. 'You two girls make sure you behave yourselves while I'm gone.' She opens the door and her dark hair immediately starts to get wet because her mam never puts her umbrella up in the house for fear of bad luck.

They watch her hurry down the path, giggling together when she leaps over a huge puddle out in the road.

'Let's go upstairs,' Lily says.

There's not much to look at on her mam's dressing table except for a small bottle of perfume they daren't touch and the tube of cherry red lipstick she keeps for best. Lily picks it up, then hesitates. A sharp elbow digs into her side. 'Go on then.' She's watched her mam – knows you have to start with the top lip then fill in the bottom before you press your lips together to even it out.

When it's Stella's turn, the girl pulls her mouth into really silly shapes. Her hand shakes too much and one side of the cupid's bow is much higher than the other. Checking the effect in the mirror makes Stella scowl because the truth is, the lipstick looks plain awful on her. 'I reckon pink might suit your colouring better,' Lily says.

'You look a bit like Snow White,' Stella tells her. 'Rub some on yer cheeks like it's rouge.'

The lipstick in the tube has softened. Using a finger, she rubs a ring of it onto each side of her face then turns her head this way and that to admire the effect.

Stella sighs. 'You look really beautiful.'

Her mirror face grows red all over because she can't say the same thing back – Stella's not daft enough to be fooled. She'll get in trouble if her mam notices how much they've used up between them.

'I've got something to show you,' she says, taking care to place the little tube back in the same place. 'Before I do, you have to properly swear on your life not to say owt about it to anyone else.'

'I promise I won't.' Stella's finger makes the required sign across her chest. 'Cross my heart an' hope to die.'

The book is still in the wardrobe although now it's up on the top shelf poking out from under a neat pile of winter blankets. Even on tiptoes it's impossible to reach so they half-carry, half-drag the chair over to the wardrobe, trying not to leave any tell-tale scuff marks on the lino.

Lily takes charge for a change. She sends Stella to listen at the door while she climbs up onto the seat and, stretching to her fullest, pulls at the spine until the whole book comes away. To be safe, they put the chair and everything back where it was and take the book into Lily's bedroom.

Stella's all wide-eyed with excitement. Her grubby finger runs underneath the words on the front cover as she reads aloud: '*Every Woman's Doctor Book.*'

They budge up on the bed until they're as close as they can get, staring down at the image of the pretty young woman on the cover. She's dressed in a blue hat with a yellow scarf and the collar of her matching blue coat is turned up like she's feeling the cold. The woman's cheeks have bright red patches maybe from illness or embarrassment. She definitely looks worried – scared even.

The doctor's sitting on the other side of his desk. Though he looks quite young – not much older than the woman – you can tell he's a doctor because there's a stethoscope lying on the desk between them and his pen's poised in mid-air about to write in his notes or maybe a prescription. The doctor's mouth is half open and it looks like he could be telling the woman something that might not be good news.

A stale sort of smell escapes from the yellowed pages when Lily opens the book. Inside, she sees her mam's name – *Flora Hetherington* – written in faded blue ink. It's odd to think that her mam was once not married to her dad.

'Most of the first part's quite boring,' she tells Stella. 'Either that, or it's, you know…' She screws up her face like she's drinking vinegar to show her distaste for all that stuff about innards and what the book calls bowels.

For Stella's benefit, she runs her finger down the index at the front. 'There it is see, Chapter Four – *The Health of the Unmarried Girl.*'

Her new friend snorts; both hands fly to her face. Lily turns to the chapter and scans the page for the particular section she's looking for: 'Preparation for Marriage.' She nudges her giggling friend.

As the better reader, Lily considers reciting the first part – after all she almost knows it by heart – but decides it would be too embarrassing; she doesn't want to have to say words like *vagina* and *hymen* out loud.

Stella continues to run a finger under every word as she reads to herself, slowly mouthing the more difficult words – sounding each syllable out. Beneath her freckles, her friend's cheeks are boiling.

Though she's impatient for her to get to the last bit, she can't turn over because Stella's only halfway down the page.

Frowning, the girl looks at her. 'It says here you're supposed to go to a ruddy doctor before you get married to make sure you can carry a baby. I should have thought anybody with two arms can carry one – I mean they're not usually that heavy, are they? Least ways not to begin with.'

Reading on, she's quiet for a while before elbowing Lily's side. 'Says here he's suppose to go see a doctor an' all.'

'And look,' Lily tells her, 'it says if the doctor was to find summat wrong with either of 'em, they've got to get it put right before they get wed so they've got no *weak spots.*'

Stella's frown lines deepen. 'What the hell do they mean *weak spots?*'

'I've thought about that, an' I reckon it's like our attic – I'm not allowed in there cos the floorboards are rotten in places, an' if you was to step on the wormy ones, you'd fall right through an' probably kill yourself.' Stella looks up at the ceiling as if someone might come tumbling through at any minute.

While she's distracted, Lily takes the opportunity to turn the page. 'This is the bit I want to show you – where it says you're not to get married if there's summat wrong with any of your relatives. If either your gran or your granddad is insane – that means if they're in the loony bin. Same thing goes if they've got something called ep-i-lep-sy.'

'What the hell's that when it's at home?'

'I looked it up in the dictionary, and it said it's when someone has fits – you know, like old Billy Grant does when he falls on the ground an' shakes all over.'

'But he were married to Bertha Grant afore she died last year.'

'Well, according to this, he should never have got married in the first place.'

Stella raises her eyebrows as she reads on. 'Did you look up *con-sump-t-ion?*'

'I did and it's some horrible disease that makes you keep coughing up blood. If the woman has that, it says right there she'd probably die if she was to get married and have a baby.'

'Yuck.' Stella shakes her head. 'I shouldn't think any lad would want to marry her in the first place, if she kept spewing blood.'

Lily pulls a matching face as she scans the page again. 'They reckon if either your mam or dad are what they call *habitual drunkards* – that means they're always down the pub – then a terrible cravin' for drink will be passed on to their children or grandchildren; so them people shouldn't get married neither.'

Stella gasps and covers her mouth. When her hands come away again, the lipstick's been smeared right across both cheeks. 'But me dad goes down the pub every night after work. On Saturday night he plays darts. An' he pops in for a beer on a Sunday before his dinner.' She turns her clown's face to Lily. 'Does that mean *I* shouldn't ever get married or have any kids?'

Lily tries to shrug off the question, not at all sure of what to say without upsetting her. 'P'raps you should ask your mam, you know, when the time comes.'

'So, if you're one of them as can't get married, what the hell are you supposed to do?'

'It says here you must dedicate your life to *useful work* instead. You know – like Miss Barratt or Miss Davies.'

'Bloody hell – I'd hate to be a teacher or a ruddy dinner lady.' Stella slides off the bed and stands scowling before her. The small hands planted on her hips make her look like a shrunken down version of her mother. 'I wish you hadn't ever showed me this stupid flamin' book, Lily Hetherington.'

She turns and strides out of the room. Lily expects her to come back laughing but instead she hears her tread on the stairs.

'Wait!' Lily leans right over the bannister and shouts down at the top of her disappearing head. 'Don't go, Stell – it's just a silly old book, it don't mean owt.'

Without even looking up, the girl walks out into the rain, slamming the front door behind her.

The book is still there in Lily's hand. The girl on the cover is only young – not much older than her cousins. She doesn't look happy. P'raps that doctor's been telling her she's got a disease and she can't ever get married and she'll have to do lots of *useful work* for the rest of her life.

CHAPTER TWO

August 1938

The Marsdens' front door is already half open but, mindful of her manners, Lily daren't enter without knocking. A shouting match is going on inside, which is nothing out of the ordinary. She knocks as loudly as she can. 'Hello!' she shouts.

The row stops and a boy's suspicious face appears round the door. She can't be sure if this one is Fred or Nobby because both boys are lanky with spots and curly red hair and less than a year separates them.

'Is your Stella in?'

'Aye, she's out back.' She thinks he's the slightly older one – Nobby; his voice is deeper than it seemed to be last time she remembers hearing him speak. He steps aside but doesn't show her through the house or anything.

In any case, she can see the garden through the open backdoor. Lily steps over the threshold and heads towards the sunlight. Behind her, the two boys start their argument where they left off – some fuss over Fred's missing catapult.

She likes the way the Marsdens' back yard is all jumbled up and overgrown and nobody shouts at you for stepping on vegetables. A few sparse-feathered chickens are clucking away in a wire coop against the bottom wall, scratting at the bare ground in search of worms and things.

Stella's mam appears with a bundle of newspapers under one arm. Alma Marsden is a stocky woman, her wraparound pinny bulging in all the wrong places, but she has a nice, friendly face. 'Stel-la!' she shouts.

Her daughter's only a matter of yards away playing hopscotch by herself. Balancing on one foot, she bends to grab a stone from its square before smiling at Lily. She jumps through the rest of the grid, her loose plaits flying out like wings.

'Them rabbits need cleaning out. I'll not ask thee again, lass.' Her mam wrinkles her nose. 'I can smell 'em from here. Lily here won't mind givin' a hand, will ya, lass?'

'Course I will,' she says.

'Alright,' Stella says. 'But can we do it later on when it's not so ruddy hot?'

Alma holds a warning finger up. 'Just make sure you do, my girl, or you'll feel the back of my hand.' She doesn't see the face her daughter pulls behind her back.

'I got summat to show ya,' Stella says pulling on her dress. She follows her over to the shed. As soon as she opens the door, Tiggs, the Marsdens' cat, leaps out of its box and runs out past them. Jumping up onto the garden wall, the tabby rolls over and spreads herself out on the warm slabs. Lily goes over to stroke the soft white fur on her belly. Her swollen teats are sticking out here and there – she does her best to avoid them.

Mrs Marsden's left the old newspapers on the garden bench and, while she's stroking the cat, her attention is drawn to the paper at the top of the pile. Tilting her head, she peers at the yellowing image of the handsome man who used to be their king. Her dad reads this same paper – The Daily Mirror – and she's already seen this photograph of the ex-king waving as he walks down some steps with his new wife on his arm. She reads the headline to herself: *On the Steps of a New Life – Together.*

Mrs Simpson is wearing a wedding dress of sorts, though

it's not a proper one. Her hat seems to have a load of fur or feathers wrapped around it; she hasn't got a proper veil because, apparently, you're not supposed to have one of them if you've been married before.

You can't tell in black and white but Lily recalls that she read somewhere that her dress had been dyed a pale blue and they're now calling that particular shade *Wallis Blue* after her. She can't imagine being so famous they'd name an actual colour after you.

Though she wishes Wallis was a lot better looking, their love story is really romantic all the same. Without intending to, she says aloud, 'If Mister Graham wanted to marry Miss Barratt, would he have to stop being our headmaster?'

Stella screws up her nose, squeezing her freckles closer together. 'I shouldn't think he'd want to marry her in the first place – she's really old and not a bit pretty.'

'What about Wallis Simpson? I mean, she's quite old, an' not very pretty neither, but the King gave up everything – his whole kingdom – to marry her.'

'Aye, I suppose so.' It's obvious Stella's not really listening because she's too busy playing with the kittens Tiggs gave birth to a few weeks back.

Abandoning their mother, Lily goes into the shed and looks into the cardboard box. 'Have you named them all yet?'

'No – we're not suppose to. Our mam says it's best we don't give any of 'em names or we might get too attached to 'em.'

'What's wrong with that?' Lily reaches in between their warm sleepy bodies to pick up the only white one.

'Because we're not allowed to keep any of 'em.'

Suspended in mid-air, the white kitten straight away opens its mouth and mews. Hardly any sound comes out.

'They've got to go off and live with other people,' Stella tells her. 'That's if we can find people that want 'em.' She's tickling the nose of one of the kittens with the end of her plait; it doesn't seem to like it much. 'Ernie Perkins is goin' to put any that's left behind into a big sack with a rock in it and drop it into a barrel of water so they all drown.'

Lily's so shocked she can hardly breathe but Stella's expression remains unchanged; she just carries on playing with her kitten, pressing down on its head with every stroke in a way that keeps pulling its tiny eyes wide open.

'But why would Ernie Perkins want to drown these poor little things?'

'Cos our dad says we can't keep any more flamin' animals – the bloody things are eatin' him out of house and home.'

There are two black kittens and three are tabbies like the mum, so with her white one, that makes six altogether that they'll have to find new homes for.

Stella reaches up to place one of the tabbies on the wall next to the stretching mum's swollen teats and it crawls across and starts to blindly feed, making its paws go up and down like it might be kneading bread.

'I heard our dad say to our mam he hasn't got the heart to drown 'em himself and Ernie Perkins will get rid of the lot an' have done with it.'

Lily decides to ask her mam if they can keep this little white one. She knows that to stand any chance of getting her to agree, she'll have to ask her when she's in a good mood and, these days, that's not often.

Going through the back door, Lily finds her mother cooking their tea. Today she seems to be happy, even starts to laugh out loud over a carrot that looks like it's got two fat legs. Lily joins in, making herself laugh as if it's the funniest thing she's ever seen.

While her mother's still chuckling, she takes a deep breath and says, 'Mam, can we have one of the Marsdens' kittens? It's such a sweet little white one. You'll love it once you see how pretty and friendly it is. I'd look after it – you wouldn't need to do anything and it would catch all the mice an' that.'

Wiping away laughter tears with the back of one hand, her mam's expression begins to darken. 'Sorry, love but the answers no; you've no notion of how hard it is scraping together the money just to feed us. We'll certainly not be getting a cat; I can't go worryin' about what to give a ruddy moggy on top the rest ont.'

'But you wouldn't need to feed it – that's the thing about cats, they go out an' catch their own food.'

'Sorry, lass, we're not be havin' one, an' that's final.'

'But Mam you don't understand – if I don't save her and they can't find a home for her, they'll give her to Ernie Perkins and he'll tie her up in a sack with the others an' drown her.'

Flora's face reddens. 'That's as may be – we're still *not* havin' it.' She points the end of the peeler at Lily. 'An' that's it an' all about it.'

Lily's tempted to argue but decides not to say anything more while her mam's in a temper. 'If you ask me,' she says, peeling the last of the carrots like she's got a grudge against it, 'they should get that ruddy cat of theirs seen-to so it wouldn't keep havin' all them kittens in the first place.'

Lily tries again a week later, and then again a few days after that, but there's no budging the woman when she sets her mind against something. When she asks her dad, he only says: 'Ask yer mam.'

In the end, she decides there's nothing for it – she'll have to bring the kitten home with her. As soon as her mam and dad see how sweet it is, they're bound to want to save it.

In their Maths lesson, she leans across and whispers her plan to Stella. The girl turns her head sideways and pulls an odd sort of face at her. 'Too late,' she says, 'they've all gone.' Stella picks up her ruler and draws two parallel lines for the answer to a sum.

Behind her hand, Lily says, 'Not all six of 'em? They can't have.'

The hum in the classroom is getting louder. 'I said no talking,' Miss Barratt reminds them. Every silent head dips down. Sideways on, she watches Stella checking the answer by taking away one finger at a time. She finally writes down a one and then a five. It's the wrong answer.

'What about that little white one?' Lily hisses.

'Oh, that one's gone off to live with a nice, old couple.' Something about the way she whispers it, the way she avoids looking in her direction, makes Lily suspect her friend is lying.

'My mam says your parents are irresponsible,' she tells her. Frowning, Stella opens her mouth to speak. Before she can, Lily says, 'Our mam reckons it's about time they got that cat of yours seen-to.'

CHAPTER THREE

March 1941

It's not fully dark when it starts – sounding like the wail of some angry monster someone's accidentally woken up again. The two of them know the drill; how they must drop whatever they're doing and leave the house. As always, Lily grabs the precious book and runs straight out of the back door.

Should her mother be stopping to lock up? There's a definite drone – not a false alarm; they're coming alright. Still her mam won't, or can't, go any faster.

It's hard to make out the gap in the hedge. She hears Mr Harkness shout, 'Hurry up you two, for Christ's sake!' This time, she remembers to duck her head as she goes inside, keep it bent until she's sitting down.

Mr Harkness and his son built the shelter themselves. Truth is it's not very comfortable – hasn't got those wide platforms you can sleep on like the one Stella's family have. Feels smaller still as soon as Mr Harkness pulls the door to. There's the usual stink of damp and other rotten things; the air soon gets stale from being breathed in and out too many times.

Two nights ago, there was a direct hit in the next-but-one street. The shock of it had ripped through her whole body. Then dirt had started pouring in. 'We'll be buried alive!' her mam had screamed. Mr Harkness had struggled to get the door open. His wife had been hopeless – muttering the Lord's Prayer with both eyes shut. He'd put his shoulder to it and Lily tried to help – both of them pushing and kicking until it finally moved and they could all run outside coughing and blinking like moles. Unsure what to do, they'd stood there in the dark until the all-clear sounded. Standing out in the open, Lily had been too scared to cry until after she was safely back indoors. As soon as it was light, Mrs Harkness had fetched a shovel to clear all the soil out. She'd heard the noise and run out to see if she could help. Lily could see she was only getting in his way. 'Tell you what, lass,' he'd said leaning on his shovel already out of breath, 'Why don't you go an' fetch us both a cuppa eh?'

They've been waiting it out for hours and yet Lily has still got a bad feeling about tonight. It's grown warmer and smellier now with the four of them squeezed in so close. She looks at the floor – at where Mr Harkness has stuffed the new gaps with old bits of rags that are unlikely to hold anything back.

Cocking her head to one side, she's fairly certain she can hear engines. Her mam starts to whimper. Louder now; sounds like there's a lot up there and they're getting closer.

Her hands go flying to her ears though it's too late to block out the now familiar sound. A deep thud makes her jump. She'd felt vibrations from the explosion run through her. Loads of dogs have started barking, some howling like wolves.

Another one lands; the ground vibrates beneath her; tin mugs rattle against each other like they're scared, too. 'Saints preserve us.' Mrs Harkness crosses herself. 'That was close.' Overhead the noise of the planes is deafening. Keep going; please, please the Lord keep going.

The next one's further off. Engines become a long drone that fades until it might only be a swarm of bees.

They wait.

It's gone quiet out there – even the dogs have stopped barking. 'Might be it,' Mr Harkness says. 'For tonight, anyroad.'

But there's no all-clear siren. Tired of all the waiting, Lily's eyes grow heavy. She starts to doze on and off, not really sleeping, willing herself to stay awake, stay alert. Lily doesn't want to fall asleep in case she has the dream again– the one where she's alone in a narrow dark tunnel and all she can see, the only thing to guide her, is a tiny light right at the end. No matter how fast she runs she never seems to get closer to it. Then comes the worst part – her panic that the light will go out before she can reach it.

They only have a half bottle of water and a few dry cream crackers left between them. If they leave things in here ready for the next time, they'd get all mottled and mouldy. The torch battery is giving up the ghost and the first of the candles has burnt down to a stump. Mr Harkness – her mam calls him Arthur though he's old enough to be her dad – is slumped against the opposite side. Lily's counted four separate rolls to his belly. He must have worked hard to clear out all the earth from the last time, so p'raps it's no wonder he's tired out. Though the bucket in the corner has a lid of sorts, she can still smell his beery piss.

Her mam's a bit calmer. So much so that she's chatting – having one of her heart to hearts with old Mrs Harkness, or Ethel as she calls her. Out of boredom, Lily pretends to be still asleep so she can listen to their conversation – like a spy. Her mam, Flora they call her, has been given the best place to sit – an upright armchair that looks like a giant's taken bites out of it. This is due to her *condition*. Lily is squatting on the floor with just a thin cushion between her and the hard concrete. Her head is resting in her mam's lap – or what's left of it. She's been listening to her stomach, the way it keeps growling as if whatever's growing inside there is getting angry.

In this light, Ethel Harkness looks like a thin witch, though she's usually quite nice – apart from being so boring.

Their chat is nothing but the usual stuff. It gets more interesting when Mrs Harkness mentions Lily's dad. For once she agrees with her mam – if only he was here how much better it would be.

'Nae, Ethel,' her mam says, 'it's been such a struggle with our Jack away.' Her mam never seems to consider how worried the Harknesses must be about their son Terry.

Ethel is sitting on a kitchen chair that's too small for her ample backside. She doesn't even try to hide her fear when the planes are overhead. When they're not, she does her best to keep things cheerful though they're stuck in here. 'They're bound to give him some leave, Flora,' she says in her old-fashioned voice, 'When thee's time comes.'

'Not always.' Her mother's breathing is getting shallower, more rapid. 'Depends on what they're up to. He'll have to apply like everybody else. We'll just have to wait and hope.' When she sighs her belly moves. '*Compassionate leave* they call it when yer wife's giving birth. Or somebody dies. Has to be yer next-of-kin.'

They'll have to light that last candle soon. Between Lily's eyelashes, Mrs Harkness's shadow keeps growing tall, then shrinking back into itself.

'Like Jack said in his letter, they might not grant his request. Depends on where his ship is at the time.' Her shiver runs through them both. 'Last time he came home, he only said they'd been on convoy duties and it were perishing cold. Reckoned he couldn't even tell me more. Mind you, when our Jack's home, he always says he'd rather not waste precious time with too much yapping.'

Outside, Lily can hear a distant rumble that could be thunder, but definitely isn't. Her mother's body tenses as the ground begins to shake like some giant ogre approaching. She shuts her eyes tight and wills it away somewhere else. It takes all of her concentration. Opening one eye, she focuses on the cover of her special book – the one she always grabs to save.

The smiling rosy-cheeked girl on the swing under an apple tree never looks frightened. This is who she was named after – a made-up storybook person. Looking at the girl's happy face, she manages to keep herself steady until the planes pass over again.

After a little while, she hears slow drip-dripping and the usual loud snores coming from Mr Harkness – his wife's right, that man really can sleep through any ruddy thing.

Her mother's body is relaxing, growing softer. As she re-crosses her legs, she bumps Lily's head out of its place in her lap. Against her ear, her mam's swollen belly is making even angrier noises and trying to kick her face away.

'Oh eh, he's a good-looking man, your Jack,' Ethel says. 'Specially in that navy uniform of his.' Lily's surprised an old woman can say such a thing.

Her mother's shadow merges with the chair to loom across the corrugated walls. 'When he was young, he was about the handsomest lad as I'd ever laid eyes on.' Her mam's voice becomes younger. 'I were just turned sixteen when I started going with him. Couldn't believe he'd singled me out. My da' never did go much on him mind – said he was way too smarmy for his liking.'

The sound of her yawn vibrates through Lily's ear. 'I had a friend at the time: Valerie – what was it now– Robins? No, Roberts. She kept flirting with Jack, brushing up against him and the like, but he never took no notice.'

Her mam laughs, but it's not the ha-ha kind. 'I used to enjoy us having a kiss and cuddle; then he starts on – would I let him touch me down there and all that.'

Lily's shocked but Mrs Harkness just cackles like a witch again; she opens her eyes just enough to check there's been no actual transformation. Perhaps this is the time to stretch her arms out, yawn or something, least ways pretend to wake up. But they've stopped talking now, so she doesn't.

She can hear paper rustling – it could be a rat in the corner.

Then Mrs Harkness says, 'This here's the last of the scran. Fancy a cream cracker, Flora?'

'Not for me, ta; though that last one seems to have settled me indigestion.' That's good – her mother's always moaning on about that. 'Anyroad, I may as well tell you the rest of the tale, Ethel.

'This one night,' her mam lowers her voice to a whisper, 'the two of us were round back of the Picture House on the High Street. Anyway, he's telling me how much he loves me, how beautiful I was; kissing down me neck and all. Next thing was, we both get so worked up with all of it, I finally let him have his way. Hurt like hell. Bit of a disappointment – no more than a couple of pushes and just like that it's all over with.'

Lily can't believe she's said all that out loud but Ethel only bites into her biscuit and starts crunching it up, as if she's not really been listening. Lily can feel her own face boiling on her mother's behalf. If only she'd stopped pretending to be asleep like she meant to. She wishes she could close her ears up with her hands; most of all, she wishes with all her heart that her mother would please stop talking this very second.

'It were just my luck to get in the family way, straight off. Course, then we had to face both sets of parents. Me dad was so upset he wouldn't even look me in the eye. He folded his arms and refused to sign the papers to say we could have permission to wed, till our mam, says – and d'you know I can still see the look on her face when she said it – *We've no choice in the matter, do we, Harry?*'

'Ah well, it all worked out for the best in the end, didn't it?' Ethel says, in her everyday voice. 'And just think how lovely it'll be when this little 'un finally makes his, or her, appearance.'

This sets her mam going again. 'I heard how it's got awful up at that hospital. Our Tilly says they're running out of damn near everything and hardly a doctor in sight. Tilly says–'

'Nay, don't thee start wi' all that fretting again, Flora love. I don't s'pose it's half as bad as that Tilly likes to make out – always been a bloody doomsayer, that one.'

'Aye, but it's not only her that says it. And with my history, it's no ruddy joke. Like I told you afore, Ethel, I woke up in a pool of blood when I lost the first 'un. Still only sixteen, an' I thought that were goin' to be it. You don't forget owt like that in a hurry.'

Mr Harkness's snoring reaches such a pitch Lily thinks he's bound to wake himself up like he usually does. If she was a fraction nearer, she could give him a bit of a nudge with her foot; instead she can only will him awake.

'I thought that was it for me – that I was goin' down to Nick for sure,' her mam says. 'Six months gone I was. My Jack runs off half-naked for the doctor. I must have passed right out. Knew nothing till I wake up in such pain. Proper agony.' She catches her breath and seems to subside. And at last Lily hears nothing except for the dripping and snoring.

But her mam hasn't finished. 'Little boy it were – so they told us afterwards. All I know is that babby had damn near seen me off an' all.' She can't believe this – her mother's never told her any of this, her own daughter, but she's more than happy to share such things with old Ethel, who's no relation at all.

Her mam doesn't leave it at that. 'Had to burn that ruddy mattress in the backyard after – it were in such a state. The doctor tells us both he thinks I might not be able to have any more young'uns.' In the lowest whisper, she adds, 'Jack was upset at the time; but I thought, on the quiet like, p'raps it were just as well.'

She coughs and Lily's sure that must be the finish of it. But her mam's unstoppable. 'Course Jack was over the moon like, when I got caught with our Lily here.'

'Well, he would be,' Mrs Harkness says. 'I mean, it's different for them that doesn't have to bear 'em. Bound to be.'

She doesn't sound surprised by any of this and Lily wonders if her mam's told her all this before.

There's a creaking sound as Ethel gets up to stretch herself as much as she can. 'Still, like I always say, as soon as they're born we wouldn't be without 'em, would we?' In the dwindling light she watches the old lady lean over the upturned orange box to light the final candle from the stub of the old one.

She smells the spilled wax, the whiff of smoke from the match. Between her eyelashes, everything disappears for a second – the voices, the shelter, everything except for her mam's breathing.

Then the new candle's wick catches and flares up. She notices the deep lines etched into the old woman's skin. Above her ear, her mother's hushed voice says, 'This might sound terrible, Ethel, and it's not meant to; but, when I got caught the second time, I thought to meself – I'm hardly twenty, I've managed to work me way up into the clerical department, I could still have made something of myself if it weren't for this new babby. Seemed to me that were it – my life, one way or other was never goin' to be the same and me with no say in the matter.'

Lily's nose is full of the smell of molten wax mixed with the faint stench of decay lurking just behind those rusting metal walls. All of it makes her feel sick to her core. Does her mother really believe she's that fast asleep? Even if she does, why say all that to Ethel when she could wake up at any minute? Was it meant as a warning?

They let her leave school early to walk all the way to the hospital. 'Your daughter's here to see you, Mrs Hetherington,' they tell her mother more than once. At first her mam doesn't appear to notice she's there. She can't stay awake long enough. 'Sorry, flower – I'm reet jiggered with this one, I'll be blowed.'

Her mam's eyes keep closing though she opens them properly for a minute to say, 'You'd best be getting back to school now, lass.'

Before she leaves, Lily does her best – tries to assure her

white-faced, half-conscious mother that the new baby is sweet and lovely, even though he's bald and wrinkled and looked exactly like a fat frog when she watched him having his nappy changed by a nurse.

'There's no need for you to worry, little lass,' the nice nurse says, walking her out. 'Your mam's still a bit poorly but at least she's out of danger. Been through the mill a bit with this one – we thought we might lose her at one stage. It'll take her some time to recover her strength. She'll be needing your help. But eh, that little brother of yours is a bonny one right enough.' By bonny she meant fat.

Lily has to sleep in the Harkness's spare room surrounded by all the things Terry, their son, had left behind when he went into the army. Though he's been gone for months, the room still smells of cheesy feet.

They're kind to her and all that, but the whole of their house seems dark, especially downstairs; it always smells of old people and Izal.

And she hates the way they do the exact same things each day of the week. With it being a Tuesday today, she knows without even asking it'll be Woolton pie for tea – which is just some fancy name for a vegetable pie with a smattering of grated cheese on the top.

She's getting ready for bed when, for some reason, Mrs Harkness comes in with a glass of water. The old lady starts to smooth down the eiderdown, her wrinkled hand stroking the same spot over and over. 'Wouldn't my boy love to be back in his old room.' Lily hears the wobble in her voice. 'Lord knows where he's laying his poor head tonight. This ruddy war…'

'I'm sure he'll be back home soon,' she tells her – the same words Mrs Harkness always repeats when her mam mentions her dad.

Ethel smiles her near toothless smile. 'Try not to worry yerself about your mother, pet. She'll be right as rain before long – just needs time to get her strength back,' she says, like a person's strength can just go wandering off. 'Good thing is, she'll never have to go through all that palaver again.'

'She might though,' Lily says, 'She might be like Mrs Kirby over the road.'

'Aye, well, for that Rita Kirby drops her young'uns as easy as shelling peas.' Mrs Harkness shakes her head. 'I don't know if I should say owt, but I think it's only fair you know.' She takes a breath. 'Them doctors decided it were best to sterilise yer mam while they were at it.'

She's looking straight at her now, checking she's understood. 'They did whatever they do to make sure she can't have no more babies. I dare say it's for the best – your poor mam might not survive if she'd to go through it all again.'

'Did Mam mind?'

'I shouldn't think so – I 'spect she's delighted to be done with that business once and for all.'

According to Ethel Harkness, her mam has been *seen to* by the doctors – just like the Marsdens' cat. She's glad the old lady told her – it's a relief. Already Tiggs has grown fat and bored – will the same thing happen to her mother?

While she's brushing her teeth, she thinks back to *Every Woman's Doctor Book.* Which bits of her mam did they take out or sew up? No wonder she still winces when she sits up. Her *weak spot* must be that she's rubbish at giving birth – not like Rita Kirby. Should a doctor have examined her mam when she was sixteen and courting her dad? Would he have told her that, like drunkards and the mad people and the other lot, she should never have had a babby in the first place?

When Flora leaves hospital she's still sickly; it's left to Lily to fit in most of her chores before and after school. She finds it's much harder to concentrate on her schoolwork after she's been up and working before six o'clock.

Her dad finally gets his special leave and is allowed to stay with them for a whole week. Together they go out to the park and take photos of him and Flora and Lily with the new baby.

They decide to call him George – the King's name – though they say it's after her mam's dead dad. The only thing Lily can remember about Grandpa George was the long-stemmed pipe he smoked; she couldn't see into his eyes behind those glasses.

In the photos they get developed, her mam looks like she's been half rubbed-out of the picture. She gets Lily to address a big envelope to her dad's ship in her best writing and they post a couple of the photographs to him wrapped up with tissue paper and both of their letters. Lily can't see how these letters and photos are ever supposed to find him if no one's allowed to know where his ship is.

CHAPTER FOUR

December 24th 1944

For once, the whole house is empty and Lily can do exactly what *she* wants – although she's not sure what that might be. For a start, she retunes the radio to the Light Programme but then turns it off because, despite it being Christmas Eve, the music they're playing is gloomy and slow and makes her feel miserable.

She's re-reading Wuthering Heights for the umpteenth time. Last time she renewed the book, the librarian had told her how the author and most of her family had tragically died of tuberculosis. The one sister to survive had got married only to die in pregnancy.

Lily's reached the heart-breaking part where poor dead Cathy is outside the window when she's startled by a knock at the door. She waits. Two quick raps followed by three spaced out ones tell her it's Stella.

Still clutching her book, she opens up. 'I've come over to hide,' the girl says, rushing in. 'Had to get away from our mam; the bloody woman's gone half round the twist 'cause some mate of our Nobby is coming back with him to stay for Christmas. They've both got forty-eight-hour passes. Not like our poor Fred – he can't get leave 'till the New Year and Mam seems to think it's more tragic than the Titanic goin' down.'

Lily shrugs. 'Why doesn't his mate go to his own home for Christmas?'

'Well, apparently, his parents live someplace abroad. Think it began with an S – Spain, Sweden – somewhere like that anyroad. Not sure if he's a foreigner.'

Lily notices again how her friend's new haircut really suits her – especially the ways she's rolled it back at the front so you can see more of her face. Her pale eyes seem more prominent – she might be wearing mascara. 'No bugger's ever stayed at our house before 'cept our gran and it's gone to our mam's head.' She's always thought of her friend as a bit on the plain side but she has to admit that, these days, Stella's looking pretty – least ways when she can stop rabbiting on. 'The woman's only had me making paper-chains – like I was still a ruddy kid. She kept nagging at our dad – bending his ear about how we've got no flamin' Christmas tree even though no one else has one.'

Stella takes a breath at last. 'Anyway, in the end, he went out and cut a big branch off some tree then whitewashed it and stuck it in a bucket so she can hang baubles on it; but she's no ruddy happier now because it looks a right mess – more like some tree that's been shat on by a load of roosting pigeons.'

She gives a long sigh. Lily goes to say something but, of course, she's still not finished. 'Our mam's still at it over there – only cleanin' the whole flamin' house from top to bottom like the ruddy King himself is stopping the night.' At long last she flops down spent on the sofa.

'Well, at least she's making an effort.' Lily's determined not to be outdone in the moaning stakes. 'Our mam keeps saying there's no point in us getting excited about Christmas when Dad won't even be here and George is too young to know any different. This morning she's been banging on about how there's nowt in the shops even if she had owt to buy presents with in the first place.' Flopping down alongside her, the two sit in companionable irritation.

Stella's first to break the silence. 'Eh, you could come over our house after tea, if you like. This chap our Nobby's bringing back is one of the actual flight crew he's got friendly with. His name's Luke – like the saint.' She nudges Lily's arm. 'Eh, he could be a handsome pilot.'

'I suppose he's likely to be single,' Lily says. 'If he weren't, he'd be going home to his wife – unless she's abroad an' all.'

'Aye, an' just think – he'll be sleeping in our Fred's empty bed on the other side of the wall from me.'

'Could be fat and old.' Lily laughs when her friend's face falls. 'Eh – he'll probably keep you awake all night with his snoring.'

'Trust you to spoil it, Lily Hetherington.'

'I'm just warning you not to get your hopes up.'

'I bet you're wrong. In fact, bet you a sixpence he's young, single an' handsome.' Stella holds out her hand. 'Come on – shake on it.'

Lily spits on her hand like she's seen her dad do. 'We'll find out soon enough, won't we?'

'I'm not shakin' that,' Stella says, 'not now you've gone an' gobbed on it.'

'Ah – well, if you don't, it's not a proper bet. It won't count.'

After their handshake, Stella keeps wiping her palm like there'd been more than a drop of spit on it.

Tea is tripe and onions in a thin, white sauce. The smell gets to Lily and she has to practically hold her nose to swallow a few mouthfuls. 'Waste not want not,' her mam declares. George looks at them both and then turns his bowl upside down. Escaping the pandemonium that follows, Lily goes up to her bedroom to get ready.

She runs a comb through her hair, experiments with parting it further over to one side and clipping the front back in a roll. She stares at her altered reflection in the mirror, turning her head one way then the other trying to decide if it's an improvement or not.

She can hear her mam talking to George downstairs so it's safe to sneak into her parents' bedroom and rub a bit of that sacred lipstick on her cheeks and along her lips – just enough to redden them a bit.

'I'm off round to Stella's.' Lily aims her words in the general direction of the kitchen. Her mother comes out into the passageway, wiping her hands on the end of her pinny.

'Aye, well, you make sure you're back before it's chucking out time, my girl. Christmas Eve or not, a woman's not safe on these streets once them lot roll out of the Feathers.'

'Aye alright, there's no need to keep going on. Message received – over and out.' She slams the door to put an end to the conversation.

Nobby opens the Marsdens' door to her. 'Well if it isn't Lily Hetherington – aren't you a sight for sore eyes.' He gives her a breath-squeezing hug in a way he's never done in his life before. The buttons on his uniform dig into her. Somehow he seems even taller though surely that can't be – he must be all of twenty these days. He's definitely filled out since she last saw him and, though he'll never be good looking, his RAF uniform really does suit him.

Their house is almost unrecognisable with everything so tidy and all the surfaces shining in the lamplight. The air in the living room is toasty warm for a change and heavy with the combined smells of furniture polish, smoke and boiled cabbage. She spots that mockery of a Christmas tree in the corner; the baubles seem to wink at her like they're in on the joke.

Nobby claps the broad shoulders of a fair-haired chap in matching blue uniform. 'This is my mate, Luke; or I should say: *Navigator* Luke Wilson.' The navigator's chair scrapes as he stands up and turns to face her. 'Nice to finally meet you, Lily.' He holds his hand out expectantly.

She has no choice but to offer her own, unsure whether she should shake his up and down or just clasp it. For one awful moment she thinks he's about to raise hers up to his lips and kiss it. Before he lets her go, Lily looks up into his face and is shocked by the directness of his gaze.

Once released, she retreats to the other side of the table and takes the chair next to Stella; aware only of how her cheeks are burning for everyone to see the effect the airman's had on her. That thought is enough to make her blush intensify until she feels sick with embarrassment and almost wishes she'd stayed at home. The conversation carries on while she recovers. She looks down at her hand – the spot where she felt his soft touch on her skin.

When she dares to look sideways at Stella, the girl's attention is, in any case, glued to their visitor's handsome face; she looks like the cat that's got the cream and is lapping it all up. Lily will have to pay her that sixpence; it seems a small price to pay for the thrill of this man's company.

Nobby nudges Luke. 'Make sure you don't play our Stella here at darts – she may look young and innocent but she's a demon shot.'

'Oh really?' Luke says. 'I'm glad you warned me.'

Stella gives a shy smile. 'Nobby hates it when I beat him. Fred too.'

'Especially if it's cricket.' Alma Marsden looks up while her fingers blindly carrying on with her knitting. 'By rights our Stella should have been a boy.'

'Nobby said in his letter you're a sergeant same as him,' Jack Marsden says.

'I understand you come from Sark.'

'Got to admit it,' Alma says turning her needle around, 'I haven't the foggiest idea where that is.'

'I'm not surprised – it's only about three miles long, mile and a half at its widest. It's one of the smaller Channel Islands, Mrs Marsden – only twenty-five miles off the French coast.'

'Well I never.' Alma's needles fall silent. 'That close.'

'In actual fact, Sark is made up of three islands; the largest two – Great Sark and Little Sark – are connected by a narrow strip of land called La Coupée.'

Stella's dad leans forward frowning. 'If they're connected, how can they be separate islands? I mean to say–'

'Luke speaks fluent French,' Nobby says, clearly as proud as punch to have such a friend. 'After the Germans invaded, he managed to escape just in the nick of time.'

Lily, Stella and Alma gasp in unison.

Nobby nudges at his friend. 'Go on, Luke – tell them how you had to run for your lives.'

Luke puts down his beer glass and leans forward. 'Not sure I'd put it quite like that. Long story short – when the British army pulled out of the islands, for various reasons, my family chose not to leave our farm. Dad even helped put up posters saying things like: "Don't be yellow, stay at home". Needless to say, I wasn't at all happy about their decision. Lucky for me, I had a pal who kept a small fishing boat moored in a tiny inlet – so small Jerry wasn't guarding it.'

'All the same, they could have been shot,' Nobby interjects.

Luke nods. 'Yes, well, I will admit it was a bit hairy scrambling down the cliffs in the pitch black and then launching her on a heavy swell. We'd have been in for it if they'd spotted us but the moon stayed hidden by clouds long enough for us to clear the coast. And, of course, it was impossible to navigate at first.'

'So how in hell did you find your way over here?' Bernard Marsden asks.

'Well, as luck would have it, Mr Marsden, I'd learnt a bit about astronomy from my Uncle Julian so, once the sky had cleared a bit and we were far enough out to raise the sail, I managed to keep us heading more or less in the right direction. Wasn't until the evening of the next day when we finally got sight of the English coast.'

'He's now a senior navigator on one of the Lancasters at the base – that's how we met like.' Nobby nudges the poor man for the umpteenth time. 'Eh, tell 'em the bit about how the bloody Home Guard took you for spies.' Lily wishes their Nobby would put a sock in it and let the man speak for himself.

'Ah yes – our little encounter with some Weymouth LDVs. Seems awfully funny in retrospect, though it was anything but at the time.'

As he continues his life story, Lily is transported; despite his la-di-da voice, the airman is everything a man should be and more – brave and so very good looking. Luke Wilson is a real-life hero if ever there was one.

CHAPTER FIVE

January 1945

They have to run for the connecting train. 'All aboard!' the guard shouts practically in Lily's ear. Catching her breath in the corridor, she's overwhelmed by the sensation that all this has happened before, it's like she's acting a part in a film of her own life; the sensation is slow to leave her.

At least this train is less crowded; they manage to get window seats facing each other in an otherwise empty carriage. Only halfway there and already it's the furthest Lily's ever been away from home. She finds she likes the regular rhythm of the wheels on the track, the faded colours of the wintry landscape. So many bare-limbed trees, the wide valleys that sweep away towards blue-tinged distant hills. It makes her wonder what it might have been like if she'd been born in a different place.

All morning the two of them have been unusually quiet because there are posters everywhere warning them how *Careless Talk Costs Lives* and they should *Be like Dad – keep Mum* and though Lily can't think of anything she knows that could be of the remotest use to the enemy, it's hard to think of anything it might be completely safe to talk about.

Several stops on, their carriage has filled up and people are standing out in the corridor. Lily is getting too hot. It's the first time she's worn her smart red coat. Her mam bought it for her at a rummage sale because it looks brand new, like it's never been worn. There's no utility mark inside, which means it must have been made before the war. Why had the previous owner given it away? Had they put on weight or hated the colour? With a shiver, it occurs to her the woman might have died.

The man next to her fails to give up his seat to a woman in a WREN's uniform. He sits there smoking one cigarette after another; his hands appear unsteady, as if he's really nervous about something. And he will keep leaning across her to get to the ashtray below the window though he could just as easily stretch to the one on the door. He doesn't say *excuse me* or anything else. Unlike the other men, he still has his hat on, which adds to her growing suspicion he could be a foreign spy.

They finally arrive at Lincoln Station and step down into a cloud of smoke and steam. Stella grabs her arm and hangs onto it. Lily soon loses sight of the nervous man as they struggle to thread a way through the dense crowd. They keep their arms linked – all smiles at sharing this great adventure together.

Most of the people milling around are in uniforms of one sort or another; the whole place is packed out with so many travellers and supplies coming and going. 'Of course it's simply impossible to find a porter when you need one these days,' a woman in a fur coat complains to her companion.

It's a struggle to find their way out of the station. With the weather being unusually mild for the beginning of January, Lily has chosen to wear her prettiest dress though it's far more suitable for summer; once they're out in the streets the biting wind cuts right through her topcoat.

The pavements are edged with painted white stripes and far too narrow and congested for them to continue along arm in arm. Lily sets the pace out in front, hoping the exercise will warm her up and stop her teeth from chattering.

In his letter, Nobby had assured Stella they wouldn't be able to miss the Saracen's Head – a large and apparently popular pub very near the South Gate of the city. She's thankful the full blackout has been lifted but the half-darkness of the "dim-out" isn't much better. She begins to suspect that like Winnie the Pooh in George's book, they might be going around in circles.

'I give up. I've no bloody idea where we are,' Stella declares.

'We'll have to ask somebody,' Lily says. 'There's nowt else for it.'

It's hard to know which of the shadowy figures hurrying past they should approach. In the end a WAAF shows them the right turning.

The air inside the bar is hot and so dense with smoke it's hard to see across the room. Lily's eyes begin to smart as she peers at a sea of blue and khaki uniforms.

'Look – there they are over there.' Stella is waving her scarf. Following her gaze, Lily recognises two of the three men standing up.

'Eh – what sort of time d'you call this, our Stella?' Nobby taps his wristwatch as he comes forward to give his sister a bear hug.

'Don't you start.' Stella breaks free to cuff his head. 'The flamin' train were late getting in an' it's taken us the best part of half an hour to find this ruddy place.'

'Aye, well, it's really good to see you both.' Nobby wraps both arms around Lily like he's taken to doing of late.

She wonders if Luke Wilson is going to hug her as well, is disappointed when he only extends his hand and says, 'Welcome to Bomber County. Good to see you both again.' Lily looks up into that same penetrating gaze; in this light, his eyes seem more grey than blue.

Having shaken Stella's hand just as formally, Luke turns to

the older man standing beside them. 'This is my friend – our pilot, Zachery Pearson – also known as Zach the Flak. I have to warn you, Zach's exploits are legendary and not just in the air.'

In the laughter that follows, the pilot steps forward. Taking the pipe from the corner of his mouth he says, 'Enchanté; a pleasure to meet you lovely ladies,' in what sounds to Lily like a Yankee accent. She notices his well-trimmed moustache and wonders at the amount of Brylcreem he must put on to keep his dark hair immaculately in place. 'The snapshot Marsden here showed me hardly does either of you justice now I see you both in the flesh, as it were.' His sweaty hand lingers on hers in a way Lily finds thoroughly discombobulating. She can't imagine how Nobby might have got hold of a photograph with her and Stella together, never mind why he would be showing it around to all and sundry.

'You're American,' Stella says, her cheeks reddened by her share of the compliment.

The pilot laughs. 'I'm a proud Canuck – a Canadian. I assure you there's a big difference.'

'Time for another round, I think,' Luke says. 'What can I get you two ladies?'

The question flusters Lily; so far, no one's challenged them about being underage, but will that change if they ask for something alcoholic to drink?

'Think I'll have half a cider,' Stella says straight out. 'Oh, an' we haven't had much to eat so a packet of crisps would be nice.' She takes off her beret and scarf and then finally her coat.

'Come on now – this is a family reunion, why not live a little?' Like a matador, Zach takes Stella's coat and drapes it over the back of the chair. 'I'm sure you girls would appreciate something a little bit stronger to keep out the cold.' His hand stays where it is on her friend's shoulder. 'What say we get you young ladies a proper drink?'

'A small sherry then,' Lily says. 'That'll do me fine.'

'How about you, sweet thing?' The pilot's smiles are all for Stella. 'If they've got it, I'm going to treat myself to a glass of Scotch – would you care to join me in a glass?'

'Why not?' Stella giggles. Lily notices her quick glance across to her brother to check he's not going to object. Nobby does look a bit uncomfortable at this turn of events though he only says, 'I'll have the same again, thanks.'

It's a jolly evening. The men tell funny stories about things that have happened during what they call *ops,* along with some of the daft or improbable things that go on at the base. The closeness of the air is making Lily sweat, despite her summer dress. At times she finds it hard to follow the conversation with all the noise around them and she hasn't the foggiest idea of what all those initials – A.T.C., O.T.U.s, Q.D.M. and so on – might stand for. She can't guess at the significance of this "clearance chit" and why it's such a problem when it gets lost.

As the sherry begins to relax her, she becomes less anxious about looking daft for not knowing. 'So, hang on a minute,' Lily says, 'just how many of you are there in this Lancaster of yours?'

'Seven altogether,' Luke tells her. 'Aside from Zach and myself, there's our flight engineer Ronnie Burrows–'

'He sits right next to me in what they insist on calling a *dicky seat,*' Zach says. They're still laughing at that when he adds: 'I'm afraid Burrows has a nasty habit of farting, which, as you gals will appreciate, ain't none too pleasant in a confined space.'

'I'm right behind the two of them,' Luke tells them. 'Fortunately for me, there's a curtain I can pull across – it's meant to help me navigate but it comes in handy in other ways.' His face grows serious again. 'Next to me there's Jenkins, our wireless operator, and then there's Jock McFarley, our mid-upper gunner, and right down the end there's Higgins our Tail-End Charlie.'

'Wait up,' Zach says, 'you forgot to mention Basher Blake our bomb aimer – the only fella who gets to lie down on the job.'

Luke interrupts. 'Before Zach gives you the wrong idea, when he's not firing his gun, Blake lies flat on his belly so he can direct us to the right position.'

Stella stops munching her crisps. 'The right position for what?'

Clearly a bit taken aback by the question, Luke says, 'Well – for releasing our bombs over the target.' In the silence that follows, he claps Nobby on the shoulder. 'We get all the exciting stuff but Marsden and his fellow mechanics are the real heroes. You blokes work day and night to patch up our kites ready for the next op.' He turns to Zach. 'Without them, we couldn't keep it up.'

Zach roars with laughter. 'Speak for yourself, pal.'

Lily smiles amid the general laughter. 'Aye – well, we try to do our best,' Nobby mumbles. 'Must say it's damned annoying when you come back with the kite in tatters.'

'Sorry for the inconvenience,' Zach tells him. 'We'll have to try harder won't we, Luke?'

Nobby doesn't reply. In their company, he's unusually quiet though he's noisy enough at home. 'Must be my round,' he says. 'What's everyone havin'?' Lily can see he's a bit unsteady on his feet. She remembers Stella telling her that, unlike his father, her brother has a problem holding his drink.

'Oh no – nothing for me.' She holds a hand over her glass. 'I've still got half this schooner left to drink.'

'So you have.' Luke smiles over at her. 'Another half a bitter will do me, mate.' He turns to Zach and, without smiling, says something in French.

The reply he gets in French is curt – as if the two are in disagreement.

Zach answers for Stella. 'We'll have the same again, won't we, honey?' He has his arm draped round her friend's shoulders in a way Lily doesn't much care for. Stella doesn't seem to mind. 'Hey, you gals wouldn't know this,' Zach says, 'but they keep what they call a *line book* in the officer's mess where folks can write down funny things other people say.'

The pilot's arm finally leaves her shoulder to hand his empty glass to Nobby like he's a waiter. Stella copies him. Zach waves the stem of his gone-out pipe in front of the girls. 'The other day I saw this hilarious one where one officer says to another after a dance.' He clears his throat before breaking into a posh English accent: 'I'm surprised you're going out with that girl, she's T.B., and the other guy replies: But she seemed in perfect health, and then the first one says: Who's talking about her health, old boy? I was referring to her figure – she's *too broad*, old chap, much *too broad*.'

Though she's not sure the story's that funny, Lily laughs along with the others. For a second she's reminded of that doctor book of her mam's that said people with T.B. shouldn't ever get married.

Nobby returns with the drinks and Lily notices the way he hesitates before handing his sister her second whisky.

'Cheers!' Luke says as he clinks his glass against Stella's.

A short lad in RAF uniform knocks into their table. 'Watch where you're going, airman,' Zach tells him.

'Sorry 'bout that.' A cigarette somehow dangling off his lip, he peers at Nobby, 'Hey, Serg, how about giving us a tune or two on the old Joanna?'

The pilot nudges Stella. 'I've always suspected that brother of yours was a bit of a dark horse.'

Lily turns to Nobby in surprise. 'I didn't know you were musical.'

Waving his cigarette towards the piano in the corner, the young airman says, 'If you can hum it for him, darlin', the Serg here can play whatever takes yer fancy.'

'I can bash out a tune or two.' Nobby looks embarrassed. 'After a fashion, that is. I'm no Duke Ellington.'

Zach leans into Stella. 'Not just handy with a wrench, he can tinkle the old ivories, eh.' Straightening up, he pulls her to her feet. 'Sounds like a swell idea wouldn't you say, sweetheart? How about we start with *Is you is or is you ain't, my baby?* You know that number, Marsden?'

Once they're gathered around the piano, Nobby begins the slow introduction with more confidence than Lily had expected. Straight away, Zach starts snapping his fingers in time. It's clear the pilot knows every word and so the rest of them stop singing and just join in with the chorus. The way Zach starts to act out the lyrics is comical. He's singing to Stella, making her the object of his attention like he really *is* asking if she's still his girlfriend or not.

'Zach's quite a performer – I'll say that for him,' Luke whispers in Lily's ear.

They give the two of them a round of applause at the end and, ignoring Nobby's contribution, the pilot takes a bow before once again draping himself all over Stella. When she looks up at him, Lily can see how besotted the girl is.

One of Nobby's mates puts a fresh pint on the top of the piano for him and he stands up to gulp down more than half. 'An' the rest,' someone shouts. Holding his head back, Nobby tries to swallow what's left, spilling most of it down his chin then wiping it away with the back of his hand.

'That's enough of that bloody Yankee music,' another airman shouts out. 'Give us a bit of George Formby, Serg.'

One of the airman nods towards Stella and Zach. 'How about *If you don't like the goods, don't maul 'em?*' This gets a general laugh. The pilot chuckles along, though, looking at his expression, she suspects he's more irritated than he's letting on. 'My round this time, I guess,' he says.

Two more pints are lined up on the piano for Nobby. After playing the next tune, he downs the first of them to a general cheer. Playing to the crowd, he balances the empty mug upside down on his head like he's just been crowned.

Slumping back down on the stool, he begins the introduction to a tune Lily recognises as *The Lambeth Walk*. Everyone joins in. Forming a long line, they strut one way and then the other. Lily collides with Luke and he steadies her with a hand to her elbow, keeping it there longer than really necessary.

Missing a fair few notes now, Nobby plays the next tune well enough for most to recognise *Down at the Old Bull and Bush* and they sing through his mistakes.

'Our passes run out at ten o'clock but I'd like to see you safely back first,' Luke tells her. 'Where are you two girls staying?'

'Nobby's booked us a room in a place run by a woman called Mrs Kenny.'

'Ah – the infamous Ma Kenny's.' When her face falls, he laughs and it's a lovely laugh that makes her want to hug him. 'Don't look so worried – this town's full of unfounded rumours. I'm sure it's a perfectly respectable establishment.'

He nods towards Nobby. 'We might have a few problems getting Marsden over there back to the base. I'm afraid they'll put him on a charge if they get wind of how drunk he is.' Like a wound-down toy, Nobby is slouched across the piano, so drunk he can't find the right keys to play another tune.

The place is beginning to empty out. Lily's relieved when a couple of men lift Nobby off the stool and prop him upright. 'Don't you worry your pretty head, darlin' – we'll see him back alright,' the lanky one assures her. The lad on his other side wraps Nobby's arm around his shoulder. 'Come on, sunshine – let's get you on yer feet; we don't want you doing jankers, do we?' He takes most of his weight. 'Better walk him around a bit, try an' sober him up before we get him into the passion wagon.'

Lily frowns. 'The what?'

'Truck they laid on to take us back to the base,' Luke says shaking his head. 'Passion wagon is wishful thinking in my experience.'

Lily smiles to hide her puzzlement. She looks around for Stella but the girl has disappeared along with the pilot.

'I expect they've stepped out for a breath of fresh air,' Luke says, taking her empty glass from her hand. Lily picks up Stella's forgotten scarf.

After all the heat inside, outside in the darkness it's freezing and she starts to shiver. 'Alone at last,' Luke says, turning her to face him. 'If you'll excuse my French, tu es très, très belle, Lily Hetherington.'

It's the first time she's ever been kissed by a man and she worries she might not be doing it right; Luke's mouth is more open than hers and she can taste the beer he's been drinking. The sensation is so much hotter and wetter than she'd imagined and yet far from unpleasant.

'You're shivering,' he says, pulling her into his chest and wrapping his arms around her. She loves the close-up smell of him; how the rough cloth of his uniform feels against her cheek. 'I've been longing to do that since I first laid eyes on you,' he tells her, echoing her exact thoughts.

'Luke's promised he'll write to me,' she tells Stella on the walk to the station the following day.

'That's nice,' Stella says, nothing more. She'd hardly touched breakfast and still looks more than a bit worse for wear.

The train's packed out and in the end they're forced to sit in different carriages. In a way, Lily doesn't mind having this time to herself.

She finds Stella on the platform and they rush to catch the homebound train. This time it's less busy and they can sit together. The whole way back Stella is strangely quiet considering the exciting time they've had – all the new things they've seen and done.

'I think I might be in love,' Lily tells her mam when she gets in.

'Oh aye.' Her mam gives her one of those looks – the sort that makes her feel guilty even when there's no reason to be. 'In wartime people can get carried away. Don't you go taking things too serious, my girl. At your age, you need to go around the bush a bit before even thinking about settling down.'

'For heaven's sake, Mam,' she says. 'Who said anything about settling down?'

Every morning before work, Lily rushes down to check on the post and most days she's not disappointed. 'Must be costing him a ruddy fortune in stamps,' her mam's fond of saying.

Over the next few weeks, she sends as many letters back to him along with a photo of herself, which she takes out of the family album without asking. It's disconcerting to look at the blank space where her image should be.

When he asks her for a lock of hair, she cuts a piece from underneath so it won't show too much and ties it up with a thin strip of blue ribbon.

By return, he tells her he'll keep it in his breast pocket over his heart. Lily can't imagine anything more romantic. She's thrilled when, with the next letter, he encloses a picture of himself and the rest of the crew linking arms in front of what he calls "our Lanc". Luke looks every inch the hero in his flying jacket. She's surprised by the sheer size of the plane they fly.

Zach is standing next to him; a small shiver runs through her at the memory of the man's heavy arm hanging round Stella's shoulder. Running her eyes along each face in turn, their smiling confident expressions suggest they're all having a jolly good time.

The week after that, Luke sends another photo of himself "in civvies" – as he puts in writing on the back. She's relieved to see he looks just as handsome without his uniform.

'He's a good-lookin' man, I'll grant you that much,' her mam agrees when she shows her. With that face on her, she can't stop herself from adding: 'Just remember, our Lily, he's a grown man – an adult – while you're still a girl, hardly more than a child.'

'You seem to forget I'm sixteen – nearly seventeen; an' I'm earnin' me own ruddy money. If he was to ask me, I'd be old enough to marry him.'

'Not without our say-so, you wouldn't.'

'That's bloody rich coming from you,' she tells her before slamming the door.

With no phone in their house and the nearest phone box down the end of Dyer Street, it's not easy to speak to Luke directly. Lily's forced to tell him she had used all her savings on their trip to Lincoln and can't afford to go again for some time.

When he offers to pay, she refuses because it doesn't seem right. Instead, they make plans that he'll come to visit her as soon as he gets a long enough pass for the round trip.

'You make sure you tell him he'll have to stay in town,' her mam reminds her, waggling that finger of hers like she's so fond of doing. 'There's no room in this house for him or any other lad you might take a passin' fancy to.'

Lily bristles at that. She finds Stella has surprisingly little to say on the subject. Every morning they work alongside each other on the carding machines. The noise makes it impossible to chat without lip-reading but that won't work if the person's not looking at you.

'What about Zach?' she asks Stella during their dinner break.

'What about Zach?'

'Is he planning to come up here with Luke?'

'I shouldn't think so.'

Stella stands up, snapping her bait-box shut though she's left most of the food inside uneaten. Lily follows her on down the passageway leading to the toilets. It's a struggle to keep up with her.

Through the cubicle door, she asks: 'Have you two had a row or summat? Has he stopped writing to you?'

At first Lily doesn't identify the sound she's hearing, it takes a while before she realises that her friend is throwing up in there. Lost in her enthusiasm, she'd hardly noticed Stella's pallor, the pinched-in look she's had about her for some time now she thinks about it. A fear grips her that Stella might be really ill. What sort of a friend is she that she's barely noticed?

Stella finally emerges, wiping her mouth with the back of her sleeve. 'What's wrong with you?' Lily demands. 'I know something's not right.'

Stella tries to shrug her off but she grabs her arm and refuses to let go. 'Just tell me the ruddy truth, will ya?'

Stella leans closer and her own stomach turns at the smell of sick on her breath. 'If you must know, I haven't heard from Zach since I wrote to him with some news he didn't much care for.'

'What was it then – this news that's put him off?'

In her ear, the girl whispers: 'I told him I'm pretty certain I'm in the family way.' Her face has a greenish tinge. 'Think I might be sick again,' she says, retreating inside the cubicle to crouch over the toilet bowl again. 'You're not to say owt to Luke when you write to him.'

Stella looks at her sideways. 'Promise me you won't.'

Though she's forced to promise, Lily decides she'll have to say something to him when he visits. His friend has to be made to do the right thing.

'False alarm that time,' Stella says, straightening up. Her face remains sheet white.

'So have you told your mam and dad yet?'

'No, I haven't.' Stella splashes her face with water then cups her hand to gulp down a few mouthfuls and rinse her mouth. When she straightens up, she looks nearly as ghostly as before.

Lily does her best to hide how utterly shocked she is that her friend could have *gone all the way* with a man she'd only just met. 'Well, you'll not be able to keep it hidden for long,' she tells her. 'I 'spect your mam and dad will understand.' She can't imagine what possessed Stella to let that show-off of a pilot have his way with her – drink or no ruddy drink.

March 1945

Of course, no one writes to tell Lily; why would they? One Saturday morning she opens the door to find Nobby on the doorstep. Doesn't smile or say hello, he just stands there turning his RAF cap round in his hands, his head bowed.

'Summat's wrong,' she says.

'Aye.' He purses his lips in that way he has. 'Got some bad news.'

'It's not Stella.'

'Our Stell's right as rain.' Looking into his earnest face, she tries not to guess what he might be about to say. Having thought the worst, she convinces herself it can't possibly come true; this is like the scene from a film – such things don't happen in real life.

'I know you bin writing to Luke Wilson – that the two of you was sweet on each other.' Nobby seems close to tears. 'So I thought I ought to let you know –' He clears his throat. 'That him and all the rest of his crew are missing in action. Their kite didn't make it back from an op.' Finally looking her in the eye he says, 'Whole lot are listed as *missing presumed dead.*'

He pulls her into his chest and at first it's hard to take in what he's just said. Then her tears and snot are wetting his uniform; the rough material harsh and unyielding against her cheek.

'Let it all out. It's okay, lass,' Nobby tells her, like she's a child that's fallen over, keeps stroking her hair though she wants him to stop doing it. Close up, the smell of him is all wrong. 'It'll be alright,' he keeps saying over and over. Lily knows it's a lie – how could anything ever be alright again?

CHAPTER SIX

May 8th 1945 – V E Day

Being the owner of the longest set of ladders, Lenny Townsend's been roped into hanging the bunting along the front gutters of the Municipal Hall. It's a bloody long way up. A shudder runs through the ladder and, looking down, he sees the chap – the long streak of piss who'd been holding the bottom – has wandered off and left him to it. He may be a window cleaner but it's not like he can defy gravity. How effing ironic if, having survived this war, his ladder were to slip now. From this height, he wouldn't stand a chance – he'd fall splat on the pavement, which ought to dampen the mood a bit.

Lenny contemplates climbing in through an open window but the gap's too small. Instead, he ties the string in his hand around the bracket in front of him and lets the rest of the bunting flutter down the front of the building.

Muttering to himself, he climbs down the ladder and lets out a sigh when his feet are finally on solid ground.

In high dudgeon, Lenny peers through a sea of heads in search of the fella in charge. Pushing his way through, he taps him on his well-padded shoulder. The captain turns round. 'What is it now, man?'

Lenny bristles at the man's high and mighty airs. To his face he tells him, 'If you want that ruddy bunting hung along the other half, some bugger is goin' to have to hold the bottom of my ladder good and steady.'

Ethel Harkness walks through the cemetery holding the lilac flowers she's just cut from his favourite tree. The heads are already beginning to wilt. When she gets to the spot she sees the soil is still mounded up on her husband's grave – hasn't yet settled into its final resting position.

Here and there the bare earth is beginning to sprout new grass. 'Well now, Arthur,' she tells him, 'seems it's all over bar the shouting.' Ethel bends down despite her arthritis to pull last week's faded peonies from the granite urn that cost more than a week's pension. There's a glass vase set into it. Tipping the brown-yellow water onto the path, she smells decay. She takes the vase over to the tap in the corner and swills some clean water round a few times before filling it up to the brim. For today, at least, them lilacs will look lovely.

She's startled when the church bells begin to ring out – almost has to block her ears being so close. Over and over they repeat the same peal, which must carry far and wide. 'Pity you're missing it all,' she tells him. Whatever the doctor says, she's convinced in her own mind he would still be here if he hadn't worried himself to death over their Terry.

Lily can hear people outside in the street – all those shoes and boots clattering on the cobbles like an army marching. 'You can't keep moping around here forever – not at your age,' her mam says laying her ironed dress on the bed. 'This'll be summmat to get you out of yerself.'

To shut her up, Lily puts on her best clothes though she's in no mood to go whooping and dancing down the ruddy road with the rest of them.

Her brother George is only three but that hasn't deterred her mam from dressing him in somebody's hand-me-down shirt that's miles too big for him. She's even found one of their dad's ties to pull the collar in tighter. 'We'll take it off before you eat owt,' she says, tucking the loose end of it into his waistband so it doesn't hang down. 'Just remember to tell me when you need a wee, sweetheart – alright?' She waits for his nod.

Flora takes a step back to survey her mismatched children – making sure they pass muster. 'Don't you both look ever so smart.' She tells them to stay put while she fetches the box brownie, gets them to stand by the door where the light is better. 'Say cheese now.'

George shrieks the word out and that makes them all laugh so much that Lily's happy face must look genuine when the shutter clicks even if it doesn't last long. 'This here's a day to remember,' Flora declares opening their front door and almost pushing her out of it.

By the front door Stella overhears her mam having words with her dad on the stairs, 'This is not the day for talk like that.' She doesn't catch his reply.

Dressed in their Sunday best, all four Marsdens step outside. She hears the strains of a brass band in the distance. Beside her, Fred is smiling again, looks proud as punch in his army uniform. She's so glad to have him back, to be on his arm heading down the road towards the celebrations.

Right out of the blue, her brother had arrived home the previous afternoon – first time any of them had set eyes on him for months. He'd dropped his kitbag onto the mat to hug them for the longest he'd ever done in his life. She'd been the last one. 'Eh – you've put on a bit of weight, our Stella,' he'd said in her ear. He'd turned to their parents. 'Which one of you has bin fiddling the rations?'

Smiles fading, they'd told him there and then and she'd had no choice but to wait for him to say whatever he had to say on the matter. It went so quiet you'd think somebody had died.

'Aye well, best get this lot sorted out,' was all that came out of his mouth in the end. Swinging the heavy kitbag onto his shoulder, he'd headed up the stairs.

'I'll put kettle on,' her mam had shouted up after him. Though she'd put the cosy round the pot, it was tepid by the time he ventured downstairs.

Now, as they near the square, the music grows louder and Fred starts to march to the beat, taking her along with him; their mam and dad are lagging way behind. 'Shouldn't we wait for them?' she asks.

'Nah – they'll be alright.' He nudges her. 'Come on, our Stell – lets you and me have ourselves a bit of fun while we have the chance, eh?'

Heading for Lincoln city centre, Nobby Marsden is squeezed into the back of an open truck, which has to be laden several times above its official weight limit. Ah well. Someone's elbow digs into his side but he pays no mind to the pain – nothing can hurt him today.

Horns keep honking like bullfrogs calling out and other drivers are answering back. On both sides of the street the houses are fluttering with Union Jacks – Lord knows where they've all come from. Hearing the strains of Rule Britannia, they bellow it back at the waves of people pouring into the road – so many that the truck is forced to a halt.

It's clear to all this is as far as they'll get. 'Looks like it's shanks' pony from here, lads and lasses!' the driver shouts.

Before Nobby can climb down, a young WAAF he's never even spoken to grabs him round the shoulders and plants a kiss on his lips – it's a real smacker.

CHAPTER SEVEN

June 1945

Stella

Another Monday morning to face. Coming back from the lav, Stella spots a pile of clothes on the bed she's never seen before. Though they've been washed and ironed, she can tell they're other people's castoffs. Her mam appears in the doorway. 'No point in wasting money on new,' she declares. 'You won't be getting any wear out of 'em.'

Last night's heat made it hard to sleep and her mam is red-faced and clearly in a bad mood – though when is she in a good one these days? Arms crossed, the woman looks like she has something else to add but then thinks better of it.

Once she's gone, Stella holds a skirt up to her reflection. It's a horrible muddy sort of colour and the style's about twenty years out of date, but the waistband looks about right so it'll have to do.

The wireless downstairs is playing Vera Lynn's *We'll Meet Again* for the umpteenth ruddy time; Stella loathes the tune never mind the maudlin, sentimental words. She can hear her dad whistling along ahead of the beat – turning it into a jaunty march as he leaves the house. He doesn't bother to shout cheerio up the stairs like he used to.

Truth is, he seems to be doing his best to avoid her these days. She suspects he hates confronting her now that her belly is making itself obvious whatever she wears. When she puts it on, the skirt looks even worse than she feared. She selects a cream blouse and, despite the weather, does it up to the neck. The label at the back makes her neck itch but she doesn't bother to cut it off. The mirror confirms what she'd expected – at a distance she could be taken for a woman in her forties who's lost her figure.

Before she leaves the house, her mam thrusts her sandwich tin into her hands. 'Make sure you finish it,' she tells her. 'Remember you're eating for two now.'

On her way to work she can sense the neighbours' disapproval as they pass silently by; all those knowing sets of eyes travelling down to her expanding waistline, the proof, if it were needed, that she's become a different person – someone who's '*no better than she should be*'.

It's less than a ten-minute walk but she'd left it to the last minute as usual. At the corner of Ridge Road and about to cross, she's brought to a halt. More than a flutter – she'd felt a distinct blow that must have been a kick or punch. Several more in quick succession cause her to hold onto the lamppost for a minute or two. She can picture it all too clearly now – the sharp-elbowed child growing inside her, put there in one brief and drunken moment of madness. Another jab tells her, *I'm here and I'm not going anywhere – you can't ignore me any longer.*

"*The quickening*" the doctor had called it two weeks back– strange word like somebody in a hurry. 'Early days,' he'd said. 'Nothing to worry about. Believe me, you'll recognise it when it happens.' Nodding with that half smile on his lips as if the bloody man had experienced it for himself. 'I assume you're claiming the extra rations you're entitled to?'

She'd nodded.

'Well then, healthy girl of seventeen,' washing his hands with a block of carbolic, 'I don't envisage too many problems up ahead.'

Stella had almost laughed in his face. 'Is that right?' she'd said though he didn't appear to catch her tone. Dressing, she'd watched the way he scrubbed at each of his fingernails to remove contagion, moral or otherwise.

And now there it is again – a poke from the half-Canadian stowaway she's carrying; he or she making their presence felt – a growing, fighting reminder of the consequences of indulging in the *sins of the flesh*.

Reaching the opposite pavement, Stella can't see anyone about. Is she late? She scurries past the double gates and down the pitch to the propped-open doors. A minor miracle occurs as she pushes her card into the top of the machine and it's stamped with 45 seconds to spare. Slotting her timecard back in the rack, she notices Lily's card is already in its place.

When she turns around, Big Lottie is blocking her path. They're all a bit scared of Lottie Smith, although the woman's been in better spirits since getting the news that her youngest, Robert, is about to be demobbed.

'I got something I want to say to thee, young Stella.' Lottie plants her hands on those wide hips of hers. She can smell her fleshy armpits. 'An' I want 'ee to listen hard.'

Stella sighs. 'Go on then – get it off yer chest whatever it is.'

Lottie takes a step forward; her massive bosom only inches from her own chest, she grabs her chin in one of her pudgy hands. She couldn't look away if she wanted to. 'You're not the first wench round here to get herself into trouble,' she says, 'an' truth on't is, you won't be the last.'

Though it's early in the day, this close she can smell pickled onions on the woman's breath; thank the Lord her stomach's not as sensitive as it was a few weeks back.

Lottie lets go, though Stella can still feel where the woman's fingers dug in – like a podgy ghost hand holding her. She goes to walk on by but it's impossible to squeeze past that wide frame.

Refusing to step aside, Lottie continues to scowl down at her. 'I seen how 'ee hardly raise that head of yourn from the ground, lass. It won't do, d'you hear me?' Stella nods hoping that'll be enough to satisfy her.

'They reckon that chap of yours got shot down an' that makes him an 'ero in any bugger's book.' She glares down at Stella's stomach. 'That there babby in yer belly is all that's left of the poor man. Think on that. Don't 'ee go listenin' to them that's all holier than thou – all them sanctimonious buggers.' She points a finger – holds it half an inch from Stella's eyes. 'An' don't let any of 'em make 'ee feel ashamed of carryin' that there innocent young 'un.'

Lottie lifts her eyebrows, waiting. 'I won't,' Stella says, aware that she'll get into hot water if the charge-hand notices she's not at her machine.

'Good.' Lottie claps her hands together. 'That's settled then.' After a huff of satisfaction, she finally steps aside; it's still a struggle for the two of them to squeeze past each other.

'Hurry along there – we're not paying you ladies to gossip.' Not wanting a run-in with Lottie, Mr Bryant, the general foreman, is hard on Stella's heels instead. 'Get a move on, Miss Marsden, you should have started work by now.'

The sun is hot on Stella's back as she walks home. Along with all the fag ends in the gutter, something blue catches her attention. Growing in the road, in the sparseness of the dust and right up against the kerb, there's a small tuft of forget-me-not – its tiny petals tremble at each passing car. How can the poor thing survive on next to nothing and still flower like that?

Squinting against the brightness of the sun, Stella looks up. There's not a single cloud in a sky that's the exact same forget-me-not blue. Their next-door neighbour is coming towards her. 'Evening, Mrs Harrison,' she says meeting the woman's narrowed eyes full on.

August 1945

Saturday afternoon and her dad comes in whistling again – a warbling version of *Don't Fence Me In*, his jacket slung over his shoulder. Some cowboy. Stella checks the pot's still warm before she pours his tea. It's stewed to a rust colour; when she splashes in the last of the milk, it makes little difference.

'Ta,' he says. Looking at the tea he laughs, 'or should I say tar.' Stella's determined not to rise to the bait. He takes off his cap before he sits down and extracts a rolled-up copy of the Daily Mirror from his jacket pocket, smoothing it out on the table.

'Look at this,' he says thrusting the front page with its black letters towards them. Government Act on Houses, Demob and Mines the words under the headline declare: "Mark my words – this country's goin' to be different now we've got Labour in charge."

His eyes dart a challenge to her mam but she only carries on warming up bubble 'n' squeak that's a darn sight more cabbage than potato.

In the silence Stella hears the clock ticking. Something's burning. 'You've certainly changed your ruddy tune, Bernard Marsden,' her mam says, scraping the charred bits off the bottom as she turns his dinner over in the pan. 'A bit back, Churchill could do no wrong in your eyes.'

She turns down the gas and lets it heat through with a lid on while she cuts a thin slice of spam. Doesn't bother to heat it up; instead, balancing it on the knife, she transfers it onto a waiting clean plate. To Stella she mutters, 'Poor man was good enough to lead us through the war. He was a bloody hero then. Now, all of a sudden, he's the enemy of the working people.'

Her dad waves his half-empty cup in the air. 'Your mother's fond of twisting my words.'

Her mam mounds up the bubble and squeak alongside the spam and plonks the plate down in front of him. 'I'm only repeating what you said this morning.' She stands back to wipe her hands on her pinny.

He shakes his head at her. 'I said no such ruddy thing and you know it.'

Both of them turn to Stella like they're appealing to the ref. 'Don't try an' drag me into it,' she tells them. 'I'm having none of it. I'm not about to argue over politics – I've got more than enough on my plate as it is.'

'Talking of which,' her mam says, 'someone will be callin' round to speak to you later on.'

'To me?' Stella frowns. 'Who is it wants to speak to me?'

'Her name's Judith and she's a very nice lady from the church.' Her mam goes back to the sink and busies herself with washing the frying pan.

Still chewing, her dad lifts his eyes from his meal. 'Why would some woman from the church want to talk to our Stella?'

'Her name's Judith Fellows. Very nice lady, she is. I had a chat with her when I was doin' the flowers last week.' That pan's certainly getting a good scrubbing. Her mam stops to clip the front of her hair back in place. 'Anyway, she said she'd call round at six-thirty this evening.'

'What ruddy business can this Fellows woman have with Stella?' her dad asks through half chewed spam.

Her mother keeps working away with the Brillo pad. 'Judith Fellows is a trained Moral Welfare Officer.'

Stella stares at her mam. 'What the hell's a Moral Welfare Officer when they're at home?'

In a clatter of cutlery, her dad stands up. 'She's a holier-than-thou busybody Catholic that's what she is. And your mother's only gone an' invited the woman into our home without so much as a by-your-ruddy-leave to either of us.'

Her mam leaves the washing up and now her parents are standing so close they could kiss if they had a mind to – although their expressions make it unlikely. 'What could Mrs Fellows possibly want to discuss with our daughter?' he says. 'Come on – out with it, woman.'

Wiping her hands on her pinny, her mother takes a step back. 'Mrs Fellows is goin' to talk through – to *discuss* with Stella – the possibility of adoption. That's all.'

'That's all!' Her dad's red in the face. 'That's all, is it?'

He looks up at the ceiling, takes a long breath in before he speaks. 'Have you forgotten that baby she's carrying is our first grandchild?' His voice is unsteady as if he can't decide whether to lose his rag or burst into tears. Eye to eye, both beetroot in the face, fists ready curled on either side.

'Aye, well,' her mam says, 'when all's said an' done, that decision's not up to you or me for that matter.'

'Maybe so.' Her dad shuts his eyes like he's praying for someone to hold him back. 'What I want to know is what the hell can it have to do with Mrs flamin' Fellows from the church?'

Her mam's lips form a thin, determined line. 'Listen to me – our Stella's barley seventeen; she has her whole life ahead of her. We've got to think of the future, Bernie. What man's goin' to want to take her with a baby that's – well you know what?'

'That's what, woman? Spit it out!'

'Illegitimate – an' that's the fancy word for it. Besides, it's not only that – we have to consider what's best for the baby.'

'Oh aye? I doubt Stella's ever spoken to this wretched woman before and you expect her to sit here and make a decision like that without us.'

'I'm only sayin' she needs to talk it through, consider what might be for the best all round, in the long run.'

Her dad shakes his head. 'Sounds like you and this Judith Fellows person have already made yer minds up about what's best.'

'Stop it will ya – the pair of you!' Stella shouts. They look round at her like they'd forgotten she was standing less than a foot away. The baby's been kicking like anything and she wonders if *he* or *she* could hear the two of them rowing. 'You'll have to tell this Fellows woman I'm not in,' Stella says. 'I'm goin' over to Lily's for some peace and quiet.'

'You can't just ignore it you know!' her mam shouts to her back.

On the threshold, Stella hesitates, door in hand. 'I'm not the one ignoring it. For your information this is *my* baby an' there's no way I'm goin' through nine months of this just to hand it over to some strangers.' She glares at her mother. 'An' you can tell that to the whole congregation if you like.'

She turns to her father. 'That goes for them pals of yours at the Crown and Sceptre an' all.' The slam is loud and satisfying.

As usual, the Hetheringtons' house is quiet and orderly. 'Mam's taken our George to the swings,' Lily tells her. They go through to the living room where the open windows are letting in a welcome breeze. Stella flops down on the sofa.

'You look tired,' Lily says. 'Here put your feet up.' She positions the footstool at just the right angle. Looking at her raised legs, Stella wonders if her ankles might be a bit swollen. She can't recall the name of whatever it is puffy ankles are a symptom of – a danger sign the doctor said she must look out for. They'd warned her it could be fatal. She raises one leg and then the other then compares the two together. Perhaps it's only because of the heat.

When Lily smiles down at her, for once her whole face is lit up. She's wearing a halter neck white cotton dress with fine blue stripes – with its full skirt it has to be an old one of her mother's from before the war; there's certainly nothing of the Utility mark about it. 'I got something to show you.' Flushed with excitement, Lily reaches behind her. She holds up a knitting needle with a few lines in yellow garter stich hanging from the centre. It looks like something for a doll. 'Can you guess what it is?'

Stella shakes her head. 'A scarf for George's teddy?'

Lily laughs good and hard at that. 'I bin thinking that, by October, it's goin' to be a lot colder and your little one will be needing some booties. I thought this colour would be alright whether it's a boy or a girl.' To her this baby is something to be dressed up – prettified. Lily smoothes the knitting out. 'Well – what d'you reckon?'

The wool she's using is wrapped in a tight ball and must have been used before. It looks itchy and the colour's all washed out. 'Perfect,' Stella tells her choking back tears.

She can smell Amami shampoo – Lily must have just washed her hair; she can see it's all shiny and smooth. 'You look really nice today,' Stella tells her. She remembers their old make-believe games. 'You know, you could still be Snow White.' Looking down at her own shapeless clothes, Stella can't stop herself adding, 'I'm more like some old crone you might stumble on in the woods.'

'Don't be daft.' Lily takes her hand. 'Cheer up – you haven't got long to go now.' Her words are meant well but a shiver runs through Stella. Whatever happens, there's only a short time left just to be herself.

September 1945

Stella wakes from a feverish dream to find her sheets warm and damp. Too damp. There's no tell-tale stench of urine as she pulls back the sheets. Out of bed, she begins to shiver.

It's too early. Through the thin curtains no light shines in. Everything's too early; she's not ready for this.

'Mam!'

She tries again. 'Mam! I think me waters just broke.'

Alma finally comes into the room rubbing at her eyes. 'A first baby's ent usually this early.'

'But me waters have gone.'

'You sure you haven't just wet yerself?'

'Course I bloody haven't.' She's trembling all over – the knot of fear in her gut making her feel sick.

Like always, her mam's not listening. 'Aye, well, I told you that babby'd dropped a bit; puts a lot more pressure on yer bladder.'

'It's not ruddy piss.' Her heart's beating like mad and despite the shivering, her underarms are running with sweat. She stares down at the growing puddle on the oilcloth. 'See, it's still coming out.' Every time she moves, more of the tepid liquid runs down her legs.

Her mam studies the floor. 'See what you mean.' She stares at Stella now like she's remiss. 'Don't look to me like you're in pain. Are you gettin' any contractions?'

'No, not really.' As if it's been listening, her stomach tightens for a moment, taking her breath away. Not painful though – no more than a feeling of muscles being flexed and then finally released; something that's been happening a lot lately. 'Least ways I don't think so.'

'Believe me, you'll know all about it.' Her mam's still frowning. 'Best thing we can do is get you strolling around here for a bit. Now the waters have broke, we need to get you started.' Makes her sound like a broken-down car. All this time her mother's been so distant and now it's *we* – like the two of them are going through this together. 'I should get to the hospital.' Stella tells her. 'You need to go an' call the doctor.'

'Calm yerself down.' Her mam's firm hand rubs at Stella's back. 'No need to panic, my girl. Take a few deep breaths – that's it. And another. There's no point in us going in there too early. I made that mistake with our Nobby; they had me shaved down below and lying flat on me back for bloody hours before anythin' started.'

The back-rubbing is starting to annoy Stella. She shrugs her mother away, checks to be sure the bag she'd packed is still by the door. It's all in there – the things she'd been told will be needed for herself and the baby afterwards. Refusing help, she'd worked through the list methodically while her mind was somewhere else altogether.

She turns to face her mam. 'They told me it would be safer if I went there at the first signs.'

'That's as may be, but you have to remember childbirth takes time. It's the same wi' animals. Humans are no different.' Her mam grabs her shoulders. 'That babby will arrive in its own time. Chances are it's goin' to be a long hard day for us all and there's no getting' round it – they don't call it labour for nothing. The first time always takes much longer.'

'This'll be the first and last bloody time,' Stella says. 'I'm never doin' this again.'

'We all say that.' Her mam wraps a blanket round her shoulders. 'Anyroad, you're better off walking around like this for a bit. Come on, lass, let's try to get them contractions goin'. Stella catches a glimpse of her own reflection in the mirror – she looks like somebody who's just been bombed out. Her mam gives her a thin-lipped smile. 'In that hospital they'll take over and their ruddy idea of helping a baby on its way is to give you a damned great enema. Best part of a quart of soapy water.'

'Shit!'

'Exactly – an' like you've never done before.' Her mam shakes her head at the memory. 'If you ask me that's the last bloody thing any woman needs to put up with before delivering a babby the size of a football through her you-know-what.'

'Everything alright?' Her dad's voice through the half-closed door. 'D'you want me to nip round to Lenny Townsend's? I'm sure he'd be willin' to give our Stella a lift to hospital?'

'Not just yet, Bernie,' Alma shouts back at him. 'We're goin' to give things a chance to get goin' a bit.'

The decision's been made for her. 'Let's get you walking.' She leads Stella by the shoulders around the bed, pausing to shout over her shoulders, 'If you want to make yerself useful, Bernard Marsden, you'll go an' fetch me a rag for this floor before the two of us go skittering.'

Her stomach only half deflated, Stella needs to sit up though every movement pulls at the stiches between her legs. Like ruddy clockwork, every four hours a line of nurses wheel in the new-borns to be fed; this time she's determined to be ready for them.

She's trying not to dwell on what happened in that delivery room – the whole thing's best forgotten. They'd made parents wait outside until it was over though the entire hospital probably heard her screams.

Her mam was allowed to see her for a few minutes afterwards. 'Nine pounds four ounces is a decent size.' She'd patted Stella's hand like she'd done something good for a change. 'You can rest now, lass – the worst ont's over.'

Her mam's advice had been right up to then but she'd been wrong about that. Wincing, Stella pulls herself up to a sitting position; the rubber-covered mattress squeaks its complaints. The ward around her is packed out with women of all shapes and sizes and despite the open windows the place smells of their combined bodily odours. There's barely a gap between the lines of narrow beds and not a bit of privacy to be had. She'd once managed to pull the curtains around her bed but they were soon yanked back again by one of the auxiliaries.

Since becoming a mother she's had to learn a new vocabulary – phrases like *latching on* and *letting-down* are bandied about while the women do their best to feed their bawling offspring to order.

The latest four hours is nearly up. Any minute the place will be filled with wailing followed by noisy sucking and the air will grow redolent with the smell of milk and dirty nappies. It puts her in mind of the time they visited her great uncle Bert's dairy farm.

Hats like folded paper yachts, the nurses sail in all smiling efficiency. They save their scowls for her alone. Being the only unmarried mother and younger than any of the other patients, she's an abomination they would glide on past if they could. There's been no let up since that first day. As her baby screams to the rafters, they never miss an opportunity to remind her of how useless she is at this. 'We'll have to give him another top-up,' they like to tell her with obvious relish. 'Poor little mite's still hungry.' They stare down their noses at her as if to say, *putting him up for adoption would be a kindness*. Then they shake their know-it-all heads, turn their backs and wheel him off to the superior discipline of the nursery. Her regular humiliation is witnessed by dozens of knowing-better eyes before they look away.

Stella's determined not to give any of them the satisfaction of thinking they've beaten her into submission – though that's exactly what it feels like. 'A prison cell would be more welcoming than this place,' she'd told her parents during yesterday's all-too-brief visiting hour.

Her mam had leant in close to whisper, 'Pay no heed – they're just silly, ignorant bitches the lot of 'em.' Stella had never heard her use that particular b word before.

Squeezing her hand, her dad said, 'Only a few more days before you and that little babby of yours can come home.'

Her mam had done her best to change the subject. 'Had any more thoughts about his name? Thomas or Ernest – what's it to be?' Funny how, after all the months of silent disapproval, with the baby's arrival the two of them had become her staunchest allies – for now at least.

She's made it to a sitting position, even props the pillows up behind her. Her dad's made it no secret he favours Thomas – his own middle name. Does have a ring about it. 'Goes way back in the family does that,' he'd said with something close to pride. 'When he's little, he can be Tommy for short. Tom once he's in long trousers. Mr Thomas Earnest Marsden – now there's a man who'll stand up tall, a man who'll take no stick from any bugger round here.'

The big clock is upright on the hour as they wheel them in. She's almost the last one. 'I have baby Marsden here.' Looking uncertain, the young nurse cocks her head, holds him to her like she's reluctant to hand him over. He's half asleep. 'This one yours, is he?'

'He's my son,' Stella says, 'give him here.' With the full weight of him in her arms, she says, 'And his name's not *baby* – it's *Tommy* Marsden.'

CHAPTER EIGHT

April 1946

It's a small triumph when, without a struggle, Stella does up the waistband of a skirt she hasn't worn since last year. Turning this way and that in front of the mirror, she almost looks like herself again.

She bumps into Nobby on the landing and he does that silly thing of dodging this way and that when she tries to pass. 'Where you off to in all yer finery?' His nose closes in and he actually sniffs her. 'You're wearing scent.'

Still in his work clothes and with his hands covered in grease, his own particular smell is essence of engine oil. 'If you must know I borrowed a dab of mam's watered-down eau-de-cologne,' she says. 'Not exactly French perfume.'

A smirk pulls at the edges of his mouth. 'Have you got a date or summat?'

'Only with Lily.' She pushes him backwards. 'She has a fancy to see Brief Encounter for the umpteenth time – wouldn't let up until I promised I'd go with her.' She sighs. 'Can't say's I particularly want to see it again but our mam keeps naggin' about how I should get out more and, let's face it, Tommy'll hardly notice my absence.'

'So how come you're dressed up in yer glad rags?' He

nudges her. 'Come on spill the beans – you two meeting up with a couple of lads?'

Stella scoffs in his face. 'Fat chance. Besides, a bit of lipstick an' a blouse not stained with baby sick hardly counts as finery.'

He's still blocking her way. 'I've not seen it yet,' he says. 'The film that is. 'Appen I might tag along if it's all the same to you, find out what the fuss is about.'

Now she's the one grinning. 'I wouldn't have thought that romantic stuff would appeal to you.' At such close quarters, she notices again how much he's filled out like men do in their twenties. Not that you'd call him fat – his waist is as narrow as before but he's put on more muscle around his chest and shoulders. His hair is less carroty than when he was younger – in this light it seems more auburn than anything else. 'You can come with us if you like,' she says. 'I'm sure Lily won't object.'

'Okay – why not?' A wide smile reaches his eyes and makes him look quite handsome – to her mind at least. 'Give us a few minutes to change.'

Tommy is out of his playpen. They've put him in front of the fire, sitting up more or less straight-backed – his latest trick. She's pleased to see someone's remembered to put the guard around this time. Her son's pudgy fingers are examining a wooden car that used to be Fred's. She hopes her mam's had the sense to give it a good scrub; either way it's too late to worry about germs with him mouthing one of the wheels.

'Hurry up!' she shouts up the stairs.

'Hold yer ruddy horses,' Nobby tells her, coming into the living room. In the last five minutes he's gone through quite a transformation. Her dad's head comes up from his crossword like a snake sensing easy prey. 'Who's the lucky lady then?'

'Take no notice,' their mam says. 'It's nice to see you looking smart, Norbert.'

Stella says, 'I'll say this much our *Norbert*, you don't give up easy.'

71

'What the hell are you on about?' With such pale skin, it's easy to spot when he's embarrassed.

Stella shakes her head. 'Nothin' – just teasing ya.' Her eyes flick up to the clock on the mantlepiece. 'Anyroad, if we don't get a shift on, Lily will start to think we're not coming.'

When she bends to kiss the top of Tommy's head, he barely responds. 'It's past his bedtime,' she says. 'I don't want him up with me half the night.'

Her mam makes that noise she's fond of making in the back of her throat like the very suggestion might choke her. Her knitting needles keep up that clickety-clacking in an unstoppable rhythm. 'Leave him to me. I'll give him his bottle shortly. Now off you go the pair of you and enjoy yerselves.'

They get to the Picture House in good time. Nobby insists on paying for all three tickets. Stella's quick to take her seat leaving her brother on the end of the aisle with Lily sitting between them.

The room darkens; a hush descends and is filled by the stirring music of the Pathé news. The newsreel is one she's seen before about Churchill and his wife setting off to visit America and some big battleship returning to Southampton. Then there's a beauty contest.

Stella's distracted by the flare of a match, which is followed by lots of crackling and sucking as the man next to her struggles to light his pipe. She wafts at the air hoping he'll blow the smoke the other way. The young women on the screen are walking around indoors dressed in swimwear with high heels; the commentator makes some quip about the judges having a head for figures.

The B film is not up to much, which probably explains why people pour in during the interval.

Finally, the lights go down for the main feature. It's hard to see the screen through the haze; makes it look like real smoke and steam pouring from screen as the trains keep arriving and leaving. Stella can feel her throat drying; her clothes will stink of tobacco in the morning.

The music is too loud for her liking. What with those clipped accents and the mutterings of some men behind she has to concentrate to catch what's being said. A strange sound draws her attention across to where Nobby is sitting with his hand clamped to his mouth in an effort to stifle his amusement.

By contrast, Lily is mesmerised, even mouthing the words along with the actors in some of the scenes. Before the end, and despite knowing full well what's coming, her wet cheeks shine in the big screen's reflected light. When heartbroken Laura runs towards the speeding express, Lily gasps and her hand goes to her mouth. Even with her eyes shut, the tears keep flowing. It's easy to guess she's thinking of Luke – her own lost-forever love.

Without saying a word, Nobby hands her his handkerchief. Lily's chest continues to shudder with suppressed sobs. His arm comes round the back of her seat until it rests on Lily's shoulders. The gesture appears to be neither welcome nor unwelcome. He leans in to whisper something in Lily's ear, touching the back of her hand but not daring to take hold of it.

As the lights go up again, Stella is left feeling sorry for Laura's nice but boring husband. That last line about her coming back to him shows the poor man had his suspicions all along but decided to keep them to himself. Though he's not nearly as good-looking as Trevor Howard, to her mind Fred Jesson is the real hero of the film.

As they step outside into the darkened streets, Lily is still dabbing at her eyes. The George and Dragon on the opposite corner is lit up; someone is plonking out *Ilkley Moor* on the piano and a handful of drunk-sounding people are singing along. 'Fancy a quick drink?' Nobby asks. 'Might cheer us up a bit.' He checks his watch. 'Pub won't shut for a good half hour.'

'Tommy's been fretful with that tooth coming through,' Stella says. 'I'd best get home but you two don't need to rush back.'

'Don't be silly.' Lily threads an arm through hers. 'Can't have you walkin' the streets on yer own, can we, Nobby?'

'Course not.' He raises his voice to mask his disappointment. 'Though our Stell can give as good as she gets.'

Lily comes to a halt. 'Oh, sorry, Nobby, I nearly forgot.' He's all anticipation. 'Here's yer hanky back. It's a bit damp.'

Her brother stares at the handkerchief like it doesn't belong to him. Lily strides off dragging Stella with her while Nobby dawdles his disappointment a few paces behind. She can hear him flicking the top of his lighter up and down, over and over like he has a habit of doing. It gets on her nerves; if Lily wasn't with them, she'd tell him to stop it.

Cold air is sweeping down from the moors – it blows right through her and makes them walk faster and talk less.

'Night then,' Lily says when they reach their front gate.

'Nobby'll see you the rest of the way home.' Stella gives him a nudge. 'Won't you?'

'Course I will.' He perks up. 'Can't be too careful; you never know who's about.' He offers up his arm.

'There's really no need,' Lily tells him.

'Nonsense.' Nobby gives her a heart-rending smile. 'Like you said earlier, can't have you walkin' the streets on yer own at night.'

She notices the way Lily hesitates before she takes his arm.

The lamp is still on in the sitting room; Stella wonders if her dad's done his usual trick of falling asleep in his armchair. 'Had a good night?' he asks, looking up from his book. The front cover tells her it's another one of those cowboy yarns.

'I'd seen it before,' she says. 'Not sure it was quite our

Nobby's cup of tea – bit too slushy for him.' For once her dad passes no comment.

'Nobby's just seeing Lily home.' She takes off her mac. The fire's gone out in the grate and there's a new chilliness to the room. Her dad's definitely got that serious face on him. 'Everything alright is it?' she asks. 'Tommy's not been playin' up or owt?'

'The lad went down without a fuss.' He turns the corner of the page down then shuts the book and sits up straighter. She waits for whatever's coming.

Finally he says, 'Thought I might have a word with you – on the QT like.' He taps his finger on the side of his nose. 'Just between the two of us.'

'What about?' It's no joke that's for sure. 'Come on, Dad – out with it; don't leave me in suspense.'

His face lightens as he pats the arm of his chair. She perches on it like she used to, like she hasn't done for a long while. Close up, more lines are etched into his skin than she's noticed before. 'Yer mother's got this notion in her head that I thought you should hear about.' His sigh is long and heartfelt.

'What sort of a notion?'

'There's no easy way to say this.' He looks right at her – unblinking. 'Yer mam thinks that, before our Tommy gets much older – learns to speak an' all that – we should maybe get him used to the idea of us, yer mam an' me that is, of us bein' his parents. Let the lad think you're his big sister.'

Stella springs to her feet. She can't breathe. There are no words.

'No need to upset yerself.' He grabs her hand. 'Alma's only thinkin' of you – of your future and the babby's a course. She reckons this would be a way of makin' thinks right.'

'Makin' things right? How in God's name could she even suggest such a terrible thing?'

'I'm not sayin' I agree with her, though it–'

'Besides, every bugger round here knows full well Tommy's my baby. Who's she hopin' to fool?'

'Alma's suggestin' we move away somewhere where they wouldn't know any better.'

'The woman's gone bloody mad.' Stella can't stop shaking her head, over and over until she's dizzy with it. 'Where the hell is she planning to move to – an' how?' She scoffs in his face. 'Come on – tell me where is this ruddy mythical place where people would be gullible enough to swallow the idea of the pair of you havin' a lad of Tommy's age?'

'Hang on a minute – we may seem ruddy ancient to you but remember yer mam's only just forty-three. Women of her age have been known to–'

'An' she's actually got you goin' along with the idea?'

'I never said that.' He waves his hands in the air like he's tamping down a fire. 'Keep your voice down, Stella. Calm yerself. Carrying on like this, you'll wake the babby up.'

'I can wake him if I bloody well want to – he's *my* son! I'm never goin' to agree to pass him off as yours – d'you hear me? Not while I live and breathe!'

A movement alerts Stella to her brother's presence in the doorway. Taking the cigarette out of his mouth, Nobby looks from one to the other. Their dad clears his throat. 'Never heard you come in.'

'I'm not surprised with the racket you two were making – I could hear you out in the street. What's all this ruddy fuss about?'

'Go on,' Stella says, 'tell him your idea, Dad.'

Her dad shakes his head, seems to find something to interest him on the rug.

Nobby frowns. 'Well?'

'If you're not goin' to tell him, I will.' She turns to her brother. 'The two of them think we should move somewhere where nobody knows us so they can pass Tommy off as *their* son – which would be a bloody miracle in itself. They…' She wipes her eyes with heel of her hand. 'They want me to pretend I'm only his sister, not his mam.'

'You've got to be fuckin' joking.' Nobby takes a step closer to his father.

Her dad curls his fists in defence. 'I won't have that sort of language in this house.'

Nobby scoffs in his face. 'You object to me cursing when the two of you have been plotting to take our Stell's boy away from her.'

'There's no need to exaggerate – nobody's taking the babby away. It were only a suggestion of yer mam's. She – *we* both meant well by it.'

'*Only* a suggestion?' The lighted tip of Nobby's cigarette is very close to their dad's face. He drops the butt onto the hearthstone and grinds it underfoot. 'Shame on you – the pair of you.'

Nobby's arms come round her shoulder. Up against his chest, she hears his heart pounding. 'I can't answer for Stella, but I certainly won't be made a party to

something so heartless.' Voice unsteady, he points a finger at his father. 'If you did do such a thing, that'd be the last you ever see of me.'

CHAPTER NINE

May 1953

Lenny Townsend is struggling with his end of the television set. Why the hell hadn't Charlie bought a smaller one – one of them that'll sit on a table instead of this ruddy great thing? With it being just shy of three-foot-high, they'd had to lay it across the back of the van and now it's all the two of them can do to manhandle it. After getting it out the back, they set it down on the pavement and take a well-earned breather.

Lenny rubs at the muscles around the small of his back. With the low sun shining on the cabinet, he notices the scratch to the side of the four brass letters below the screen. E K C O – like echo misspelt. He runs his finger over it – not too deep; ought to more or less disappear with a drop of varnish.

Wiping the sweat from his forehead, Charlie says, 'Her indoors will be like the cat that's got the cream when she claps eyes on this. I just hope the ruddy thing works.'

'Either way, I'm not luggin' it back there,' Lenny tells him.

'She's bound to invite half the neighbourhood in to watch the coronation.' He grabs Lenny's arm. 'Now don't, whatever you do, breathe a word to her about how I came by it.'

In the carding shop the maintenance men have half-heartedly draped a load of sagging bunting overhead – high enough so there's no chance of it getting caught in any machinery. It's hard to see it against the sunlight shining in through the roof; even squinting; there's nothing cheery about it.

Lily's not fussed about the idea of a street party – their neighbours are a pretty boring lot at the best of times. Some of the girls here have been talking about catching the train down to London to watch the coronation procession. She's thrilled at the idea of visiting the capital for the first time, seeing all the places she's only read about in the papers – Buckingham Palace, The Mall, Westminster Abbey – names that seem like places from a storybook. Even for those who could afford it, there's no chance of finding anywhere to sleep. The trains will be packed out so they'll have to set off dead early and then stay up the whole night – another thing she's never done in her entire life before. Lily can't wait.

Stella shakes her head before she's even finished. Lily's shoulders droop. 'Why not? Your mam can look after Tommy.'

The only answer she can get out of her is a curt, 'Thanks but I'm not interested.' When her mouth sets into a hard line like that – something she gets from her mam – there's no reasoning with her.

When someone mentions the idea to her, Big Lottie scoffs. 'What go all the bloody way down to London just to watch the high and mighty dressed up in their finery to look down their noses at the likes of us?' Hands planted on those massive hips, for good measure she adds, 'Besides, weather forecast's not up to much; 'appen you'll come back wi' the flu an' who knows what else besides.' Trust her to put a damper on every-one's mood.

Nobby Marsden shuts the bonnet of the Morris Minor 1000 he's been working on and jumps into the driver's seat. It brings a smile to his face when the engine catches at the first turn. He revs it a few times to be certain then leaves her running for a couple more minutes to check the tick-over.

She purrs away, filling his workshop with fumes until he finally turns the ignition off and, wiping the grease from his hands, goes out into the street for some fresh air.

The eldest Kirby girl saunters by and smiles up at him. Pretty girl – slender at the waist unlike the rest of her family. Fanning her face with one hand, she says, 'Afternoon.'

'And the same to you.'

'It's really hotting up now, don't you think?' It takes him a moment to understand she's only referring to the weather.

He looks up into the pale blue of the sky. 'Aye, you're right.' Expecting her to walk off, he carries on wiping at the ingrained grime on his palms.

Her feet haven't moved. Raising his head he finds her still there smiling up at him. He notices her teeth – how white and uniform they are; the front two have a faint red line to match the lipstick she's wearing. Olive – that's her name; he's just remembered – like Popeye's wife. Olive Kirby. She keeps swinging her shopping bag to and fro. 'Sort of day that makes you glad to be alive,' she says.

'You're not wrong,' Nobby tells her.

Stella hasn't told anyone here she's thinking of leaving. Due to the noise levels, like the rest of the women on the shop-floor, she's had to learn to lip-read, which makes it easy to keep her head down and ignore what's being said around her.

She could do this job in her sleep – the same damned thing day in day out with no let up. With Tommy already seven going on eight, it's time she tried to make something more of herself. A week back, she'd spotted that advert in the paper for nursing orderlies at the Royal. She'd had to pretend to be ill to attend the interview. Thinking about her own miserable hospital experience, she'd told the formidable matron, 'Being in here – well, it's a worrying time for the patients. I'd enjoy making them a bit more comfortable while they're stuck in bed. Sometimes a friendly face can make all the difference.'

Stella wasn't sure how well that had gone down until, standing up like she'd had enough of her nonsense, the matron had said, 'The job's yours if you'd like it, Miss Marsden.' That was it. They wanted her to start on the eighth, which means she's got a couple of days to decide one way or the other. Her mam and dad think she should take it. Which just leaves Lily to worry about.

Brian Bagshaw doesn't like school anymore. All week he's had to sit next to Peter Jenkins who's been moved from the back row because he threw an ink pellet. The boy smells like stale milk and has a funny habit of holding his head on one side like he's trying to see something just behind you.

Today, their teacher, Miss Greenwood, hasn't set them any sums or spellings, instead she's been telling them all about the coronation and now, heads down, they're supposed to be drawing the new queen sitting on her throne.

Though Miss Greenwood had held up a picture of the Abbey, Peter's blue crayon is scratching away as he colours in the sky above the new queen's head. Brian wishes she'd given them a page of sums instead. Miss Greenwood is out of her chair patrolling and so he'd better make a start. 'Let's make these really colourful,' she says, 'As befits such a joyous occasion.'

His mind blank, Brian draws a red circle, gives it two blue dots and a curved red mouth. He picks up the black then drops it again. Peter's now finished colouring his sun so he can give their new queen rolls of yellow hair to make quite certain she looks nothing like his mother.

CHAPTER TEN

August 1953

Will

Will Bagshaw walks into each empty room in turn checking everything is gone except for one or two items he'd agreed to leave – for a price of course. In Brian's room, he thinks he can still smell something of his son though there's nothing left – no trace except for the outlines left on the walls where the lad's aeroplane pictures used to be and the two brighter rectangles on the lino where the wardrobe and chest of drawers used to sit.

With no job and no living relatives, when he leaves here today he'll be severing every last link with the city.

In their bedroom – *his* room of late – something's catching the light down by the skirting board on the far wall where the bedhead used to be. He bends to pick it up; it's one of Violet's lipsticks. Turning the small tube over he reads the words printed on its base: Heart Red by Gala.

Not sure what he should do with it, Will lays it back down on the floor exactly where he found it.

In here the smell of damp is more noticeable than it was.

Walking over to the window, he notices the brown ringed stains that have bled from the side of the frame into the roses on the wallpaper. Ah well – someone else's problem.

He takes a last look through the windowpane at the row of identical houses opposite. On this bright, clear day, beyond all the buildings and mill chimneys, he can see the hazy blue outline of the moor. He tugs the curtains tight together before he leaves.

He's already checked everything is gone from the front room and kitchen so that only leaves the bathroom. Since the night Norma died, his son has point blank refused to go in the bathroom; the lad swore blind his mother's ghost had appeared behind him in the mirror. Nothing would shake his certainty. Will had borrowed an old-fashioned chamber pot for the lad to use in his bedroom; it's been the devil's own job having to keep emptying it. That's something he's not going to miss. It was decent of the neighbours to let Brian use their bath a few times.

Satisfied that he's left nothing upstairs, he walks down the stairs of number 17. There's nothing more left to do except lock up and leave.

It takes a couple more minutes for him to pull the warped back door tight enough to lock and bolt it. That's it – all done with.

He walks through the house and out of the front door for the very last time.

Whilst he's locking up, he turns to see Mrs Hutton watching him from her front room window. He'd gone over and said an awkward farewell to her and Fred yesterday evening. They'd not much to say in return except to ask after Brian and wish the two of them better luck in the capital. 'Never been there, never want to,' she had declared.

Their two cases and a couple of cardboard boxes are wedged in the back seat and stable enough for the journey. After checking the boot's closed, he raises his hat to Mavis Hutton knowing he'll never see the woman again.

Will leans across to place his trilby on the back shelf and then climbs into the driver's seat. Across from him, Brian still won't look up, doesn't say a word. He's noticed that, along with his reluctance to speak, the lad has a new habit of keeping his head down as if something on his shoes is fascinating him.

A week or so back, his normally hard-faced teacher, Miss Greenwood, had called him in to discuss this change in his son's behaviour. She'd made a point of meeting him in the classroom where she'd led him over to a colourful display of the children's drawings of the coronation. 'This one is Brian's,' she'd said, pointing to a drawing that showed their new queen not sitting in a carriage but laid out in an open coffin being drawn by black horses. 'Need I say more, Mr Bagshaw?'

Unlike his classmates, Brian had given the queen bright yellow hair. Lost for words, he'd cleared his throat and said, 'I see.'

Miss Greenwood had returned a sharp look that indicated that wasn't good enough. 'In class Brian used to have his hand raised all the time; he barely utters a word these days. At play-time, we've all noticed he no longer runs around in the yard with the other boys.' She'd shaken her head. 'I'm afraid they've given up trying to include him.'

Sighing from the depths of her heavy bosoms, she'd clearly felt the need to add, 'Mind, it's hardly surprising after what happened to your poor wife. Such a tragic event is under-standably hard for any child to comprehend let alone make sense of.'

Despite the woman's usual reserve, she'd touched Will's arm as they stepped outside. 'We all feel for the boy; I'm sure it's an equally worrying time for you, Mr Bagshaw.' She'd walked with him towards the playground where he'd left Brian on his own bouncing a ball over and over against the tarmac. 'Perhaps this fresh start you're planning will help matters. I do hope so.'

She hadn't left it there but had halted at the gate deliberately standing in his path, giving a quick glance to check the lad was out of earshot. 'He's mentioned that the two of you might be emigrating somewhere abroad. That would certainly provide excitement for the boy. I'm sure such an adventure would help him to forget recent tragic events.'

'Who knows what the future holds,' Will had told her.

He starts the car and watches the needle on the fuel gauge spin round to full. The boy doesn't look up, doesn't take one last look at the old house. Will notices he's busy playing with something – not a proper toy but one of those folded paper things that seem to be all the rage.

'What you got there?' he asks knowing the answer.

'I can tell your fortune with this,' Brian tells him.

'Oh aye,' he says. 'That could come in handy.' Will lights a cigarette, holds it in the corner of his mouth while he puts the car into reverse. In his mirror, he catches sight of Mrs Hutton waving at them from her front step. He winds the window down to give her a half-hearted salute then flicks the ash off his fag.

As he pulls away, his mood begins to lift; it's hard to take in that he's leaving this town and everything in it behind him. Good riddance to the lot.

He glances across at his son. Brian has hardly said a thing about this move. Even when they were packing up his toys and all his clothes, he'd made no comment about leaving his bedroom, their house or his school. Never mind about them heading down to London. It's like some part of the boy has switched itself off. He hasn't dared say a word about Ivy though the lad is bound be meeting her soon enough. Best to give him a few days to settle in, let him get used to things one step at a time.

'You've got to choose a colour,' Brian says, coming to life a bit and poking the paper thing up in his face. 'If you don't, I can't tell your fortune.'

Will's eyes flick down. 'Okay, then I'll go for red.' At the junction, he pulls out into the main road, has to be careful to avoid a wobbling cyclist.

'There's no red, see,' the boy tells him, 'just blue, green, yellow or brown.'

Will looks up into the summer sky. 'Blue then.'

'B-L-U-E.' The paper crackles as the boy snaps the thing to and fro four times to spell out the letters.

'Now you've got to pick a number out of this lot.'

'I can't ruddy see, I'm driving.'

'Right, well – do you want the two, three, six or seven?'

'Seven,' Will says. 'That's always been my lucky number.'

The boy slowly counts to seven moving his paper contraption to the beat. 'Now, this is the last one – do you want one, four, five or eight?'

'What – I can't just have seven? Have I got to choose again?'

'Aye, you do – them's the rules.'

Will's looking for the turning that will take him to the building society where he's got to hand over the house keys. He'd better check they've got his new address to send any remaining money on to.

'Dad! You've got to pick another number – one, four, five or eight?'

'I'll have eight then, if I must.'

'Right, it says –' Out of the corner of his eye, he watches the boy bend forward to lift the flap of paper up.

'Oh.'

'Well then – what's it say? What does my future hold?'

Brian folds the whole thing up and puts it away in his pocket. 'It's a stupid game – don't mean anything, not really. I just made them up meself.'

'That's as maybe – tell me what it said will ya? I want to know.'

He has to strain to hear the boy's mumbled reply: 'It said, *you are going to die.*'

CHAPTER ELEVEN

December 1953

Lily

With little money to spare, Christmas in the Hetherington household is a subdued affair, though they try to make a bit of an effort for George's sake. Amongst other things, her dad had bought him a giant Meccano set he's been wanting for ages. Being eleven, he'd shown less excitement when he unwrapped it than he would have a few years back.

'If I can't spoil me own son, it's a poor state of affairs,' her dad says more than once. He seems so defensive, Lily wonders if her mother's had words with him about being too extravagant.

It's meant to be the *Festive Season* but Lily's never felt less festive in her life. On Boxing Day, she makes an effort to play with her brother; they sit on the floor in front of the fire and between them have a go at constructing something that's meant to be the Eiffel Tower. Afterwards, they all have to pretend it looks exactly like it.

New Year's Eve is soon upon them. Her dad goes off to the pub promising to bring a quart of cider back, 'Once I've quenched me thirst.' From lots of little gestures and mutterings, it's obvious her mam's got some sort of bee in her bonnet and yet, for once, keeps it to herself.

At seven o'clock on the dot there's a knock at the front door. 'Can you go an' see who that is, Lil?' her mam says, hardly looking up from her darning. When she opens up, Stella is standing on the doorstep dressed in her finery.

'What the hell–'

'I thought you could do with some cheering up,' her mam says coming up behind her. 'A good night out will sort you out.'

'If only it was that simple.' Lily feels a pang of guilt seeing the disappointment in their faces. 'Besides, where would we go?'

'Well, as it 'appens, I've been invited to a party by my friend Kathleen – one of the girls I work with. She's looking forward to meeting you – they all are.'

Her mam puts her arms around both their shoulders and pulls them in close together. 'I'm goin' to say summat you girls may not thank me for sayin'.' These last few months more grey has worked its way into her mam's dark hair.

Lily pulls away. 'Oh aye, and what's that?'

'Things may not have worked out for either of you like you might have imagined or wished for, but you mustn't forget how to enjoy yourselves.' She eyes them both in turn. 'When all's said and done, you're only given one life; you need to make the most of it.'

Stella grabs Lily's hand and starts to swing it back and forth like they're little kids. 'Yer mam's right. On New Year's Eve you're meant to say goodbye to the old year and all it's brought and look forward to the start of a brand new one.' Lily can smell her perfume, notices the she's made her eyes up more than usual with a thick sweep of dark eyeliner along her eyelid that's flicked up at the ends. It really suits her. 'Come on, Lily love, what d'you say – shall we give it a go?'

They catch the bus into the town centre and find a seat upstairs so they can get a better view of the Christmas lights. For the first time in a long while, Lily's wearing lipstick and stockings along with a proper frock – a really smart one she bought in a sale last spring and hasn't yet had an occasion to wear. It's in fine, dark blue rayon and fits her much better than she was expecting. Though she's wearing her thick coat, she's still shivering. Stella looks lovely though her dress looks a bit dated. Of course she wouldn't dream of saying that to her.

They walk around for a bit amongst the swarms of people and eventually find the turning that leads to the girl's house. It's a detached place – her family must be well to do. On the threshold, Lily's nerves start to jangle at the thought of walking into a room full of strangers. 'Are you sure they won't mind me tagging along?'

'Course not.' Stella gives her shoulder a shake. 'I promise you'll enjoy it.' The door is on the latch, they follow the music to what looks like a sitting room; they've wisely moved out most of the furniture. It's lively inside but not packed like she'd feared. Even so, they have to shout above the din. Someone puts on *I saw Mummy kissing Santa Claus* and a few people are trying to dance to it.

Lily notices they have a help-yourself bar – she could do with a drink in her hand. A tall girl with shoulder length brown hair comes over to give Stella a big hug. She smiles. 'Hello, I'm Kathleen.' The girl looks younger than she was expecting. 'You must be Lily – I've heard all about you.'

'You're here!' A redhead pushes her way through to give Stella another hug. 'I'm Debbie.' Her lit up face is awash with freckles. The three of them fall into easy conversation; Lily only has to put in the odd word. She feels oddly put out that Stella should be such good pals with two girls that she's never met until now. Of course she's not jealous – that would be childish.

Kathleen leans in. 'You know the chap I was telling you

about last week – he's over there by the window; whatever you do, don't look now or he'll know I'm talking about him.'

Helped by a couple of glasses of punch, Lily begins to enjoy herself. The music changes – she recognises Guy Mitchell's new song *Chicka Boom*. They join in with the silly words of the chorus. She notices how Stella is already beginning to slur her words.

Lily makes her way over to the young lad in charge of the music. 'Have you got *She Wears Red Feather –*'

'*And a huly huly skirt*. I certainly do.' He puts his head on one side. 'I'll only put it on if you'll dance with me.'

He's still at that spotty stage – can't be more than eighteen. 'Why not,' she says.

Coming up for air she locates Stella deep in conversation with some big bloke who looks like he might play rugby. Though she's quite certain she'd never do anything like that again, Lily is keeping half an eye on her.

Later on she begins to worry when she can't see her anywhere. She weaves her way out of the room to where she can hear people cheering. They're crowded round the threshold. She can just see a dartboard on the opposite wall.

'It's nearest the bull,' someone says. The man Stella was talking to earlier throws the first dart; it misses and hits double top instead. 'Just getting' me eye in,' he says. With the bit between his teeth now, the next one lands in the outer ring of the bull. The crowd give him a rowdy clap.

'Move over,' Stella says. 'You've had two chances – now it's my go.' She elbows him in the ribs. The first dart bounces off the edge and gets the man jumping out of the way. 'Here, watch it, sweetheart!' one of them shouts out. Stella stares at the board and concentrates as she takes her aim. This time the dart sails straight as a die and lands right in the centre of the bullseye.

They all clap and jump up and down. The men are slapping her on the back like she's one of their own. One of them, a tall chap with a nice face says, 'If you can do that again with the next one lass, I'll give you five bob.'

Lily shakes her head; Stella wasn't so drunk after all.

CHAPTER TWELVE

April 1956

Will

He's thumping on the wood so hard it's bruising his fist. 'Arthur! Arthur! For God's sake wake up!' Will carries on banging on the door until a light finally comes on upstairs. He shouts up at the window, 'Arthur! I need your help!'

More light pours out into the garden; footsteps on the stairs, in the hallway, a key finally turns in the lock. 'Whatever is it?' One eye and a nose come round the doorframe at him. Hetty. 'Is that you, Will?'

'Aye, it's me.'

She opens the door a touch wider, her curlers a semicircle of zeros. 'Whatever's the matter?'

'It's our Ivy.' He takes in a long breath before he adds: 'I think she might be dead.'

'Don't talk so bloody soft–'

'No, I'm serious, Hetty. She's not breathing. Where's Arthur? He needs–' He doubles over to catch his breath: 'He has to run for the doctor quick as he can.'

'Good Lord above!' She yells up the stairs, 'Arthur get down here!' She tries to tie her dressing gown cord but her hands are shaking too much. 'I'll go over and see her for meself. I'm sure I'll–'

'No.' Will blocks her way. 'You don't want to see her like that.' He shouts round her, 'Arthur!'

The man's bare feet finally come into view on the stairs. 'Hold yer bloody horses, will ya?' He pushes his way past his wife to confront him. 'What in hell's name's all this fuss about?'

'It's our Ivy; I think she's dead. I'm pretty sure of it.' Will pulls on the man's pyjama sleeve, tugs him on towards the house. 'I need you to fetch the doctor.'

'How in bloody hell's name can she be?' Arthur stands his ground, scoffs in his face. 'She were as right as rain when I saw her this morning. She can't just have upped an' died.'

'Come and see for yerself.' He tugs harder until Arthur gets the message, pulls on his boots then grabs his topcoat from the hook by the door.

Will's front door is gaping wide open. He flicks the light switch as they step inside to reveal Ivy lying at the foot of the stairs in her nightie.

'Flaming hell!' Straight off, Arthur's face changes. He bends right down, stares from one of her fixed eyes to the other. 'Christ Almighty! Ivy! Ivy – wake up, lass!' He doesn't give up, slaps her cheeks and shouts, 'Wake up, will ya!'

Will wishes he could stop those fat, trembling hands from touching her face and now stroking her hair, stop him looking down at her body all twisted like it shouldn't be. 'Best leave her to me now,' he tells him. 'You need to fetch Doctor Blackhurst; see if he can do owt for her.'

Left alone again, Will stares down at his late wife. Her skin has turned the colour of an approaching storm. She looks much smaller; almost like a child; except the black centres of her open eyes seem much too knowing. He wants to shut her eyelids. He moves his hand towards her face, but then stops himself, thinking it would be better not to change a thing from what Arthur has just seen.

The doctor lives only a few streets away but it's bound to be a bit of a wait. No good, he can't keep still; he's all nerves. A weird silence has enfolded the house. Alert for the slightest sound, he can almost hear her soft footsteps descending the stairway right behind him. He goes into the kitchen. Cup of strong, sweet tea – that's what he needs.

Finding himself back in the front room, Will paces back and forth. The doctor is certainly taking his time; even in an emergency, he's the sort of man who would insist on fully dressing. Will gulps down the dregs of his tea. In the hall again, he's almost convinced Ivy has moved. Resting the cup on the bottom step, he gingerly checks her neck for a pulse.

Nothing. Standing up, he rakes his hair back, does it over and over trying to slow his thoughts down, to anchor them in what's going on right this minute; he mustn't let his brain spin out his control.

A squawk from the gate hinges and then the two men are rushing in on him. He's a tall man, the doctor – threadbare grey hair with quite a stoop to his back. 'Mr Bagshaw I presume. And the patient…'

'Right there.' Will's arm goes out to the side like he's introducing an act on the stage. 'She must have fallen down the stairs.'

The doctor throws his overcoat across the banister and knocks the teacup sideways with his leather bag; there's a dull crack as it lands on the hard tiles.

'Oh, dear me.' He bends over her as he goes through all the usual checks. 'Dear me.' A heavy sigh. 'I'm afraid the poor woman is beyond my help.' His fingers search her flopping neck – double-checking there's no pulse. Ruefully shaking his head he looks at Will and says, 'She's in God's hands now.'

Straightening up, the doctor's hands come together like he's about to pray. Will touches his arm. 'There must be something you can do for her, surely?'

'I'm afraid it's too late.'

Arthur staggers back against the wall. 'I can't ruddy believe it. This morning she were right as rain; humming a song to herself she were. "Morning Arthur" she says –' A shudder runs through the man. 'As bright as a daisy. "Is that the jumper your Annie was knitting?" – she were smirking like. "Just right on you, after all" she says, laughed out loud, in that way of hers.'

'Best you get back to your missus now,' Will tells him. He doesn't like to see a man, any man, cry like this. 'I can handle things from now on.'

He follows Arthur out. Will watches him shuffle up the path and out of the gate like a much older man.

'This is a sorry business.' The doctor moves his bag onto the table by the open door. His hooded eyes turn to Will. 'For a young woman in the prime of her life to fall like this – it's nothing short of a tragedy.'

He shakes his head several more times. Another long sigh, then, almost as an afterthought he says, 'I'm afraid the police will need to be informed. Don't concern yourself, Mr –um – Bagshaw, I'll make the necessary phone calls when I get home. In the meantime, I must insist you don't disturb anything here until you're given permission to do so.' Up close, Will catches a faint smell of whisky on the man's breath. Nodding, he hands him his hat and quietly closes the door behind him.

In the sitting room, the mantelpiece clock taps away at the silence. He drops down into his usual armchair then perches on the edge of the seat, his legs juddering.

His throat is rough as bark and still he draws hard on a cigarette he can't recall lighting. He's trying to think, though it's difficult to remember, if Dr Blackhurst offered his condolences. With Violet they all seemed to feel the need to press his shoulder while they said their '*so sorrys*' and the rest ont.

Headlights shine in through the gap in the curtains. He

hears gravel spray as a car pulls up sharp in the road outside. The engine dies then two doors slam one after the other – each echoes like gunshots around the cul-de-sac.

When he opens up, two uniform policemen are standing on either side of the doorframe. 'Mr Bagshaw?'

He nods.

'I'm Constable Fenner,' the big one says through a heavy moustache. 'This here's P.C. Clarke. Tragic business – may we offer our deepest condolences, sir.' He walks on in without being asked. 'We've been sent to safeguard the premises. Routine measure, like, when a death is sudden like this.'

'Mr Bagshaw.' On the threshold, the younger one takes off his helmet and rakes back his hair. Sergeant Clayton will be along directly.' He turns to guard the open doorway and the path beyond. His colleague, PC Fenner, carries on along the hall, steps around Ivy with barely a look and climbs the stairs and parks himself squarely on the top landing, legs splayed apart like a fielder as he bars the way.

Before long, another car pulls up. A man knocks on the open front door and strides in. 'Mr Bagshaw?' He takes off his hat as he steps into the hall. 'I'm Detective Sergeant Clayton, City Police.' Stiff back and severe haircut of an ex–soldier. An officer's voice. Not in uniform but wearing a jacket and tie beneath his gabardine.

'She's there.' Will nods towards the foot of the stairs as if it were needed. Clayton strides past him and squats down right beside Ivy. 'The poor woman,' he says. 'Such a tragic end to a young life.'

Will leaves him to it. In the front room he's up and down like a jack-in-the-box. After a bit, the boards above his head creak where they must be poking around up there. Muffled voices – he can't make out what they're saying.

It goes quiet for a bit and then one of them is off again. This time the footsteps come right overhead and Will realises they're snooping around in his own bedroom. The feet move on.

He hears them on the stairs – can't make out much though it's clear instructions are being given. Will sits down in his usual armchair and waits.

The sergeant comes into the room holding one hand out as if to push him away: 'No need to get up, Mr Bagshaw. Don't disturb yourself.' He lowers himself into Ivy's chair; greying temples, narrow eyes peering at him. 'I'll need to take a full statement from you but we can do that later,' he says, with only a dart of a smile. From an inner pocket, he withdraws a small notebook. 'Just a few preliminary questions if you wouldn't mind.'

He wants names, ages and so forth, then, looking at his watch, he says. 'I understand your wife's physician – Doctor Blackhurst – called earlier. Chap lives nearby, so I'm told. At this stage, I believe it'll save us all time if I go and have a word with him directly.' Clayton springs to his feet like a much younger man. 'Stay where you are, Mr Bagshaw – I'll be back shortly to take a longer statement from you.'

Defying orders, Will follows him out into the passageway. A sharp draught sneaks round the door in the sergeant's hand. 'Please leave everything just as it is for now, Mr Bagshaw. Procedure, you understand?' The man's coattails fly out after him.

Suddenly dog-tired Will goes into the kitchen and sits down at the table to rest his head in his hands.

He must have fallen asleep because he wakes with a start when the door opens and Sergeant Clayton comes in. 'Ah, there you are, Mr Bagshaw – you had us thinking for a moment you'd upped and disappeared.'

Will sits upright. 'Why would I go an' do such a thing?'

'Quite so.' Leaning heavily on the table-top, the sergeant pulls another chair out. 'Right, Mr Bagshaw – let's begin at the beginning shall we?' Will notices the way the man's narrow moustache lines up exactly with the edges of his mouth.

'My lad's away camping – he's just joined the boy scouts. I was asleep in bed, woke up at around ten when I heard a strange noise.'

Clayton keeps looking down – seems to be fascinated by Will's hands of all things. The policeman follows every movement as he picks up his pack of cigarettes and tips one out. 'P'raps it were quarter past ten; hard to be exact.' The match won't strike and Will has to try two more before he can finally light up. 'Anyroad, it were around that–'

'I understand Ivy was in fact your *second* wife – or so Doctor Blackhurst informed me. Is that correct?'

Surprised, Will says, 'Aye, that's right.' He's back up on his feet searching for the ashtray. When he walks behind the policeman, Clayton's head flicks round after him. 'Would you mind telling me a little about your first wife, Mr Bagshaw?'

'What's that got to do with owt?'

'If you'll allow me to ask the questions, Mr Bagshaw.'

Will shrugs. He's ready with all the facts. 'Her name were Violet. Violet Kenton afore I married her. She were taken ill all of a sudden and died in the Royal.' He shakes his head: 'Only thirty-three. Coroner's inquest said it were due to encephalitis. That's when the brain–'

Clayton holds up a hand. 'I'm aware of the condition, Mr Bagshaw. Tell me – when was that *exactly*?'

'Call me Will, please – everyone does. It were in the spring about two years back.'

'The *exact* date, if you wouldn't mind.'

'Twenty-seventh of May 1953. Not a date I'll forget in a hurry.'

'I see.'

'And you married Ivy when?'

'November thirtieth, 1953.'

Clayton's raised eyebrows say it all. 'I see.' The sergeant leaves a full minute before filling the silence. 'You appear to have gotten over your grief remarkably quickly.'

Will sits down to face the bugger fair and square. 'Look, Sergeant – Violet and myself, we'd been planning to part – to go our separate ways. But we'd been putting it off – couldn't decide what we were goin' to do about our Brian. I met Ivy when I were down in London visiting an old army mate. The two of us hit it off right away – you know how it is?' One of Clayton's eyebrows seems to be stuck a good half-inch above the other.

'I'll be honest with ya, I'd already been seeing Ivy on and off when I could; we'd been to the pictures and that. Then, out of the blue Violet was taken ill.' That pencil of his keeps scribbling at that notepad like a mouse scratching behind plaster. 'So you see, our wedding wasn't as hasty as some might think – if they didn't have the full picture, that is.' He takes a drag of his cigarette. 'After Violet died, me and my lad moved down to the smoke but neither of us could settle there. I married Ivy and applied for a senior nursing job at the Royal. The three of us moved back up here about eighteen months ago.'

Peering straight at him, Clayton says, 'How very tragic that your second wife should have passed away after only two and a half years of married bliss.'

Before he can answer, Constable Fenner knocks at the door. 'The pathologist has just arrived, sir.'

'Good. Show him in.' It's no longer Will's house. He stands up beside the sergeant; smells the cloying stench of whatever's holding the man's hair in place.

Clayton strides towards the door. 'I'd like you to join us, Mr Bagshaw, if you wouldn't mind. It won't take a moment.'

A bald-headed man appears in the doorway. He nods towards the sergeant,

greets him with a single word, 'Clayton.'

'This is the deceased's husband,' the sergeant says, 'William Bagshaw.'

'Sad business,' the pathologist says in place of a greeting. Behind his wire-rimmed glasses, the man's eyes seem too small for his round face.

The three of them squeeze into the narrow hall. The other two men are wearing raincoats; Will is out-of-step in his dressing gown. They all stare down at Ivy. She could be asleep if it wasn't for her colour and the awkward angle of her limbs.

'I'm sorry to ask this, Mr Bagshaw,' Clayton says, 'but could you please state for the record, whether your wife is in the same position you discovered her in?'

'No, she's not. She's more in the hallway than when I first found her.' Will's not sure if he should go on with his story but does. 'I had to drag her a bit – so I could give her artificial respiration. I tried to get her breathing. I'm a trained nurse so I know how to do it right. Couldn't lift her up properly – the weight of her was too much. To tell you the truth, I could see there weren't much chance, that it were already too late, but I did me best.'

The pathologist fellow is peering at the floor then up the staircase. Turning his attention back to Ivy, he bends right over to look directly into her black eyes. 'I see.' Looking up at Will he says, 'Please excuse us now, Mr Bagshaw.'

CHAPTER THIRTEEN

Will's been trying not to pace out his impatience with all the toing and froing of the undertaker's lads. From what's been said, it's clear they're getting ready to carry her body out. Unbidden, he pictures Ivy's laughing face as he stumbled over the same threshold with her in his arms. 'Your new home, lass,' he'd announced. He remembers her shrieks, head right back: *'For pity's sake put me down, darlin' or we'll both take a tumble.'*

From the doorway, he watches them slam shut the doors of the hearse and pull away. Already, the birds are warming up to begin their morning chorus. He looks up towards the moors where there's a low glow across the sky.

Chinks of light are evident from every house in the street; all of them must have been up watching when the undertaker's van arrived; they must all be awake wondering what might happen next.

Stifling a yawn, he checks at his watch; still time for a few hours kip before he'll have to go to collect Brian and doubtless face yet more prying.

A voice from the landing says, 'That's it for now, Mr Bagshaw.' P.C. Fenner has his helmet back on. 'Been a long old night eh? Thanks for the tea and that. I expect we could all of us do with a bit of shut-eye now.'

Will steps aside. 'Aye.' He's out of words, hoarse from answering all their questions. He seems to have said more tonight than he's done in years.

The constable hesitates like he wants to say something more. He puts a hand on Will's shoulder and squeezes his reassurance: 'You take care of yourself and that lad of yours.'

Earlier on, the burly policeman had shown sympathy when Will had cried over Ivy's photo. After the grilling Clayton had given him, the two of them had exchanged a look. Though it wasn't Fenner's place to say anything about the way he was being treated, the man looked uncomfortable – guilty even. Later on, Will had overheard him say to the young PC that anybody with eyes in their head could see Ivy had tripped on the landing. He'd muttered something about Clayton being a hard-nosed sod – how the man had a reputation for being a stickler, insisting on doing things by the letter of the law whatever the circumstances.

The younger man had confessed this was the first time he'd ever seen a dead body and it had given him the heebie-jeebies, and Fenner had warned him that, in their line of work, he'd have to get used to seeing corpses. 'Mind you, we all get upset when they're young like this poor woman,' he'd said. 'Untimely,' he'd said – odd word for a man like that to use. Untimely implied this wasn't the rightful time for Ivy to have died.

Behind him now, PC Fenner clears his throat. 'We'll keep you informed, sir. It's over to the pathologist now.' As Will follows him out he says, 'If you have any questions or owt, you'd best phone the station an' ask to speak to Sergeant Clayton.' A decent chap – not like his bastard of a sergeant.

'Can't think straight right at this minute,' Will tells him. 'The shock I expect.' They leave it there. He's dying to shut the door and the wind catches it; he can't stop the sound of that final slam echoing into the street.

Will locks up and slides the heavy top bolt across. Does the same to the back door, putting the keys in his trouser pocket for safety. He climbs the stairs, goes into his bedroom and opens the window before pulling the curtains closer together. Most of the lights in the close have gone out.

Ivy's clothes are still piled up on the chair: the beige skirt, her white blouse, those two nylon stockings dangling over one arm ending in the two flimsy silhouettes her feet have shaped.

He tells himself it's all over. Before he left, Sergeant Clayton had said, 'Right you are, Mr Bagshaw. That would appear to be it.' An odd note to finish on. With them coppers you could never be certain of anything.

CHAPTER FOURTEEN

May 1956

Though she'd known it was happening, it's a shock when Lily walks in through the front door and barely recognises her own home. The kitchen table has vanished along with all four chairs; even the rag rug from the floor – the one her gran had made – is rolled up and resting on a pile of boxes. How the colours in the scraps from clothes the family had once worn have faded over the years. Her eyes travel to words scrawled on the sides and tops of boxes. *Pans. Cutlery/ Knives. FRAGILE (underlined twice) Best Crockery.*

No chance of a cup of tea then.

By the sink, her mam is red-faced, hair tied in scarf with a wet rag in her hand. 'It's not too late you know, Lil.' She drops the cloth into the sink and wipes her hands on her pinny. 'You can change your mind and come with us.' There's more grey than ever in her escaping curls.

'We've been through this and I've made up me mind.' Lily sighs. 'I'd feel lost living in the middle of nowhere – can't think of anything worse than looking out on nothin' but muddy fields in every direction.' She shudders.

'But it's so beautiful up there – you'd soon get used to it.'

'And what would I do for work? Besides, I already paid Mrs Ferguson a month's deposit.'

There are footsteps overhead – she can't tell if it's her father or George walking around up there. This last year her brother has shot up and now the two of them are almost the same height and build. Nodding at father and son, people are fond of saying how the apple hasn't fallen far from the tree. She shuts her eyes and tries not to think about how much she's going to miss George.

Lily isn't expecting the hug – to be standing in the kitchen pressed up so awkwardly against her mother for the first time in goodness knows how long, to breathe in the familiar smell she'd recognise blindfolded. 'Nothing stays the same for ever,' she tells her mam. 'If someone had asked me a year ago, I'd have said the last place I'd end up working was in a ruddy hospital.'

Her mother is sobbing – the skin on Lily's neck is damp with her tears. 'Don't fret,' she tells her, remembering all the times it was the other way round. 'I'll come an' see you – I promise. Besides, it's about time I was out from under your feet.'

Instead of wallpapering the bedroom, Lenny Townsend has nipped round next door to watch the Cup Final on their telly. Face like a wet weekend, not for the first time Madge had voiced her disappointment, trotting out the old adage that shoemakers' children are the worst shod.

The armchair he's offered, like all the others is swathed in embroidered clothes. No ashtrays so he daren't light up. In many ways he'd rather be listening to the match on his wireless.

'Of course Birmingham are the favourites by a mile.' Stan Goodman nods, cocksure his team are going to win.

'So they say.' Time for a bit of fun. 'P'raps you'd care for a little wager?'

'Seems hardly fair to take yer money.'

Lenny holds out his hand. 'Five bob on Manchester.' Stan's happy to shake on it.

Three minutes in he's on his feet as Hayes puts City in the lead. 'Early days yet,' Stan mutters. Smiles like a Cheshire cat when they equalise fifteen minutes in. 'What did I tell you?'

Before the half-time whistle, Mrs Goodman comes in; her wide arse blocks the screen. 'Cup of tea, Lenny?' It's impossible to see round her.

How could he have forgotten the pair of them are teetotal? 'No, ta,' Lenny says cocking his head to peer around her. It's as much as he can do to be polite.

She comes back in balancing a tray with yet another embroidered cloth on it.

After stirring in three sugars, Stan dunks a biscuit in his tea and sucks at it. 'Aye, everything still to play for.' Once his missus has left the room he leans in. 'Care to make it double or quit, Len?' Not that virtuous after all.

'Why not make it a quid?'

'Aye – why not.'

Sixty minutes in the picture starts to roll and Stan gets up to adjust the horizontal hold. A shout from the commentators suggest someone's scored but there's no way of knowing who. It takes a further minute before it's clear it was City. The picture steadies at last and then a couple of minutes later they go and score again. 'Three one.' Lenny rubs his hands together. 'Looks like you owe me that quid.'

'Game's not over,' Stan tells him. For some reason the men on the screen aren't running around. A change of angle shows City's goalie is lying out on the pitch. 'Looks like he's bin knocked out,' he says with obvious relish. 'Don't fancy their odds without him.' Stan frowns. 'Troutman, eh – what sort of a name's that?'

'It's Trautmann,' Lenny tells him. 'He's German.'

'German eh? Well that explains it.' He's pleased Stan doesn't elaborate. They watch Trautmann get to his feet though he looks anything but fit to play on. His head looks wonky. Even on a ten-inch screen you can see the man's in real pain. Despite his injury, he makes two further saves.

A few days later Lenny waves the Daily Mirror sports page in Stan's face. 'Says here, City's goalie – our German friend – played on with a broken neck.'

Before she leaves the house, Alma Marsden stoops to pick up the airmail letter lying on the front mat. It can only be from Fred. The damp has made the thin paper go floppy and she opens it with care the way she's learnt to. It never ceases to amaze her that from the other side of the world he can describe in his spidery handwriting all manner of things that have happened to him and she can read about it a matter of days later.

As usual, he begins: *Dear Mam & Dad, Nobby, Stella & Tommy, Hope this letter finds you all well.* What would he do if one of them got seriously ill? Since he'd met that girl of his – Margery Hope – there's been no more talk of him coming back. With a bus to catch, she scans through the contents just in case. Like always, it's all *we* did this and *we* did that. Margery – Madge more often now – is by his account a lively sort of girl. Reading between the lines, it can be only a matter of time before a wedding's on the cards. Thinking back to when he was a little boy, it would never have occurred to her that someday he'd be getting married to an Australian girl and none of them would be there to witness it.

Stella hears the music from out in the street – inside it's almost deafening. Her mam and dad must be out, that's for sure, or they'd never put up with the racket.

In the living room, her brother is bobbing around to *Zambezi* while Tommy is trying to snap his fingers to the beat but not getting it right. After the final shout of *Zambezi* the record finishes. Nobby already has another a disc in his hand; he takes it out of the sleeve, holding it by the edges like a precious object.

The crackling ends followed by a click as the arm lifts off the disc. 'You know this one,' he tells Tommy, no longer needing to shout. As always, her son looks up at him with undisguised adoration.

She coughs and their two heads turn together. *See You Later, Alligator,* Bill Haley sings out and they all sing the next line back. Nobby gives her a sideways smile, grabs her by both hands and, despite her protests, pulls her into the centre of the room. 'Come on, Stell, let's see you rock and roll.'

She's not much of a dancer but he spins her around this way then that like she hasn't done in ages. As the record ends, out of breath and dizzy, she flops down on the sofa.

Tommy jumps up and down. 'Can we have this one next?'

'Your lad's quite a Bill Haley fan,' Nobby tells her with a wink. When he tries to take the record from him, Tommy snatches it away. 'I want to put it on. I'll be careful. Please.'

'Aye, alright but mind you don't scratch it.'

She peers at her brother. 'How come you're in such a good mood?'

'Why not? I just sold that Austin for a tidy profit. Things are looking up.' Stella's pretty certain his high spirits have very little to do with selling a car.

CHAPTER FIFTEEN

Lenny

The rousing strains of "Abide With Me" drift across the churchyard. At a respectful distance, Lenny Townsend is sitting on a damp bench finishing off a cheese and pickle sandwich. In truth, his back's not really up to grave digging these days. It's cold for May. The weather's been changeable all week and he'd like to get this poor woman's grave back-filled before the forecasted heavy rain arrives and makes the upturned subsoil all claggy.

Since the end of the war, he's taken on more and more household work to make ends meet – a nice bit of money to be made. Grave digging's more of a sideline these days and not a very profitable one at that. Still, he's glad there are fewer young ones to bury than during the war.

When the vicar had given him the chit, he hadn't recognised the address of the deceased straight away – that part of town isn't on his window-cleaning round, not yet anyway. He'd read about her accident in the local paper a week or two back. There'd been a photo of the poor young woman before she'd tragically fallen down the stairs to her death. Nice looking she was. A sudden death usually meant the coroner's investigations delayed the burial. Makes him feel sorry for the relatives – having the funeral hanging over them for so long.

An unfortunate accident, so the account in the paper had said. Chewing on the last few mouthfuls, Lenny reflects on what a strange business it is that someone so young and healthy should up and die just like that while others last well beyond their allotted three score years and ten.

Recognising the strains of the Purcell march – the one the organist usually finishes on – Lenny puts away his bait tin to stand, cap off and head bowed, while the mourners file out of the church and gather around the graveside.

He spots the copper straight away – man about forty-odd with a ramrod back. He's positioned himself on the periphery. Legs planted apart, he starts to rotate his hat as the ritual of the interment begins.

The vicar likes to keep this part mercifully short. A few umbrellas are opened against the drizzle. It's a scant crowd – not much of a send-off. A good half of the mourners have already turned their backs; dabbing at their faces, they walk past the copper towards the lynch gate. Lenny's close enough to hear one woman say, 'I heard she'd been drinking.'

'Shh! For pity's sake,' a grey-haired woman tells her, 'Now's not the time.'

The rain is setting in. He's pretty sure he recognises the widower from his picture in the paper. With his dead wife not yet fully interned, the man walks away from the graveside without so much as a second glance.

Freed of their own obligations, the remaining mourners begin to depart. Lenny overhears various mutterings about where they should go to warm up and a nearby pub is suggested. A few more follow their lead, peeling off one at a time.

The policeman's head turns to study each of them though his attention keeps wandering back to the widower already some distance away, leant against the high stone pier of the cemetery's smaller gate. Lenny narrows his eyes to watch how, with unsteady hands, the bereaved man is lighting a cigarette.

He reluctantly transfers the fag to his left hand to accept the patted handshakes from each man in turn. The women hug him to their sombre best coats.

Lenny's too far away to hear anything – no doubt it'll be all the usual words of condolence. The vicar finishes up, clasps a few hands and then walks off towards the vestry.

He can't get on with his work because two women are lingering at the graveside; one of them holding a small posy. From the colour he'd hazard a guess they're harebells or forget-me-nots though he can't be certain from this distance. They both look young – though it's hard to see their faces under their mourning hats. Both bend their heads as one drops the flowers into the open grave.

A piece of white paper breaks free, flutters up for a moment before it too falls into the void. He recalls how the Victorians had a whole vocabulary of flowers and their meanings – for-get-me-not was obvious enough. The two women blow kisses into the grave.

Not for the first time, he ponders the question of why have so many women taken to attending funerals these days. A few years back, it wasn't the done thing – aside from widows and daughters, only the men would go to the service. The women used to busy themselves preparing the spread they'd come back to; that way they were saved the ordeal. Nowadays, so many things seem to be changing for no good reason.

Over by the lynch gate he hears raised voices – not something you'd expect in the circumstances. The policeman soon strides over to see what the fuss is about.

Clutching her friend's arm, the woman with the flowers finally turns from the grave. As they pass him, the church clock begins to strike, the racket stealing some of her words '.... miss her... he's got... of her... We all...'

Once the last deep notes have faded the graveyard lapses into a respectful silence.

Everyone's left but the policeman hasn't moved. Lenny

hangs back with his spade in hand. The man takes out his notebook – the rain must be making the paper damp; Lenny wonders if the pencil is still making its mark.

Notebook in hand, the copper approaches the graveside and peers down into it.

Lenny's taken by surprise when the copper strides over and says, 'My name is Detective Sergeant Clayton.' No handshake. 'Would you mind retrieving that scrap of paper for me? See it – just there on the lid of the coffin.'

Frowning, Lenny reluctantly follows the direction of the pointing finger. 'Seems to me such a thing would be wrong,' he says. 'I don't hold with violating the sanctity of the grave.'

'Nonetheless, I require your assistance.'

Lenny daren't argue – not with a copper. He goes off to fetch his ladder. It's a bit of a caper to clamber down into the grave, not exactly the normal thing to do with the coffin lying in its final resting place.

The sergeant offers no help as he struggles back out again – doesn't want to get his own hands dirty. Lenny hands over the scrap of paper unread. Thanking him, the copper presses a more-than-generous two bob bit in his palm.

Leaning on his spade, he watches the sergeant scrutinise the note before laying it carefully inside his notebook and snapping it shut. 'Carry on, man,' he barks, like he was back in the army, then strides off to his nice warm car.

Lenny pulls the layers of damp sacking off the mounded-up earth and begins to shovel the soil down into the hole. The heavy clods thud onto the coffin lid and soon cover any trace of the small, blue posy.

For the next hour the graveyard continues to ring with the blunt echoes of his shovelling and the sound of falling earth.

CHAPTER SIXTEEN

September 1957

Lily

They're in the lounge bar of the Blue Moon on the corner of Cable Street. It's unusual for them to be out on a Wednesday evening but they'd had quite a day of it on the wards and Stella had declared that a couple of drinks after work would do them good.

Lily thinks she can hear Dean Martin singing *Memories are Made of This* but it can't be playing on the jukebox in the public bar – not when the place is stuffed full of men. With only a bedsit to call home these days, she welcomed any change of scene; instead of being in there with the men, the four of them – Lily, Stella, Kathleen and Debbie – are stuck in this dingy room because Kathleen insisted on it; according to her, only *common women* drink in public bars.

Lily stares down at the fire; the coal isn't properly alight and a trickle of smoke is escaping to hang in a thin layer along the ceiling. It's starting to sting her eyes. If she could see a poker, she'd knock the coals together and get it going.

Every so often a raucous noise erupts from the public bar

– cries, or cheers, or roars of laughter from jokes too far away to hear. More than an hour's passed since they shared a round of drinks. Lily's half a cider is nearly gone and Stella's already polished off her gin and orange. Debbie lights a fag while Kathleen is idly running a finger round the rim of her empty glass, making it ring like she's summoning a genie.

'Our Fred's chuffed to be a dad – though neither of them expected it to happen so soon.' Stella gives a throaty laugh. She opens her handbag and gets out a couple of dog-eared snapshots to show the others; Lily's already seen them. 'Course, with them being in Australia, we haven't seen him – nor likely to more's the pity.'

Recently Lily's had this strange sensation like her life is running backwards and not forwards. She's the oldest amongst them – Kathleen and Debbie are still in their early twenties and even Stella is a couple of months younger. Just a few weeks shy of twenty-nine; it seems she's well and truly on the shelf.

Debbie sighs. 'I don't know why that ward sister keeps picking on me. Other people get away with murder but she notices the slightest damned thing I…'

While she's going over old ground, Stella leans across. 'They're going to call him Luke – the babby that is – after … well, you know.'

'Oh.' Lily can't say more; it's a shock to hear his name again after all this time. After the war she'd held out hope that Luke had miraculously survived – that he'd only been taken prisoner. How often in her daydreams had he turned up on her doorstep making a joke of yet another daredevil escape?

Debbie is describing how some old bloke on the Diabetic Ward was putting his hand right up her skirt while she was making his bed. 'I reported it to Doctor Jordon, and guess what he said?' She doesn't wait for a reply. 'He said I shouldn't make a fuss, because the poor bugger will likely be dead in a month.'

'That's not the point,' Kathleen chips in. 'He may not be long for this world, doesn't mean he can try to feel you up and expect you just to smile back.'

'Too bloody right. Anyway, I said to him: "Dr Gordon, I'm a respectable young woman and, if any man, young or old, dying or otherwise, tries it on with me, he'll get a good slap on the face for his trouble".'

Doing her best to show an interest in their conversation, Lily asks, 'What did Dr Gordon say to that?'

Debbie shakes her head. 'The man just laughed out loud – right in my face. Far as he was concerned it were a flamin' joke.' This doesn't surprise Lily; even the doctors try to take liberties and not just the young ones either.

Another cheer goes up next-door and she wonders if there might be a darts match on. She knows Stella would love to be in there taking them all on.

They fall silent, nursing their empty glasses.

Lily jumps when the outside door opens. A tall man in a leather jacket walks in. At first, she doesn't recognise him out of his work clothes; it takes a moment for her to remember his name's Will – not Bill for some reason – and she's seen him a few times at the hospital. It's not easy to miss a male nurse when there are only two of them.

Funny job for a man, she'd thought. They'd spoken a couple of times in passing – the odd word or two but no more.

No hat; he rakes back his hair before rubbing his hands together. 'Can I buy you ladies a drink?' As he reaches inside his jacket pocket for his wallet, she wonders if he isn't being a bit flash.

Trust Kathleen to answer straight off, 'I'll have a gin and tonic, ta very much.'

Stella has the brass-face to ask for the same. 'Well, he did ask,' she whispers behind her hand. Deb tells him she'd like a small sherry though Lily's never seen her drink sherry before.

When he turns his attention to Lily, she's struck by how different he looks out of his nurse's uniform – younger; especially with his hair combed back like it is. He's a good-looking man when he smiles.

'And what will you have, Lily?' He's remembered her name. Even his voice is different – more posh than he sounded at work.

'Just a half of cider will do me.' Lily colours up; has to look away from the way he's looking back at her. 'I'm on duty first thing in the morning,' she reminds herself out loud.

'Me too.' He gives her a sideways smile like the two of them are sharing a secret. 'It's half an hour till closing time. Have something a bit stronger – live a little.'

She can't think straight. 'Seeing as how you insist,' she says, 'I'd love a Babycham.'

He walks over to the bar and Kathleen nudges her, whispers: '*I'd love a Babycham*' and she realises it's the exact words they use in the adverts at the cinema and it must have come out just like that.

Lily studies him from across the room. When he turns sideways she notices the blue open-necked shirt under his leather jacket, the way his trousers are tapered and quite stylish.

He comes back with the drinks. 'Here we are, ladies.' As he hands them round his eyes keep singling her out. They clink glasses and say 'Cheers' like there's something to celebrate. To be different, Stella waits a second and then says 'Bottoms up!' and follows it with one of her silly laughs. Will's smile is a bit forced.

The dingy light gives him a mysterious look. His eyes are dark and moody – like a younger Tyrone Power.

'Drink up, ladies,' he insists. 'There's time for another one, if we're quick about it.' He won't let them pay a thing towards it. 'What kind of a man would I be if I let any lady buy her own drink?'

And then he's up at the bar buying another round.

When he comes back he sits down beside her. They shake their heads when he offers round his fag packet. Though he seems relaxed, she notices how his hands are restless; the tips of several fingers are stained yellow with nicotine. He's careful

116

to blow smoke sideways so it doesn't end up in their faces. And he keeps turning that smile in her direction.

It's late when they leave and Kathleen and Debbie dash off to catch the seven minutes to. Will crooks his elbows for her and Stella to take an arm each. 'Allow me to escort you two lovely young ladies to your doors.' It annoys her when Stella laughs too loudly at his put-on accent. A little lightheaded now, she's reminded of Dorothy arm in arm with the Tin man and Cowardly Lion in the Wizard of Oz. Up close his hair cream has a sweet but pungent smell.

The Marsdens' house is in darkness except for a light still on in Nobby's room. They wish Stella goodnight and watch her stumble up the path to the front door.

As she disappears inside, he pulls Lily in tighter. 'Alone at last,' he says – the exact same words Luke used all those years ago.

Without warning, the streetlight in front of them goes out. She can see only the dark outline of him now. He laughs. 'Bloody lights – they turn the blighters off just when you need 'em.'

The rest of the streetlights go out one after another until the two of them are in complete blackness. Perhaps it's the drink that makes her unconcerned to be alone in the dark with a virtual stranger. She finds herself excited by the possibilities.

Their footsteps fall into a rhythm. Her eyes have adjusted and she can make out the wavering line of the pavement's edge where it meets the road. Rounding the next corner, they catch that cold wind straight off the moors. She can't hide her shivering. His arm leaves hers and goes up around her shoulders instead.

Headlights come splashing towards them and Will raises a hand, hiding his eyes from those fierce, twin beams. They stop walking and wait for it to pass, watch it disappear around the next corner. The engine dulls into a long, low whine before it fades completely.

Newly blinded, she slowly makes out the shape of his head and it strikes her he could be any man. The warmth of his breath tells her their faces are close. It's such a delicious shock when she feels his lips on her mouth. The heat from him seems to spread itself around her, taking her out of the street, out of everything but this moment in the darkness. Their kiss goes on and on until she's tempted to break away but doesn't want to break the spell.

He's the first to pull away but only to kiss down the side of her neck; then his mouth comes back to hers and she feels his wet tongue begin to probe – asking her to let him inside. He tastes of smoke and whisky. His mouth is pressing so hard, his teeth catch on the edge of her lip and she tastes something steely that could be blood.

It's too much all at once: she has to push back on his chest and turn her head away to breathe freely again.

A hot whisper in her ear: 'What is it, Lily? What's wrong?'

'Nothing. I just need a moment, that's all.'

'Don't worry, lass.' One hand runs down her back to push her body back against his. 'Shut your eyes – you can trust me.'

CHAPTER SEVENTEEN

Will

Outside her digs a soft light is shining through the half-open curtains, allowing him to see her face more clearly. 'I love the colour of your eyes,' he tells her.

Lily disentangles herself, takes a step backwards. 'Don't look now,' she says. 'Mrs Ferguson is bound to be peering out of the window.'

'Your landlady – what's it to her? You're a grown woman after all.'

'Tell you the truth, I'm not sure she approves of men. No one seems to know if there was ever a Mr Ferguson. Some of the girls think she just made him up.'

Head back, Will laughs out loud. 'Then let's give the old girl something to look at.' He lifts her chin to tilt her head towards him. She doesn't resist though she's less responsive than before. Almost pushes him away as she says, 'Better go,' and with that retreats up the steps. She gives him a wave then lets herself in.

There'd been no talk of them meeting again; p'raps it might be for the best. All the same, on the way home he can't stop smiling – tonight's been quite a turn up for the books.

The Blue Moon isn't one of his regular watering holes. With

the weather improving, he'd gone for a bit of a wander. If he hadn't been almost out of fags, he would have walked straight past the place. Funny how things can sometimes hinge on the smallest coincidence – a moment's decision.

He'd hesitated on the threshold – the place had been crowded for a weeknight; the smoke so thick it had made his eyes smart. Inside, it was close and sweaty and damned noisy to boot. There was a darts match on making it quite a scrum – he'd had to force his way through to the bar. He'd knocked some bloke's pint arm and had to apologise more than once before tempers could flare.

In the long wait to be served, he'd nodded over to a couple of men he knew by sight. Away from the dart players, it was quieter – you could hear yourself think. His hair had been damp from the drizzle and, looking into the big mirror behind the counter, he'd smoothed it back into place. As if there wasn't enough noise, a young lad had squeezed past him to feed coins into the jukebox, peering in to watch the big machine rotate and drop his choice. He'd watched as the arm moved across to the edge of the disk until the needle released a soft and slow female voice…

'Evening, Mr Bagshaw,' the barman cut into his thoughts. 'What can I do you for?' He was surprised and a little annoyed to be recognised. Couldn't recall the man's name but remembered seeing the chap a few times in the bookies on Long Street. The barman seemed a bit put out when he'd asked for twenty Kensitas tipped because, unlike Woodbines and the like, he hadn't got them to hand.

The song on the jukebox kicked away from its slow introduction and he followed the antics of the skinny lad as he tried to jive back to his chums, all of them raising their voices to join in with the deep '*boom, boom boom's'* behind Rosemary Clooney's lead.

Though the beat of the music wasn't enough to give a damp Wednesday night a carnival atmosphere, Rosemary had done her best and managed to bring a genuine smile to his face.

'Here we go, mate, sorry for the wait.' The barman placed a new pack in his hand and that might have been it if a movement in the mirror behind hadn't caught his eye. He could see through into the lounge bar and straight away recognised one of the women as Lily Hetherington. He'd seen her at the hospital; hard for any red-bloodied man not to notice such a good-looking woman. Her figure had been remarked on more than once in his hearing. Lily – pretty name, quite an exotic sort of flower. One of the consultants had dubbed her Luscious Lily and there had been general agreement it was a flaming miracle that a woman like her was still single.

Will already had the pack of fags there in the palm of his hand. That would have been it if some impulse hadn't made him put them back down on the bar. 'Oh, and I'll have a box of strikes an' all,' he said. 'Nearly went off without 'em.'

As the barman was getting his matches, he had a chance to study Lily's image take a sip from a glass. 'That'll be tanner.'

Searching his pockets for change, he'd watched her mouth break into a smile. Something must have been said to make her laugh outright and he'd noticed how she raised her hand to hide her mouth. What was it she was hiding?

'Thanks a lot, mate.' On that note of finality, he turned his back and wormed his way out of the bar. Closing the door dampened down the noise – gave him time to think.

There'd been a moment when he wasn't sure. As he was standing there, a car had flew past and the spray had just missed his newly polished shoes. He'd pulled the wrapper off the new pack and let the cellophane fall down onto the wet tarmac.

Mrs Wright from next door was keeping an eye on his lad. He'd told her he was only going to stretch his legs for half an hour – how he was in need of a bit of fresh air. Squeezing his arm she'd said, 'Off you go then, pet. Take your time.' She was a good sort – a woman who understood how a man could unintentionally get caught up in things and lose track of time. Besides, it wasn't exactly a deadline, more an indication.

Outside the pub, he'd taken his time, weighed up the situation as he lit a cigarette. With that first lungful of smoke, he realised he'd already decided. A few more hurried drags before stubbing it out half-smoked to head off towards a different door. He'd pulled it open before he had chance to regret it.

The lounge bar was dimly lit and decidedly chilly compared to the ferocious heat next-door. Four nurses were gathered around a fire that was giving out no warmth. A collection of glasses sat on the copper-topped table – all of them empty apart from a couple of drowned lemon slices.

Their young faces had turn towards him expectantly – each giving him a smile of recognition. 'Hi, Will,' they said almost in unison. At that very moment a cheer had gone up from the public bar and it felt like the lads in there were egging him on. He crossed the room, pulled a chair away from one of the empty tables ready to sit down. The women had been quick to accommodate him – moving sideways on the sticking carpet to allow him into their circle.

On purpose, he'd sat opposite Lily Hetherington and she'd smiled at him before he even said a word. Seemed to him it was a secret, inviting smile. 'Well now,' he'd said, 'what can I get you lovely ladies?' None of them had refused his offer.

It's now too dark to see his watch face but he guesses it must be well after eleven. So what if he gets back a bit later? He'll give Mrs Wright a few bob for her troubles and she'll be happy as Larry, as his mate Brigsy used to say; all things considered it's a bargain. Where's the harm in him having a bit of a dalliance with an attractive woman? He's a free man after all.

CHAPTER EIGHTEEN

October 1956

Lily

This morning Mrs Ferguson is bent over to one side. 'My back,' she explains when Lily asks. 'It'll right itself soon enough – always does.' Wincing with each step, the woman carries on running the Ewbank over the runner in the hallway – keeping up standards. *I don't hold wi' doctors* is one of her many sayings so there's no point in even suggesting it.

After checking her watch, Lily offers to walk Ruffian before her shift.

It's barely light outside and unexpectedly cold. The fog wraps itself around her and she's glad to have the wolfhound trotting by her side though, in truth, he's a soppy old thing.

She hears a car engine before its lights come through the fog. It's a black Ford Consul – an easy shape to recognise even in the murk. The car passes by and then pulls in a few yards further along.

With the dog padding noiselessly by her side, her footsteps on the pavement are the only sound breaking the silence in the street. It's near impossible to make out if she's heading in the right direction. She's relieved when a lorry goes past though the fog soon closes in again. Ruffian's impatient – keeps sniffing the ground and pulling on his lead in his enthusiasm to be off.

An idling engine makes her turn around; she's caught in its headlights. Another black Consul – it looks like the same car as before.

Lily picks up her pace and the dog lurches forward hoping she'll break into a run. She's determined not to. A few yards behind, the car's lights illuminate the edge of the kerb, keeping pace with her – she daren't look back.

Up ahead, she thinks she can see a break in the railings. The park's main gates will be padlocked so the car won't be able to follow her inside. But the driver could. Engine thrumming, the car is still idling along right behind her. On balance, she's safer out here.

Lily pulls the dog to her side and turns to face the car that has now stopped.

Along with the engine, the headlights are switched off. A person gets out – she hears the door slam. It's a man. He raises his hat and says, 'Lily Hetherington – I thought it was you.'

Will Bagshaw– she knows his voice. Since that night she'd caught sight of him in the corridor a couple of times but he hadn't looked her way, hadn't sought her out and she wasn't about to make the first move. Maybe he didn't want to set off rumours but such coldness wasn't what she'd hoped for after such a passionate albeit brief encounter.

As Will comes nearer, Ruffian gives a low continuous growl. The closer he gets the more noise the dog makes until he's all out snarling and it's as much as she can do to hold him back.

At a safe distance, Will nods towards the dog. 'Quite the protector, isn't he?'

'Following us like that, you must have frightened him,' she says. 'Despite his size, he's normally a big softy.'

'If you say so.' His hat is a dark grey fedora – the sort Clark Gable wears. 'I wanted to be sure it was you – hope I didn't scare you.' His smile disarms her, the way it transforms his face. 'Believe it or not, I'm not in the habit of approaching strange women in the street.'

Ruffian drops down onto his haunches – he could be relaxing or planning to spring at Will given the slightest chance. 'I would offer you both a lift,' Will says, 'but I don't think the Hound of the Baskerville there would be too happy about it.'

'He hasn't had his walk yet.' She looks at her watch but it's impossible to make out the hands. 'I'd best get on – got to be at work soon.'

'If you're not otherwise engaged, Miss Hetherington, would you care to meet me this evening?' The same posh voice she remembers from that night. As himself, he adds, 'We could go to the pictures if you like.'

Lily's still struggling to hold the dog back. She wishes she could see into Will's eyes to be certain. Ah well – like her dad was fond of saying: nothing ventured, nothing gained. Over Ruffian's low growl she tells him, 'I'd like that.'

'Right – well, I'll leave you and Fang to it.' He tips his hat. It suits him. 'Pick you up at your digs at seven.' His eyes flick down to the dog. 'Might be safer if I don't come in.'

She's about to respond but the fog has already swallowed him up.

Will arrives bang on time. 'We'll have to walk,' he tells her. 'Damned car's playing up again.' Lily's on the point of recommending Nobby but thinks better of it.

The film he takes her to is a comedy – a farce with Brian Rix and Sid James. She'd had hopes for something more romantic. After the pictures, he suggests they call in for a drink.

They pass several pubs but he continues to lead her away from the main road. He's very quiet as they stroll side by side; Lily notices he doesn't take her arm this time.

She's never been in the Black Swan before – it's a funny little place tucked down a side street. Between all the heavy black beams the ceiling droops so low Will has to duck down several times.

His choice is a table in the far corner and he pulls out one of the chairs for her to sit while he stays on his feet. He puts his hat down on the tabletop like he's staking a claim. 'Let me guess,' he says, 'you'd love a Babycham?'

'Aye, I would.'

Watching him from behind, she concludes he really is a fine figure of a man – dresses well, slim but not skinny, tall without being lanky.

Looking around, she realises she's the only woman in the place; the sly glances of the other customers mark her out as an object of curiosity. Lily studies the hat on the table hoping they'll lose interest.

Over at the bar, Will's raised his voice. 'Why ever not?' With a full pint of bitter sitting on the counter in front of him, has to be her drink that's causing the problem.

The barman shrugs. 'Not much call for it round here.'

'Maybe if you stocked it, there might be.' Will leans over the counter. 'Have you thought of that?'

People are beginning to stare. Lily goes over and nudges his arm. 'I'm more than happy with half a cider,' she tells him. Pouring her drink, the barman looks at her and gives a sideways wink she hopes Will didn't notice.

He carries their drinks back to the table; the other drinkers are openly staring at them. 'Cheers then,' Lily says in an effort to lift the mood. When she raises her glass, he reluctantly does the same. 'Tell me, Will,' she says. 'What made you become a nurse?'

He leans in towards her. 'In the army I got to know a few of the medics.' He shakes his head. 'Couldn't help but admire the way they went above and beyond – risked their own lives day in day out to save a life or some poor bugger's leg – if you 'scuse my French.'

She smiles away his concern. A light comes into his eyes. 'They were the real heroes amongst us.' He's fiddling around with an unlit cigarette, turning it over and over. 'After I got demobbed, I saw they were advertising for people to go into nursing and I thought to meself: I might have missed the boat when it comes to becoming a doctor but I can still join the medical profession.'

Lily says, 'I suppose it were the same for me in a way. I mean–'

'You know, of a night, when most of the staff have gone home to their beds and it's just me in charge of the ward, I think to meself – I'm the one responsible for keeping these people alive; just me, standing between life and death.' He takes a sip of beer and sits back in his chair. 'It's quite a thought.'

December 1956

With the festive season coming up, Lily agrees to work extra shifts. In a letter to her mam she says she hopes to see them between Christmas and the New Year – *weather and Matron permitting.*

They meet up in the canteen between opposite shifts. 'I'll drive you up, if you like,' Will says when she mentions her plans. He puts his knife and fork together and sits back. 'We can easily get there and back in a day.'

'Must be a good sixty miles or more,' she says stirring her tea. 'What about the petrol – the rationing?'

He scoffs. 'Not a problem – along with the doctors, I'm exempt from all that. Besides, it'll give me chance to give the new Rover a good run out.'

'You've changed your car?'

'Aye.' He lights a cigarette, draws hard before blowing it

out through his nose. 'Couldn't rely on that Consul, so it had to go.' Through a haze of smoke, he says, 'You don't look too keen on the idea.'

'Just a bit surprised, that's all.'

His arm goes round her waist. 'Won't it be nice to take a trip together – just the two of us?' He lets go. 'Unless you're ashamed of keeping company with me.'

'Course not – don't be daft. Like I told you, our house is in the middle of nowhere.'

'So?'

'You might find it a bit boring.'

He takes her hand. 'If you're with me, how could I be bored?'

'They've certainly taken to country life. In her letters, our mam goes on about the pickles and homemade wine they've been making. Dad's bound to want to show you Winston, his cockerel – so-called because he definitely likes to rule the roost.'

Will lowers his voice. 'I don't mind if he wants to show me his cock.' His laugh is loud enough for nearby heads to turn in their direction. When he can get the words out, he splutters, 'Do I have to show him mine?'

Stifling her own amusement, she prods him in the ribs. 'Ow,' he says. 'That hurt.' Face suddenly sober, he stubs out his cigarette. 'That's all settled then.'

In her next letter she names the day. *My friend Will has offered to drive me up – just for the day mind. He's working the next morning.*

So, you've got yourself a young man, her mam replies. *And about time*!! How Lily resents those two exclamation marks.

By reply she tells her, *I haven't known him for long, so don't you go running ahead with the idea and embarrassing us both. Besides, he's hardly a young man – though he's not exactly old either.* It occurs to Lily she has no idea of his precise age. Using Will's own phrase, she adds, *He's a medical man – a senior nurse at the hospital where I work. I'm sure you'll all like him.*

They're lucky with the weather except for a few icy stretches. There aren't many cars on the roads; they pass a lot of cyclists and quite a few horses. With the help of a map, they find the cottage on the edge of a hamlet surrounded by fields full of sad-looking sheep.

Lily's taken aback by how rundown the cottage looks. The photos they'd sent her were taken when there were blue skies and flowers in bloom; now the front garden is home to piles of building material.

Will's forced to park on a patch of waste ground outside the gate. They step down into mud. Before they reach the front door, a couple of hens run off squawking. Looking round she spots the footings of the extension her dad is planning to finish come the better weather.

The front porch is full of boots and raincoats. Instead of knocking, she opens the door and shouts, 'We're here.'

It's all hugs to start with. Such a show of affection almost has her in tears.

George squeezes the life out of her. 'Missed you so much, Lil. Christmas weren't the same without you.'

She steps back. 'I swear you've grown a couple of inches.' The low ceilings make her brother seem even taller.

Hat in hand, Will waits to be formally introduced. 'And you must be Will,' her dad says holding out his hand. 'Nice to meet you at last.'

Will is full of charm – even shakes her brother by the hand and says, 'How d'ya do, young man.'

Their old furniture is crowded into just one room – quite a contrast to the neat orderliness of the old house. Through one of two small windows, Lily looks up at the heavy clouds shrouding the hills. At least it's warm – a fire is roaring in the hearth releasing the pleasant smell of wood-smoke instead of coal. A bunch of holly hangs above the fireplace and familiar paper garlands droop from the beams. No room for a Christmas tree if they'd wanted one.

Taking off her coat, she hopes her disappointment doesn't show.

'This place might not look up to much now,' her dad says, 'but come next Christmas it'll be twice the size.'

'Really?' Will's eyebrows go up. 'Lily tells me you're planning to do all the work yourself.' Voice all formal, he adds, 'Seems quite ambitious.'

''Spect I'll be helping him out at weekends,' George says.

Looking over at her mam, her dad says, 'An' Flora's not averse to a bit of hard graft, are ya love?'

Will frowns. 'I wouldn't have thought heavy building work appropriate for any woman.'

Her dad stares at him. 'I meant wi' the lighter stuff – the painting and such like. Rest assured, I'll not be asking any wife of mine to help me lay blocks or owt like it.'

'Sit yerselves down,' her mam says, 'I'll go an' put a brew on.' Poking her head round the corner, Lily surveys the small kitchen-cum-scullery. She would offer to help but there's not room for two in there.

'We made good time,' Will tells them. 'Lucky I've just had a brand new set of tyres fitted or we'd never have made it up some of the hills.'

'Good,' her dad replies – just that. Never one for polite conversation, the next thing out of his mouth is, 'What d'you reckon to this damned Suez malarkey then, Will?'

Will clears his throat. 'I make it a rule not to get involved in politics, Mr Hetherington. Whoever's in power, I believe in leaving them to do their job just as I get on with mine.'

Her dad nods – not the sort of nod that suggests agreement. 'Must say, I was surprised when our Lily said you'd be *driving* up here – what with the petrol shortage an' that.'

Will moves her mother's knitting out from behind his back. 'As a medical man, I'm exempt from petrol rationing. Vital work, you see.'

Her dad leans forward in his chair. 'Wouldn't have thought they made that exception so you could go off on this sort of a jaunt.'

Cups rattling, her mother comes in with a laden tray. She's used the best china. 'Can't tell you how grand it is to have our Lil home at long last. Thank you for bringing her, Will.'

'Mam's made one of her fruit cakes.' George winks. 'I saw her put gravy browning in it.'

'Take no notice of him,' her mam says. 'It were only a few drops just to add a bit of colour.'

'Made with our own eggs too,' her dad pipes up. 'Mind you, thanks to this cold weather, the old girls have gone on strike.'

'Nice cup of tea, Mrs Hetherington,' Will is sitting bolt upright, awkwardly balancing the delicate cup on its saucer.

Her mam's smile is trying hard. 'Seeing how you're such a good friend of our Lily's, p'raps you'd better call me Flora.'

Her dad looks away – doesn't suggest Will should start calling him Jack.

'I hear you have a little lad,' her mam says.

'Not so little now,' Will tells her. 'He was ten last birthday.'

'We were expecting you to bring the lad with you,' her dad says. 'Is he poorly?'

'No – he's full of beans.' Will's smile fades. 'I thought it might be best not to drag him way out here. Better for him to stop at home with the neighbours keeping an eye on him.'

'I see,' her mam says.

The conversation continues in fits and starts. Lily never would have thought she could feel this uncomfortable sitting by the fire surrounded by her family. But then again this is their home, not hers – not anymore.

Once they've finished with the sandwiches and cake, Will springs to his feet. 'We'd best be thinking about getting on our way.'

'So soon?' Her mam's shocked. 'But you've only just got here.'

Will shakes his head. 'They're forecasting more snow. The last thing we want is to get stuck in a snowdrift out here in the back of beyond as I'm sure you'll agree.'

Her dad stands up. 'Aye, you're not wrong there.' Looking only at Lily he adds, 'We wouldn't want you taking any kind of risk with your life.'

CHAPTER NINETEEN

January 1957

Stella

Stella wakes – her heart arrhythmic, sweat soaking the back of her nightdress and a terrible fear knotted in her stomach.

A recurring dream – although she might have dreamt that too. All those people crowded round with their queer, fixed smiles. Always the same young, frightened woman lying on the bed, the life bleeding out of her – so dark a red it's almost black; breath rattling in her throat as she forms words the old lady sitting by her side has to bend to catch.

Vision clearing, already, Stella can't be sure of the woman's identity or what she was trying to tell her. It was a warning – she's sure of that. Could it have been Lily? She has no clear recollection of the dying woman's face. Has she dreamt this before? Her gran used to say that dreams are the way the dead communicate with the living.

A shiver runs through her. Sitting up, she tries to shake off such foolishness. It's not difficult to guess what brought on this nightmare.

Her bedroom walls are tinged green where the streetlight

is shining through the thin material of her curtains – it makes the room look like it's underwater. Stella throws back the blankets to cool herself though it doesn't stop her going over what she recalls of the dream – the precious little that's left.

It can't be very late – the streetlight outside is still on. Right on cue it goes out plunging her into darkness. Blinded, Stella's hand creeps across to turn on the bedside lamp. The hands of her watch are at eleven minutes past eleven.

Feeling cooler, she stares at the edge of the lampshade, at the spot where the fringe is coming away. Her eyes are drawn further in to the bare bulb at its heart.

Her alarm clock wakes her at twenty to six. Squinting against the room's unnatural brightness, she reaches to switch off the lamp she must have left on.

Trying not to wake the others, Stella creeps down the stairs, is mindful of not making a noise as she draws the bolt back. In the back yard the moon is casting long shadows between the houses. She can see darker patches on its silver surface.

She reaches up to the washing line to unpeg the stockings she'd forgotten to bring in. They're cold from the damp night air.

Back inside, she drops them on the kitchen table before pouring herself a cup of tea and stirring in two sugars. When she puts the overhead light on all the objects on the table are illuminated. She stares at the pile of papers pushed up against the wall – old bills, copies of her shift timetable and Tommy's drawings. She picks one up and sees it's just a scribble, a waste of good paper. The one underneath is better – a careful diagram of the Davy lamp with a glinting gold star attached

Her tea is too hot to drink so she sits – head in her hands, both elbows on the table – watching the wisps of steam peeling off the liquid's spinning surface. The bananas she bought yesterday sit untouched in the blue-banded fruit bowl. Beneath the outer rim lies the tiny wing of Tommy's Airfix plane – a Spitfire. Her mam must have found it on the floor. Alongside it, she's left out a couple of farthings for the boy's piggy bank.

The skin of the bananas is already darkening and beginning to slacken. Soon enough the brown patches will merge together – already she can detect a whiff of the sweet sickliness that begins the decay.

'No smoke without fire,' Kathleen had said and it was hard to deny. A wave of sorrow overwhelms her. The moment passes; she straightens up – there's no time for this, she can't afford to be late.

Stella wipes her wet face with the back of her hand and sets about searching for two unladdered black stocking from amongst the heap.

As usual, Ward 6 smells of a mix of carbolic and San Izal. To Stella, the place seems different, though she's hard pressed to say exactly how. Everyone's friendly enough; she tries not to speculate about the hushed conversations just out of her hearing, can't begin to think about what's being said.

In the lavatory mirror, Stella checks the position of the bobby pins holding her hat in place ready to return to the ward. If sister catches her, there will be words about her going off to spend a penny so near to the end of her shift. Her stomach's rumbling again, though it's only been a couple of hours since her break.

They're behind with everything due to the influx of new arrivals. Matron has been stalking the place with a face on her that could cut steel; she's not best pleased that it is well past midday and they haven't finished all the bed-baths.

Stella's thankful she's only on duty one weekend in three.

Her mam is bound to spoil Tommy rotten today; after a belly full of sweets, he won't want his tea.

There's only Mr Smedley to see to next and then they'll be done in here. 'I could jump straight ower top of any gate on our farm when I were a lad.' The old man's spent arm flops back onto the bed. 'Now look at state of me.' His wheezing is worse than ever – thirty years down the pit have stolen his breath. She swaps to the other arm. 'That water's not as cold as it were last time.' He gives her a gummy smile. 'You're a good lass – not like some round here.'

'That's grand, Mr Smedley, can you lean forward a touch more?' From what she can see upside down it's one, thirty-five. 'Just stay like that for a sec.' She almost has to shout, but tries not to. Most of the time the old man's calm like this unless he mistakes her for Vera, that mouthy daughter of his, then there's all hell to play.

'Stella!'

'I'll be finished in a minute, Deb.'

'Stella.' The girl lumbers through the curtains, eyebrows in a huddle. 'I don't know what's going on but a reporter from the Argos has just come in. Matron's told him to leave but he's having none of it. He's bin kickin' up a right fuss.'

'From the old T and A, is he?' The old man chuckles, 'I won't be telling you young wenches what we used to call it down the pit.'

Stella tries not to laugh. Having finished both marbled arms, she rinses the flannel before moving on to his back. 'Don't suppose it's owt very earth shattering,' she tells Debbie. These days they use Lux, not carbolic, but it can never wash away that sour vinegary sort of smell. She takes the towel and dabs at skin that's as pale as a frog's belly.

'Something must have happened?' Deb gives her a nudge. 'Don't pretend you're not curious?' The girl puts her dry hand on Stella's wet one. 'I'm in Matron's bad books but you could go and find out what's goin' on? I can finish off here.'

Stella continues to dab at the old man's skin. She could do with a break. 'Aye alright,' she says. 'That's your top half done, Mr Smedley.'

'That's settled then.' Debbie smiles down at the old man and the blood rises behind her many freckles. 'You've not done his bottom half?'

Stella shakes her head as she dries her hands.

'Lucky me.' The girl wrings out the cloth. 'Okay then. Alf, can you lie back on the bed?' Stella's told her off more than once for using their first names, but she can't be bothered with that just now.

Debbie's hat is coming adrift on one side. She leans across and pins it onto her marmalade curls so the ward sister won't have another go at her. The girl holds still for a moment. 'Now stop yer mothering and go and see what that reporter wants. And mind you come an' tell me.'

'Maybe our Nobby's been arrested for setting fire to next door's cat again?' Stella says, deadpan.

'He never did?' The girl's all eyes.

'Course he didn't.' She flicks at her backside with the end of the towel. 'Ya soft ha'peth!'

Lily is standing in the corridor by the door. Breaking her week-long silence, she says, 'Alvita just told me Charlie Howard from maintenance has gone an' won himself a fortune on the pools.'

'The lucky blighter,' Stella says. 'How much?'

'Heard it were twenty-five thousand pounds.' Lily widens her eyes. 'Leastways, that's what one of the nurses reckoned; though, as some of us know to our cost, this place is full of false rumours.'

'Look out behind.' Stella touches her shoulder. 'Bandits at six o'clock.'

Too late. 'I won't have my orderlies standing around chatting when there's work to be done,' Matron barks. Someone else's good fortune has evidently upset her.

'If you've finished here, you can help out on Ward 7.'

The staff nurse they report to wants them to start with the side ward. Mrs Wilson – the only patient in there – shuffles off to the toilet. They strip her bed before unfolding the clean sheets. Stella concentrates on getting her corners neat.

When she looks up, Lily is holding her mouth like she does when she wants to get something off her chest. Finally, she's out with it. 'I talked to Will and, guess what, Kathleen's got everything round her neck, as usual.'

Her voice breaks with emotion. 'Folks round here should be feeling sorry for Will instead of making up such terrible stories about him. If anyone's broken the law, it's them that are spreading such awful slander against him.'

Biting her bottom lip, Stella pulls at the pillowcase to check it's on straight before she puffs it into shape. It's no good – she has to say it. 'I know you didn't like hearing it but I only said that *if it were me*, I'd be suspicious. The man's not yet forty and he's already buried two wives.'

'But it's not up to you, is it?' Lily shakes the sheet out and it comes sailing past her head.

'I'm just saying –'

'Some bloke like Charlie Howard wins the pools against all the odds but nobody reckons that's suspicious. Don't you think other people can have terrible luck through no fault of their own?'

It's all Stella can do to stop herself saying, *the luck of the devil.*

'His first wife, Violet, died in hospital – he weren't even there at the time.' Lily's voice is sharp with indignation. 'Poor man was just as heartbroken when Ivy tripped and fell down the stairs.'

'That's another thing,' Stella says. 'Both his wives had flower names the same as you. Don't you think that's peculiar?'

Lily rolls her eyes. 'Ivy's not even a flower.'

'It has flowers all the same.'

'A coincidence. Besides, plenty of people have names like Rose, Daisy, Iris and that. Me mam's called Flora, for heaven's sake.' Lily shrugs away her concern. 'Will was fast asleep when poor Ivy had her accident. Think of the number of people who come in here after falling down the stairs at home. It can happen to anyone.' Stella feels the tension in the pull of the sheet. 'It's easy to think the worst of people when you don't know them properly.'

'And whose fault is that?'

Hands on hips, Lily says, 'You can all say what you like, I'll not change my mind about him.'

Stella objects to being lumped together with everyone else. It's a struggle to soften her voice. 'It's only that I don't want you doing something rash – something you might regret.'

'Rash, eh?' She hasn't had a chance to tuck her end in properly when a blanket comes sailing past her nose. 'Must say that's bloody rich coming from you, *Miss* Stella Marsden.'

There's thirty seconds of wounding silence between them before Lily adds, 'I'm sorry – I shouldn't have said that. I mean, I know it weren't exactly your fault you got caught with Tommy.'

'Not my fault eh?' Stella feels her cheeks burning. She wants to shout but is mindful of the consequences of doing such a thing on the wards. 'You're talking about my son.' She takes a breath to calm herself. 'Don't you stand in judgment on me, Lily Hetherington.'

'Aye, well, then maybe *you* shouldn't go doing the same with no reason.'

Lily's already turned away when Mrs Wilson comes back from the toilet. Red-faced with anger, Stella helps the old lady into bed. After that, they continue to work together in silence. On her side, Lily's face is set hard – determined not to back down, already under Will Bagshaw's spell.

Stella stares into the fire going over what Lily said about luck. Why should it favour one person and not another? She knows about bad luck – hadn't her own life been marred by what her mam calls *the hand of fate*? A single lapse at sixteen, when she knew no better, had changed the course of her life forever. To top it all, with the war almost over, Zach Pearson had upped and disappeared into thin air. If he'd made an honest woman of her, Tommy would have had a dad and she wouldn't have had to carry on living in her mam and dad's home all these years.

It wouldn't have been ideal. A shotgun wedding they'd have called it – though it was more like a shotgun conception. How folks would have whispered behind their hands at their wedding with a cardboard cake they'd have to pretend to cut for the photos. Looking into the flames, she tries to picture them boarding a ship on their way to a new life in Canada. Big, open country they say – not like the closed-in one here.

Along with everyone else, she'd read the postcard Doctor Hargreaves had sent from New Zealand a few months back. A few scrawled words full of excitement about the opportunities over there. "*They're crying out for doctors and nurses in the new world.*" Seems they get just as ill despite the space and sunshine. A fine opportunity for the likes of him, a pipe-dream when you're only an auxiliary – not a proper nurse. They're hardly crying out for unmarried mothers and their fatherless children. No, her only real choice is *this* life in the same old world. Luck meant making the best of the hand that's been dealt you.

She's staring into the embers and doesn't hear Nobby come in. 'Everything alright, Stell?' he asks from the doorway.

'Why wouldn't it be?'

'Only asking.'

'I suppose you've been out with Olive again.'

'Aye, as it happens I have.' He sits down in the chair next to her. Touching her arm he says, 'You've had a face on you all weekend. Tell me what's wrong.'

'Wouldn't do any good if I did.'

He smiles – always had a kind smile on him. 'How d'you know if you don't say owt?'

Hoping to stem the tears, Stella shuts her eyes. 'It's Lily.'

His tone changes, 'Has summat happened to her?'

'No – least ways not yet anyroad.' Stella turns to him. 'Why couldn't you have married her when you had the chance?'

She regrets her words as soon as they're out. Visibly stung, Nobby lets go of her arm and stands up. 'So that's what's bothering you – this new chap of Lily's.'

He walks off towards the door and then turns. A muscle on the side of his face twitches as he tries to master his feelings. 'She's been spending all her time with him and that's made you jealous.' He glares at her. 'Truth be told, it's not just me that's been in love with her all this time.'

'Course I love her.' Getting to her feet, Stella stares right back at him. 'Though not in the way you're suggesting. I do miss her company, I'll grant you that, but I'd be the first to be happy for her if she'd found herself a decent enough man and not that – that bloody snake in the grass.'

'Maybe your judgement's clouded. P'raps no man would ever be good enough for her – not in your eyes?'

'That's where you're wrong – *you* would be. It might not be too late.'

He shakes his head. 'It was always too late. I would have asked her years ago if she'd given me even an ounce of encouragement.'

CHAPTER TWENTY

March 1957

Lily

It wasn't a conventional proposal – he didn't get down on one knee or anything like that; far from it. Kicking at a stone, Will makes various odd remarks as they walk back from the pictures. 'Having a younger brother, you must be used to young boys and their ways.' Then a bit later he says, 'You must be fed up with being cooped up in that bedsit. 'Spect you'd rather have a home of your own.'

Lily waits. When he says nothing else, she's forced to ask, 'What are you driving at – exactly?'

Sending the stone hard against a wall, he says, 'Just that we could make things legal, if you like.' From what she can see of his face, there's no hint of a smile, no indication it's a joke. Not exactly the stuff of dreams.

'Are you asking me to marry you?'

'Aye, I am – that's if you'll have me.'

Pulling on his arm, she insists he does it properly. He touches her face, strokes her cheek ever so gently. 'Lily Hetherington, will you do me the honour of marrying me?' She's surprised by how unsure of himself he seems as she gazes into his eyes. How relieved when she says, 'Yes, Will, I will. They laugh before sealing it with more than a kiss.

'Best we keep things simple,' Will tells her once the wedding itself is on the cards. 'No need to make too much fuss, eh?' he says a couple of days later. 'Not at our age.'

That stings Lily more than she lets on. She laughs it off. 'Eh, I'm not yet thirty you know.' Secretly, she thinks a bit of fuss might be justified when this is meant to be the happiest day of any woman's life but, looking at his expression, she judges it best to leave such sentiments unspoken.

She's does her best to comply. The dress she's about to stand up in is quite different from the one she'd imagined she might wear on her wedding day. It's smart enough – a plain cream material with a fitted top running down to the clinched waistband above a full skirt. 'Demure' was the word the shop woman kept using, along with 'elegant' and 'a la mode'. Lily had only needed to nod in agreement. It's short of floor-length – stops at her calf because any longer would be inappropriate, she can see that.

She'd wished Stella could have been there to help her choose. After lots of umming and aahing, she's bought it then worried herself sick that Will might consider the neckline too low or he wouldn't like the way the stiffened layers of her petticoat lift the skirt's hem up round the edges.

She showed Debbie a few days later and the girls had said that, in all honesty, the material could easily pass for silk despite being only a rayon mix.

In daylight, anyone can see it's not white – though perhaps it's more ivory than cream. To be safe, she's added a wide, pink belt, which shows her narrow waist off. Mindful of the old superstition about it bringing bad luck, she hasn't let Will see the dress until today.

The weather forecast said it's going to be changeable and on the chilly side. They weren't wrong about that. Lily's decided to wear her short pink jacket – for outside only – for fear of creasing the material she won't be buttoning it up. Standing back, she takes a last assessing look in the mirror.

'You'll have to do,' she tells herself out loud.

Descending the stairs, she feels like someone else. 'You look a picture,' Mrs Ferguson declares and holds her hand to her heart. 'We're all going to miss you.'

The two of them are beginning to tear up when the doorbell rings. Her brother George is standing there looking lanky in their dad's old-fashioned suit. Only fifteen, and there's already talk of him getting engaged to Lena his new sweetheart. Behind him, the taxi he arrived in is idling in the street. Aside from the driver it's empty. Red in the face, George explains that their mam and dad are still laid up with the flu. Lily wishes she entirely believed him.

The taxi driver comes round to open the car door for her. 'Not too late to change your mind.' George puts on an I-didn't-really-mean-it smile.

'I'm as sure as anything,' Lily says, smoothing the back of her dress as she climbs into the rear seat.

In no time the taxi is pulling up outside the registry office. She's relieved to see Will standing there. His face breaks into a wide smile when he spots her. As the others gather round hugging and kissing their good wishes, he leans in to whisper, 'You look lovely – the perfect bride.'

The waiting room is packed with people waiting for other weddings. It's quite a squash. Clasping her shaking hands, Debbie and Kathleen tell her how lovely she looks. They're forced to stand just inside the room while they wait their turn.

There's a bit of a commotion outside; someone is struggling to open the door. Everyone giggles when Stella almost falls into the room. She looks hot and flustered but at least she's turned up. Brigsy – Will's old army mate – says in a stage whisper: 'What's black and white and red in the face?'

Stella hugs the breath out of her. 'You look beautiful,' she tells her. The dog-check pattern of her jacket is already jangling Lily's eyes like a migraine.

Stella starts gabbling, telling everyone some long story about walking in through the way out and getting mixed up with another wedding party. The others are finding her tale hilarious, but Lily's too nervous to laugh along. It's so hot – the walls are closing in and she wonders if she's about to faint.

At long last the inner doors open, their names are called and they're ushered inside a large room that's all waxed panelling and parquet floors. They sit down in the front row of chairs. The smell of all those layers and layers of polish begins to turn her stomach. On a table at the front there's a lone vase of flowers that might not even be real.

At least there's more space – too much really with only the nine of them to fill it. Lily had wanted to invite the other Marsdens but Will had pulled a face – after all he's hardly spoken a word to them.

The side door opens and a middle-aged woman comes in, her footsteps echoing against the floor. She gives them the briefest twitch of a smile and then strides over to turn on a tape machine in the corner. Its twin reels turn to release a reedy and solemn tune.

The registrar enters and his footsteps echo as he walks across to position himself in the centre of the aisle facing them. Without a word, he surveys the whole wedding party. 'May I have the happy couple?' Lily and Will go to stand before him.

She can see a shower of dandruff along the man's pin-striped shoulders. His half–moon glasses are casting green shadows below his red–rimmed and watery eyes. Probably has a touch of blepharitis. In a grave voice he reminds them of the seriousness of what they're about to do. Lily grips her bouquet of spring flowers; the sweat from her hands is making their heads droop.

The registrar turns to Will. She can't take in much of what

he's being told to repeat. When he gets to *I know not of any lawful impediment,* someone behind them coughs more than once; it doesn't sound genuine. Lily holds her breath until the registrar moves on.

It's her turn. She can't help but sway back and forth as she prepares to speak. It seems they're all waiting for her to repeat what he's just said. 'I declare that I know not of any lawful im...' Her dry mouth is refusing to say the damned word.

'Impediment,' the registrar prompts her. 'Im-ped-i-ment.'

She manages to get it out at last; her flowers shaking with it all. And still the old man is craning forward, red eyes peering at her over his wire glasses. 'Why I, Lily Joan Hetherington,' he says, which strikes her as daft because he isn't her.

Will touches her elbow. It seems she's said all that must be said. They're told to go over to sign the register. 'That's the worst on't over,' Will whispers in her ear.

The registrar hands her a pen and his finger points her to the space above the box where someone had already written the word *spinster.* She writes her name out in small, neat letters.

Next to hers, Will's signature is an indecipherable scrawl above the word *Widower;* and, although the fact of it is no surprise, she's disturbed to see it written there in black and white.

Outside on the steps of the building, she's thankful for the air. Everyone hugs them; her cheeks are getting covered in lipstick.

Lily turns to look for Brian and sees him standing by himself, head down. She goes over to pull his stiff little body into a hug, tries her level best to find the right words. 'You know things will still be the same, don't you? The two of us just need to get to know each other. I hope we can be good friends. You won't have to call me mummy or mam or owt like that. Not unless you want to like – later on. Plain *Lily* is just fine with me.'

The boy is like a shop dummy; letting her adjust the red carnation someone has pinned to his school blazer. She strokes his hair back out of those sad eyes but he looks away from her, down at the pavement, and it all flops across his face again.

It's starts to drizzle. She tries to remember what they say about rain on your wedding day – is it meant to be lucky or unlucky? Davy – Will's other army mate – has gone to get his new car to take them to the reception.

When someone calls her over, she nudges Will to go and have a word with Brian and he does. 'Okay, son?' she hears him say. He gives the lad an awkward squeeze. The lad soon shrugs him off and walks away, standing far too close to the edge of the road and its swirling traffic.

A flashbulb goes off and then another as the photographer takes pictures of the two of them. Despite the weather, she takes off her jacket – hands it and the flowers to Stella.

Will links arms with her and they smile at each other. She thinks he's going to kiss her on the lips but he plants it on her cheek instead.

Her new husband certainly looks handsome in the new suit he's treated himself to. Several times he's mentioned how it only cost ten bob over eight weeks and, for that, they even threw in the tie.

'That's enough now,' Will says, pressing some notes into the photographer's hand. Her brother George comes over. 'Con-gratulations our Lil – married at last, eh.' Kissing her cheek, he says, '*Mrs Bagshaw*' like he's finding it hard to believe. He holds both her hands and says, 'I hope the two of you will have a long and happy life together.'

He lets her go to offer Will his right hand, which is something at least. They shake without much enthusiasm. Her brother's smile couldn't look more forced. 'I'd best get back shortly.'

Lily's open-mouthed. 'You're not going already – you'll stay for the do?'

'Plenty of room for you at our house,' Stella tells him. 'Can't have you rushing off – not on Lily's big day.'

George opens his mouth then shuts it again.

From behind a deep voice says, 'Can I add my congratulations to the happy couple?' Today's the first time she's set eyes on Brigsy and he really is a giant of a man. He takes her hand and raises it to his lips. 'I see you've bagged yourself a real beauty.' She could be a fish.

He shakes Will by the hand. 'You always were a jammy bugger, Bagshaw.' Then his other old army friend, Davy, honks from the roadside; the two of them wave as they run down the steps to his car.

Along with the white ribbon on the bonnet, they've strung pairs of old boots and some saucepans from the bumper. Will opens the door for her, bowing like a flunky and she's excited as they clatter their way through the damp streets, her hand clutching his.

Everything's been arranged in the snug bar of the Queen's Hotel. He makes his friend drive around for a bit so the others will get there ahead of them.

'Happy, Mrs Bagshaw?' he asks, squeezing her hand.

Lily smiles up at him. 'Happiest day of my life.'

CHAPTER TWENTY-ONE

A cheer goes up when they enter the room. Brigsy tips his hat to them both and insists on buying the first round of drinks. No one argues with the big man. He slaps George on the back and hands him a full pint. 'There you go, son, get that down ya.'

Once they've all been served, there's another round of toasting. They carry their glasses over to a big table that's been laid next to the unlit fire. Will and Brigsy remain at the bar with their pints – understandable when they haven't seen each other for so long.

A bowl of plastic red roses graces the centre of the table; they would look more life-like if someone gave them a good dusting.

Despite encouragements, Brian won't sit down with them. Kathleen puts her arm round his shoulder. "Spect the lad just needs the lav after all that standing about. Come on, love, I'll show you where it is.'

Lily holds up her schooner of sherry. 'Thank you all for coming – for making this day so special for us both.' She looks over at her brother and adds, 'To absent friends and family.' The haphazard clinking that follows sets them all giggling.

'Here's wishing you both a long and happy life,' Stella says, squeezing her arm.

'Amen to that,' Davy says. She sees Debbie nudge him.

Stella's made her eyes up with green eye shadow and thick mascara and that must be what's making her look so pale. Her hand appears to tremble as she passes round a packet of menthol cigarettes. "'Spect we could all do wi' a gasper.' Lily decides to take one even though she wouldn't normally. Someone gives her a light; when she inhales, it tastes really odd – like chewing gum at the same time.

'Eh, but it's a bit parky in here,' Debbie says, rubbing her arms. The line of smoke rising from between her fingers is curling into Lily's face. She takes another drag then snorts out in a noisy way that makes them all start tittering. After that, every damn thing seems to set them off again.

A nervous-looking lass in a starched white apron goes back and forth with the food Will's laid on. She places a large platter with rows of sandwiches cut into triangles in the centre of the table. Someone's balanced three sprigs of parsley on the top. Some are filled with a layer of pale egg, others grated cheese; the rest have something pink inside that's probably fish paste. The girl returns with some quartered pork pies and a plate of cocktail-sized sausages rolls – also with sprigs of parsley on top. Finally, she brings bowls of crisps and a plate of shortbread.

Across the table, Debbie starts taking charge – like she has a habit of doing in the ward – distributing the plates and their interleaved paper napkins. The girl is wearing a new green suit that doesn't suit her. Her copper hair has been strained back into a stiff bun that makes her look a bit like she probably will when she's middle-aged.

George and Davy are the first to fill their plates up. Lily watches the comical way Davy's moustache moves up and down when he's chewing. Although she's not in the least bit hungry, she nibbles at the pork pie segment someone puts on the plate in front of her. It tastes of a salty nothingness.

Though he's hardly touched his food, Davy jumps up to buy another round. 'I'm in the chair this time,' he says, which Lily thinks is funny because he's standing up.

He's soon back wobbling a tray laden with overfilled glasses. He places what looks like a very large gin and orange in front of her. 'Get that down you, lass,' he says, like she's just had a shock or something. When he sits back down on the bench next to her, the whole thing wobbles under his weight.

Davy keeps inching nearer. He keeps putting his hand on her arm whenever he says anything, leans in so close she can smell the sweat not disguised by his aftershave.

When she looks up again, Will is standing there in front of her. 'Thought we best come and get somethin' to eat before it's all gone.'

He looks at Stella. 'Mind if I sit beside my new wife?' Like she's been stung, she jumps up to give him her place. It sounds so peculiar to hear herself described as *my new wife*.

Squashed in as she is between the two men, there's hardly room for Lily to breathe. She leans into Will, rests her newly-ringed hand on the warmth of his thigh.

Debbie whispers something to Stella that makes the two of them burst out laughing.

'Them two are off again,' Will says to Brigsy. 'Always laughing like a couple of blocked drains.'

That shuts them up; shuts everyone else up.

Lily watches Brigsy build a pyramid on his plate.

'Excuse me.' A spotty streak of a lad is standing over them. 'Would you like owt else? P'raps a few more rounds of sandwiches?'

'I think we're okay, ta very much,' Will tells him.

'Hang on a minute.' Lily isn't used to drinking gin – probably a treble – and it's starting to get to her. She has to concentrate on not slurring her words. 'This lot's almost gone an' I for one am still hungry.' With a loose arm she gestures across the room. 'And what about Brian and Kathleen – they've had nothing yet. He's a growing lad – 'spect he could eat an horse.'

The waiter colours up: 'Would you like me to bring the same again, madam?' The way he says "madam" sounded so queer Lily has to stifle a giggle.

'Hold up,' Will tells him. 'There's no need to go mad. A few more rounds will do us fine. And mind it's just the sarnies – there's plenty pork pie left.'

Will fills a plate with pie and crisps and carries it over to where his son is standing with Kathleen. Brian won't even meet his father's eye. He's taken off that buttonhole and is shredding its red petals one by one onto the carpet. Will touches his shoulder and says something she can't hear. The boy keeps shaking his head.

Leaving the plate on the nearest table, Will starts to walk back but Kathleen catches his arm and says something into his ear. Lily can't hear but she can see their lips – working at the mill has taught her to lip-read. Her friend says, 'Don't worry, he'll come round. Leave the lad to me; I'll see if he'd like a game of cards or summat.' Kathleen says something else though Lily can't see her mouth move.

Will's expression has changed for the worse. Kathleen must have gone too far because she's now blushing to her roots. Her eyes dart over to the rest of them. She says, 'The boy'll get used to the idea.' Then something else Lily misses before, 'She'll win him round in the end.' She pulls Will further aside though she's quick to withdraw her hand from his arm. Lily sees her say, 'You should go an' enjoy your wedding day.'

There's a commotion in front of her – they're moving aside the plates and glasses to spread a newspaper out to look at photos of some film star's wedding.

Will comes back with a weary expression on his face.

'He's nothing to look at.' Debbie's leaning so far across, she can see right down her bra. 'And a darn sight older than forty-two if you ask me.' She touches Will's arm; 'Not that I was suggesting–'

'Here, hang on a minute.' Will tries to say it with a laugh, holding up his hands in appeal. 'I'm only thirty-eight, you know.'

Brigsy snorts but says nothing.

'Look at the two of them together – just awful.' Debbie leans across to grab Lily's arm. 'A producer it says, though we've none of us ever heard of him.'

'She's the same age as me,' Lily tells them. 'And now we've married on the exact same day.'

Davy nudges her. 'She's not nearly as good-looking as you are.'

She digs him with her elbow: 'Bloody flatterer.' That starts the girls giggling again.

'It were last week they got married,' Stella says, bringing the paper closer. 'See here it says – where is it now – ah yes; "it was a quiet wedding as the bride and groom wanted".'

'Same as us.' Lily knows her voice is louder than it should be. 'Pity we don't have her sort of money, eh?' She waves her drink, notices again the way the light is catching her wedding ring. She wishes they'd put that bloody newspaper away because this is meant to be *their* day and no one else's.

'A tenth, no, a *twentieth* even, of what she's worth would set us up for life,' Will says into his pint.

'Still, money's not everything, is it?' Lily pushes her hair up at the back and holds it unsteadily in place, then leans in to kiss her husband on the cheek – a big smacker that leaves a lipstick print on him. 'P'raps I should dye me hair platinum blonde like her – what d'you reckon, Will?'

'I think you're fine as you normally are.'

Drunk as she is, Lily notices the disapproval in his voice; she can see it written all over his face too. Can he smell the gin and tobacco on her breath? Is he thinking how unattractive she looks with her cheeks flushed like she can feel they are?

She leans on him; stroking his hair as a wave of affection runs through her.

Stella is offering round those foul cigarettes and Brigsy is laughing and pulling a face. Will keeps inching away from her until their legs are no longer touching; all his warmth disappears with it.

She notices how he uses both his hands to smooth his hair back the way it was before she touched it. He removes the carefully folded handkerchief from his breast pocket and wipes her lipstick from his cheek, folding it in half again to hide the red smear. He stuffs it back down into his pocket so that, instead of the previous neat triangle sticking up above the pocket, only a tiny corner is now visible.

CHAPTER TWENTY-TWO

Stella

Once the newlyweds have left, the others start to make a move. Stella finally locates George out the back leaning against a wall with trails of vomit down his front. The lad opens his eyes. 'Stella.' Before he can say anything else, he starts to retch. Lord knows how many pints they must have bought him.

It's as much as she can do to walk him round to the front of the building. Shaking his head, Kathleen's dad reluctantly agrees to give him a lift. Stella has to sit in the back between the boy and Debbie. Though it's a cold night, they open all the windows due to the smell and the likelihood of him being sick again. Head half out the window, he mutters, 'My big sister just got married.'

'Aye, we know, lad,' Kathleen says from the front. Turning to face the road she adds, 'More's the ruddy pity.'

Her mam doesn't exactly make light of things. 'Oh, my word – would you look at the state of the poor mite,' she declares.

'Mite? The boy's fifteen,' Stella reminds her.

'But where's Flora? Where's Jack? Why aren't they looking after him?'

'They didn't come. Laid up with the flu, apparently.'

'Oh, that's bad luck when your own daughter's getting married. Reckon I'd have dragged meself there somehow. Not that I'm likely to get the chance.'

George begins to sway and Stella tightens her grip on him. 'You'd best sit the lad down before he falls,' her mam says. 'Good job yer father's out or he'd go mad. Let's get his jacket off.' She inspects the material. 'I doubt them stains'll come out in a hurry.'

George's head flops sideways against the arm of the chair, his face deathly pale. He opens his eyes. 'Eh, our Lily just got married, Mrs Marsden.'

'Aye, we know, lad,' her mam says. Turning to Stella she asks, 'So how was it – everything go off alright?'

'Well, they did the deed if that's what you're asking. An, of course, Lily looked a picture.'

'I bet she did.' Her mam does that thing with her head – rearranges it along with her thoughts. 'Shame we couldn't be there to witness it.'

Stella sighs. 'Well, in any case, she's now got what she wanted – she's officially Mrs Lily Bagshaw.'

'And the best of luck to her.' Her mam looks up at the ceiling. 'Nobby! Come an' give us a hand down here, will ya?'

Between them, they get the boy up the stairs and steer him into her brother's room. As soon as they sit him down, George falls sideways onto the bed.

'He's not sleeping there,' her brother says. He nods at the floor. 'I'll make up something for him down there.'

Hands on hips, Stella says, 'He's not a ruddy dog.'

'Would you want him sleeping in your bed?'

'No, but –'

'Exactly. At least we'll be able to mop the oilcloth if he throws up again.' He squeezes her shoulder. 'Don't look so worried; he's a young lad – he'll do alright down there for one night. I'll even sacrifice my pillow.'

When she comes back with a couple of blankets and a bucket, the boy is already on the floor and snoring.

'How did it go today?' Nobby asks. As soon as she looks at him, he turns his face away. The question seems to hang there between them.

'Well now – what can I say?' Stella sighs. 'It went off without a hitch. Lily seemed to be nervous, to begin with anyway. She looked really lovely – more like a film star.'

He clears his throat. 'I bet she did.'

They both stare at the floor for what seems like an age.

'She's leaving the hospital,' Stella tells him. 'Left already it seems. Gave her notice in last week. I only found out when I overheard Will telling one of his friends about it.'

'And she'd said nothing to you?'

'Not a sausage and I'm supposed to be her best friend. Kathleen and Deb said they knew nothing about it either.' She shrugs. 'I suppose she thought we'd disapprove.'

'Is Lily giving up work altogether?'

'Oh, no – she's already got herself a job in a laundry, of all places. Will told his friend that now she's got a house and family to look after, the hours will suit *them* much better than hospital shifts.'

'Put like that, it sounds reasonable enough, I suppose.'

'Maybe, but why didn't she have the guts to tell me to my face? How could she do something like that and not mention it to any of the people she works with?'

'Don't ask me,' he says. 'That girl's always been a mystery to me.'

George is mumbling in his sleep. 'The floor's got to be mighty hard on the poor lad's back,' Stella says.

'D'you honestly think he's goin' to notice?' Nobby rubs at the stubble on his chin. 'P'raps it's for the best – Lily leaving that is.'

'In what way?'

'You two haven't exactly seen eye to eye of late,' he says.

'Maybe you've been too close for comfort. P'raps you'll get on better with a bit of distance between you.'

'You could be right.' Stella sighs. 'In any case, you'd best help me move the lad onto his side in case he throws up again. An' we'll need to put something against his back so he can't roll over onto his back again; don't want the poor lad choking in his sleep, do we?'

Nobby gives her a mock salute. 'Yes, nurse.'

Perhaps she has been too caught up in Lily's life at the expense of her own. Maybe she needs breathing space.

CHAPTER TWENTY-THREE

Brian can't remember ever being inside a taxi before. He sits in the front next to the driver while the two of them sit in the back. The windscreen keeps misting up and the man has to wipe it over and over so he can see.

From the sloppy noises going on, he can tell they're kissing again. Yuk. It's only a short distance to their house – they could have saved money and caught the bus instead.

He gets out and stands on the pavement waiting. They take an age getting out; his dad does something from behind that makes Lily shriek and then giggle. In the dark Brian can't tell what colour note his dad paid with. The way the taxi bloke says, 'Thanks very much, sir' he guesses his dad must have given him too much.

Instead of letting them in their house, his dad bangs on the neighbour's door with his fist. He could have used the knocker. 'Good evenin', Mrs Murphy,' his dad says in that voice he has when he's drunk but trying not to show it.

'Look at you!' Mrs Murphy makes an odd sort of squealing sound in her throat. 'I'm so happy for the both of you. And my word don't you look a picture together.' She hugs first his dad and then Lily though neither of them seems all that happy to be squashed up against those enormous bosoms. Thank goodness she leaves him out.

His dad's arm comes around his neck and Brian finds himself propelled forward against his will. He's still praying Mrs Murphy's not planning to hug him. 'Here he is then,' his dad says. 'Send him round in the morning but makes sure it's not too early, eh?'

For some reason that makes Mrs Murphy laugh though she puts a hand over her mouth like she ought not to find it funny.

'Why don't I give the lad his breakfast,' she says. 'Then there's no hurry – we're not going out or owt so take your time. Just knock on the door once you're up and about.'

'Thanks, Mrs M,' his dad says. 'You're a godsend as usual.'

When Mrs Murphy smiles like that you can see she might have been prettier before her face got all saggy.

Letting him go, his dad messes up his hair in that way he likes to in front of other people. Brian tries to flatten it back down again. 'Be a good lad,' he says. 'We'll see you in the morning.'

His dad opens their front door and then picks Lily up and carries her inside. She seems to find it funny. Tonight he's good at making everybody laugh.

'Come on then, Brian,' Mrs Murphy says, shooing him inside her house and shutting the door. 'We'll leave those two lovebirds to themselves.'

He'd never thought of his dad as a lovebird – whatever sort of bird that is. If he had to draw Lily like a bird, he'd make her a dove dressed up like that. He'd draw his dad bigger and darker – more like a crow.

Looking down on the sleeping boy, Nobby is surprised by how much he resembles his sister. Sharing the same dark hair and fine features, there would be something almost feminine about the lad's looks if it weren't for the dark shadow along his upper lip.

The boy's snoring keeps Nobby awake – that and the fact that he's got no flamin' pillow under his own head only a rolled-up towel. In truth, his thoughts won't let him settle. It's an open secret that Jack and Flora Hetherington have taken against Lily's new husband. Young though he is, the lad had been more open-minded – less eager to condemn the man.

Stella had warned Lily off Bagshaw – if he knew his sister she'll have done so in no uncertain terms; Lily had stuck to her guns and gone ahead and married the man. She must really love him. He himself is courting Olive and she's a lovely girl – no doubt about it; he has no right to feel like this.

He turns his back on the boy but it doesn't help. They're married and that's the end of it. No point going over the what-ifs and the might-have-beens. Over the years since Luke's death, she's had plenty of admirers, plenty of chances to settle down. She must see something in this Bagshaw to have fallen for him – something other people can't or won't see.

He pulls the blankets over his ears. P'raps Lily will be the making of him – third time lucky as they say. For her sake, he hopes so.

It's so romantic when Will lifts her in his arms and carries her over the threshold. He kisses her and it's such a tender kiss. 'Welcome to your new home, Mrs Bagshaw.'

'You better put me down now,' she says. 'Don't want you hurting your back.'

'You're light as a feather,' he tells her. 'I hardly know I'm holding anything.'

He sets her down on her feet. She expects him to lead the way upstairs but instead he walks down the hallway. Lily follows. It's strange when she thinks about it that she's never been here before.

The front room looks cosy enough though it reeks of spent

cigarettes. 'Sit yerself down,' he says, like she might be any visitor. 'Anywhere will do.'

Lily chooses the nearest of the two armchairs – part of a dark green three-piece suite that looks more or less brand new. The sofa has the same cream antimacassars cloths draped over the back – more like a woman's touch than a man. A dark old sideboard has been squeezed in behind the sofa. In the centre of the low coffee table there's a large glass ashtray that's overflowing. The table sits on a swirling green and brown rug that's not to Lily's taste – feels like she's looking down into a muddy brook. Over to one side there's the usual tiled fireplace, though the real focus of the room is the Bush television balanced on a low table underneath the window. She can't suppress a small shudder.

'You look cold,' he says from the doorway. 'Why don't I make us some tea – fancy a cup before we go up?' He's rubbing his hands together like a barman waiting for an order.

'Um, yes, why not?' She's relieved to slip her shoes off at last; hopes her feet don't smell as she massages the ball of each foot through her stockings.

'Let me have those.' Will picks her shoes up along with the ashtray. He's got his hands full. 'I'll just empty this,' he says. 'We usually put our shoes in the rack by the door.'

'Oh, but I can –'

'Stay right where you are, Mrs Bagshaw.' He holds the hand holding the ashtray out to stop her getting up. 'Just relax. This is our special night – I want to spoil you. Be back shortly.'

She can hear him rattling cups in the kitchen. Looking around, Lily focuses on the framed photographs hanging above the fireplace. She crosses the room to take a closer look.

The one at the front is of Brian. From the gaps in his front teeth she guesses he must have been about five or six when it was taken. The other photograph is of Will and a dark-haired woman. Judging by the bunch of flowers she's holding and the confetti lodged in their hair, it must be their wedding day. The previous Mrs Bagshaw's open smile contrasts with the altogether more reserved expression on her new husband's face.

Flora Hetherington is listening to the wind rattling the window frame. It doesn't let up. Shutting her eyes, sleep won't come. That damned noise; she can feel the icy draft up round her neck. Jack's aiming to replace the windows once he's finished the extension though Lord knows when that will be. Funny how the weather never used to bother her much; out here you're exposed to it day and night whether you like it or not.

Never in a million years would she have imagined missing her own daughter's wedding. The two of them had been poorly – laid up with the flu, no word of a lie, but that was a couple of days ago. Both of them were walking round like washed-out rags and yet they could have got there all the same if Jack hadn't been so adamant. 'Everyone else can see the man for what he is – bar our Lily,' he'd declared more times than she cares to remember. 'I'll not stand up in front of the vicar with a false smile plastered on my face.'

'It's a registry office,' she'd reminded him over and over. 'There won't even be a vicar.'

He'd shaken his head at that. 'Makes no odds. You can please yerself, Flora but I'll not be made a hypocrite.'

She'd put off writing to Lily in case her father came round at the last minute. Posted too late – her letter won't have got there in time. If she'd known Will's address she could have sent it there instead.

Nobby Marsden had rung the people down the lane and they'd come up to tell them not to worry that George was stopping the night with them. Lord knows how they got the number. Nice boy that Nobby – always been considerate.

Rattle bloody rattle – damned thing won't stop. There's no telling what Lily will have made of their absence.

She should have left Jack to it and gone there with George. No matter how much she wishes she'd done just that, the die is well and truly cast; it's too late to change any of it now.

CHAPTER TWENTY-FOUR

June 1957

Lily

Damp walls closing in. Someone's behind her, breathing heavily – catching up. Waking with a start, the darkness slowly gives way to a sliver of moonlight shining in through the crack in the curtains.

Afraid to give in to sleep again, Lily lies on her back turning everything over and over in her head and only managing to make a cat's cradle of it all.

It's some relief when daylight begins to filter in through the curtains and the birds start to sing. She's able to pick out first one and then another, identifying each bird by its distinctive song just as her dad had taught her to all those years ago. One particular thrush is singing louder than the rest; she knows it's designed to stop other birds from entering his territory, nonetheless he seems to be pouring out a song of pure joy at being alive on such a fine, new morning.

She's tempted to get up and make a cuppa but instead she continues to lie within the shadowy confines of the bedroom listening to the sweet cacophony of the dawn chorus until the clamour of so many songs is almost too much.

On her walk to work, she calls a greeting over to Eddie the milkman. 'Morning, flower,' he answers. Looking up into the unbroken blue of the sky, he adds, 'Reckon it's gonna to be a bonny one today.'

He takes away the empties from the Murphys' doorstep and replaces them with a couple of fresh pints. Almost as soon as he puts the new bottles down, the boldest individual in a group of sparrows hops towards them. Eddie shakes his head. 'Will you look at that – the bare-faced cheek of it. Them spuggies'll be at the cream afore I turn me back.'

He's right. Despite being late, she stops to watch the comical way the lead bird bounces ever closer to the nearest bottle until its beak is tap-tapping against the foil top. The rest of them crowd round for their turn.

Lily checks her watch. 'I best be getting on or I'll be in hot water.' She flings out a 'S'thee, Eddie,' behind her.

Moving on, the milkman begins to whistle; the melody carries in the clear air. With the pale sunshine promising greater warmth to come, Lily begins to hum the same tune until she realises it's only that silly song from the Ovaltine advert.

In the laundry's clocking-in queue, a few women turn to look her up and down. 'Someone's in a better mood today,' Renee Elder says. 'That's more like it, gal.' There's general admiration of her cherry-patterned skirt – one she hasn't worn since last autumn.

The single girls are in a huddle near the back of the line, new home-perms hidden under their knotted headscarves, giggling over their weekend plans with only a four-hour shift before they're off home with that precious pay packet weighing down their handbags. Lily recalls the delight of all that lipsticked laughter.

'You's looking canny alreet this mornin', hinny,' Geordie Babs tells her in the locker room. The others have departed leaving a soapy, sour smell that's beginning to turn her stomach. The two of them have taken off most of their clothes and are standing in their underwear. They put on their wraparound aprons – threading one strap through the hole and then crossing the front flap over before they tie both ends in a bow at the back.

'Mind, wuh's al ganning hayam early, eh?' Babs reminds her.

'Aye, pet, thee's reet,' Lily shoots straight back, not quite mimicking the woman's accent.

'Ah, ho'way and shite!' Babs turns her back in mock indignation. For no good reason they both laugh out loud – real belly laughs that have them bent over; they can't even finish wrapping their scarves around their hair.

There's a knock behind them. The bald head of Cyril Blythe, the foreman, appears round the door. He's on the prowl for any slackers. 'Six minutes past, ladies.' Creeping further into the room, he taps the glass face of his wristwatch. 'You should've started work by now. Get cracking – or I'll be forced to dock you a quarter.'

'Right you are, gaffer.' Babs gives him a mock salute.

Ignoring her, he gives Lily an appraising glance. 'Glad to see you're looking a bit more like it this morning.'

So they'd all noticed.

When he's gone, Babs mutters, 'Little bloody Hitler that one.' She clicks her heels together and does a Nazi salute to his back.

Thought it's not yet summer, the humidity hits them as they walk through into the main body of the building. Babs touches her shoulder in a farewell gesture and she continues on through, waving at one or two of the other women. They're already heads down and hard at it, loading up the big machines and emptying the overhead drying racks.

It's much quieter in the tiny back room where she works alone. Will was as pleased as punch when she told him she'd be earning another sixpence ha'penny an hour for dealing with the finer quality shirts and blouses and so forth – the hand-finishing they pay extra for.

At first, she'd found the work satisfying; turned out she was a dab hand with the lacework and ironing the awkward angles around the yoke and back pleats of the men's shirts. She'd been pleased when Cyril went out of his way to sing her praises, telling her she was doing a much better job than Shirley Claybourn ever did. A month back, with everyone watching, Shirley had shoved two fingers in Cyril's face and strode out shouting: 'You can stick yer flaming job up your arse'ole.' Lily's heard she's now working in a bakery off Inkerman Street. Though the pay wasn't nearly as good, she'd told Babs she was "happy to be out of that hellhole they call a laundry".

Lily's mood soon darkens. She's missing the company of the others. It brings a lump to her throat if she thinks of her friends back at the Royal – Stella, Kathleen and Debs all carrying on their lives without her.

She notices again how much worse her hands are looking – as if they belong to a woman twenty years older. Though she hasn't yet started work, they're already swollen – her wedding band's gotten so tight it won't come off however hard she tries. These days the skin around the joints of her fingers is permanently sore. She's tried all manner of cream and yet, by the end of the every day, they're usually bleeding. She needs to be careful her blood doesn't stain the fabric.

The maintenance men have been whitewashing the overhead windows to help block some of the sun's heat. It's completely changed the light coming in the room, makes everything seem unreal. Recently, Lily's had this silly notion in her head that she's acting in a film of her own life. Not that anyone else would have the patience to watch it.

Encouraging her to take this job, Will had mentioned the

regular hours, pointed out how it meant she'd get back only a quarter of an hour after Brian got in from school. 'The lad needs more company.' In Will's mind that responsibility had been passed to her.

Today being a Friday and a half-day, most of the women will have made plans to nip into town this afternoon. Once she's called into the grocers, Lily will be going straight back home to start on the chores ahead of the weekend.

At ten o'clock on the dot a loudspeaker crackles into life and band music echoes around the building; the morning goes a little quicker as she works to the jaunty rhythm of each tune. She's careful not to lose her concentration or, sure as eggs is eggs, that eagle-eyed foreman will notice anything not up to standard.

By the end of her morning shift, she's emptied the two carts they'd left by her workstation. Due to the monotony of the movements involved, the usual ache has set into her shoulders; standing on the hard concrete makes the soles of her feet burn; it makes her think of penitents forced to walk on hot coals.

She knows better than to complain to Will, if she so much as mentions any aches and pains, he acts like she's deliberately getting at him. 'If I was ever lucky enough to win the pools, you'd never have to work again.' How often had he said those words to her?

When the final hooter bellows, the whole workforce jostles to clock out before scattering in every direction. Along with everyone else, Lily calls out her goodbyes. In too much of a hurry to respond, everyone around her seems to know exactly where they'd rather be.

Lily has no desire to hurry home. Brian will be happy

playing with his friends in the street. She dawdles along in the general direction of the grocers; she's relieved that, for a while at least, she can drop all pretence.

CHAPTER TWENTY-FIVE

July 1957

Lily gets to the café a few minutes after half-three. They'd warned her it might be nearer twenty-to by the time they could get there. Going over to their old table, she sits down. When the waitress arrives she orders a tea. She wishes she hadn't noticed the creases on the woman's white collar, the small jam stain on her starched apron.

It's five-to four and still they haven't arrived. The place is busy – she can see the waitress eying up the big table she has all to herself. Everything seems different though she can't pick out any obvious changes. Perhaps it's her that's changed.

It was a struggle to get here – not easy to wash two big sheets by hand and get them out on the line without leaving puddles everywhere. They'd hardly begun to dry when the rain started and she'd had to fetch them back in and leave them draped round the fireguard, though they won't be lighting the fire in this weather.

Brian had no sooner got in than he was off out again. Still, she's glad he has friends to play with. Will's due back early today; she's left a pot of spuds ready for him to cook with some bacon for their tea. She'd lied to him – said she was visiting a sick neighbour in this part of town; he's hardly likely to find out Mrs Harkness died some six months back

Lily's made an effort to look nice – changed her blouse and put on her pale blue cardigan. Along with a bit of powder, she'd even applied the red lipstick she keeps for best. Once her chores were done, she'd put cream on her hands and carefully painted each nail with varnish – a cheap bottle from Woolworths.

Looking down she sees the edges have chipped already. Without thinking, she starts to pick off little bits – even scraping at the more stubborn areas with her teeth.

The tea in front of her has gone cold. Lily glances up at the minute hand on the big wall clock and sees it's crept even closer to the twelve. She picks a stray speck of the bitter varnish off the tip of her tongue. When she looks down, the spotless tablecloth is covered in a rash of red specks; she brushes the evidence onto the floor.

The woman at the next table is looking across between mouthfuls of Battenberg, eating in that exaggerated way people do with false teeth. Below the table Lily can see the woman's thick ankles – they remind her of earthworms.

The doorbell pings and they walk in together. They come across and hug her to their cold cheeks and it's so lovely to see them she has to stop herself from bursting into tears.

'We'll get a big pot between us.' Before her dogtooth jacket of is half off, Stella adds, 'Oh and some of them fancies on that stand.'

'Sorry we kept you waiting, Lily,' Debbie says. 'Ruddy bus was late and Stella kept dawdling cos she's got a blister.'

'Massive it is,' Stella says. 'It's these damn shoes! Me other ones were filthy. I tried to clean them but I knew Matron would spot any muck right off. So it was these or nothing. Shall we get a selection – how about eight of them small ones between us?'

'I've not been here long myself,' Lily says, though the pale surface of her half-drunk tea gives her away.

Debbie's distracted by the tower of cakes over on the counter. 'I bag one of them coffee ones I had last time.'

Kathleen's cut her hair and it really suits her shorter. She leans forward. 'Well now Lily, how's it going in the laundry?'

'Fine. I've been put on the fancy hand-finishing work. You know, the lacy things and all that.'

'That's nice,' Kathleen says, looking away towards the young couple that just walked in. 'Having Friday afternoons off must be handy before the weekend.'

Lily knows this is the only thing they can think of saying about her job. 'Yes, it gives me a chance to make a start on the chores and that.' Her tears won't be held back. She sniffs. 'Something in me eye.' She gets out her hanky to cover it.

The tea arrives and they start clattering plates and dishing out the cakes. The sight of all the pastel icing makes Lily's stomach lurch. 'Not for me, ta – had some toast afore I came out.'

'Eh – I've brought a photo of our Luke. I'll show you it in a sec,' Stella says. 'Running around all over the place he is, such a bonny-looking lad – though Lord knows when we'll see him.'

'Are you sure you won't have one of these cakes? Look how titchy they are – hardly likely to spoil yer figure.' She hears the concern in Kathleen's voice. 'Will's alright, is he?' She's peering at her now – sensing something. 'Brian any better?'

'They're fine; it's fine really; you know–' Lily can't do anything to stop the tears spilling down her cheeks.

'Oh eh, what is it, pet?' Debbie rubs her back. They find another hanky and make her do a big blow and laugh when she practically trumpets and every head in the place turns towards her.

Stella pours her a fresh cup. 'Go on, get that down ya,' she says. She does as she's told. The tea warms her throat but nothing else.

The others have gone quiet while they finish their cakes. Finally, Stella sits back in her chair and wipes the corners of her mouth with her napkin like a toff. 'So, come on, Lily – tell us what's wrong.'

The words get stuck in her throat. 'I think.' She sniffs, takes a deep breath, 'I've missed me monthly; I'm pretty sure I'm in the family way.'

They seem to be relieved, smiling at her and each other. 'Oh eh, it'll be all them hormones making you weepy,' Kathleen tells her. The girl's engagement ring bites into Lily's hand as she squeezes it. 'It were the same with our Rosie: bawled her eyes out for the first four months – eyes like a panda's.'

'It's not that.' Lily looks round at all their grinning faces. Making sure to whisper, she says, 'It weren't even planned.' She looks at Stella. 'I don't want to have it.'

'Don't talk so soft.' Stella pulls her chin in. 'Course you want it, you silly hapeth. You just need to get used to the idea.' Lily might have known she'd begin the case for the prosecution.

Lily refuses to be shushed. 'You know me better than anyone, Stell. You know I wouldn't say such a thing lightly.'

'But that's daft talk, Lily,' Debbie decides. 'You'll feel different once you've had it. Once you hold its little–'

She puts them straight. 'I'm not going to bloody have it.'

Stella leans in even closer. 'Don't be stupid – course you are. What about Will – have you told him yet? I 'spect he's chuffed he's going to be a dad again.'

Shaking her head, Lily looks down at the remains of Kathleen's cake. 'No, he won't be – we'd not been planning to have one–'

'Planned or not – it's not the sort of thing you can ignore for long.' The know-it-all tone in Stella's voice is starting to make her really angry. Why aren't they listening to her properly; taking her side?

She's determined to stick to what she'd planned to say. Leaning further in, she whispers, 'I thought that between you,

you might know of something I can take. In the laundry they reckoned Pennyroyal or quinine ought do it but I've already tried both of them and it hasn't made any difference.'

Debbie grabs her arm. 'You're not saying – you're not thinking? Surely not?' Voice so quiet she can barely hear her, she asks, 'Tell me you've not bin trying to get rid of it.'

Lily nods. Each of their faces is arranged against her. The crumbs on the cloth blur together.

'I'm going to the ladies',' Stella says, standing up like she's just been stung. 'I expect in your condition you need to go too, Lily.' It's not a question.

She follows Stella down the stairs and watches her bang the doors back on both cubicles to make sure they're unoccupied. Then she stands with her back to the entrance door and pushes her foot up against it for good measure. 'For Christ's sake, Lily.' Her pupils are so wide her eyes seem almost black. 'That's got to be the stupidest idea you've ever had.'

She looks right into her and it makes Lily wants to push her away and escape. 'Doin' anything like that – it's bloody dangerous. We've all seen what can happen at the Royal.' With an effort, Stella stops herself right there. 'If you go down that road you're gambling with your life – you know that. And, what's more, it's illegal.'

'I'm only talking about a few pills – it'd just be like a normal monthly. No one would know I'd ever done it. Who'd find out?'

'Well, I for one don't know of anything you can take, and, even if I did, I wouldn't help you. It's just plain wicked, Lily, that's what it is.' Stella spits the words into her face.

'Less wicked than bringing a child into the world that's not wanted.'

She can see Stella is struggling to control her anger. Any minute she might cross herself for protection against evil. Her best friend in the world spits out, 'I'm not going to stand here and listen to talk like that. Think yourself bloody lucky you can have one.' Stella takes a breath and tries to calm herself.

'Surely you knew it was bound to happen sooner or later once you were married? What did you expect?'

'I didn't expect a lot of things,' Lily tells her. 'Besides, I've been using this Dutch cap thing the Family Planning let me have. It was supposed to make it safe. The doctor said it would. I did everything he told me to do – *exactly* like he said.'

'Aye, well, that's what they say about French letters but our Tommy's living proof you can still get caught.'

Stella hesitates like she might be counting to ten. Lily recalls the night all those years ago when Tommy was conceived; this is the first time she's ever explained what had happened. It was the same night she herself had kissed a man for the very first time. What a stupid little romantic she'd been back then.

'Whether you planned it or not, you'll have to make the best of things,' Stella tells her, in the way Lily would have expected if she'd thought about it for a bit longer. 'Believe me, you should count yourself bloody lucky you're a married woman.'

Hearing footsteps, Stella moves away from the door. Slowly her face returns almost to normal except for the red blotches on her cheeks. She says, 'I'm going to have a wee while I'm here. Been needing one since before I left the hospital.' She shuts herself in the left-hand cubicle.

Left alone, Lily wants to walk right out, but the peeing noise makes her want to go too. After they're done, they wash their hands side by side in silence.

When they get back to the table, the others try to look like everything's normal; they've even got a fresh pot they're passing round.

'Look how good you've been with Brian. I know you'll make a great mother to this little one,' Debbie says, 'once you've had a chance to get used to the idea.' Her smile is kindly meant. She squeezes Lily's hand. 'Why don't we all settle down and enjoy our tea?'

Bloody tea – the answer to everything. She sits in a hurting silence while they concentrate on their ruddy cupcakes. With a tiny piece of icing still clinging to her lip, Kathleen says, 'I wonder if they make this with Camp or real coffee?'

'I always use Camp, it mixes in much better,' Stella tells her with an effort. 'I swear no bugger can tell the difference.'

Debbie puts down her fork. 'Eh, why don't we go on to the pub after this? What Lily needs is a drink or two to steady her nervous. It'll do us all good. Will won't mind if you're back a bit later, will he, Lil?'

He'll mind all right. She hasn't been out by herself since they married. If she's not back for tea, chances are he'll pop Brian round next-door and go down to the boozer. With luck, he'll be out when she gets back and she can pretend to be asleep.

It's an effort to force a smile to her face. 'It's payday – I 'spect he'll pop out for a pint. He likes the Red Lion round the corner – the beer's a bit cheaper.'

They others laugh too hard at that.

CHAPTER TWENTY-SIX

July 1957

Outside it's still a sunny, breezy sort of a day – not that you'd know in the closeness of the kitchen. She's sitting there mesmerised by Will's every movement – how he's laid out everything on the table as if he's back on the ward. Satisfied, he sets about boiling the glass and metal syringe up in that old black-bottomed pan.

Lily knows she should have turned the key in the front door as she was told to, but in all this cramped heat, she's not thinking clearly and now she's not sure she remembers doing it.

Before she can begin to raise herself from the stupor she's in, there's a sound outside; she can only watch as the door handle begins to turn.

A gust of wind rushes into the room and their visitor calls out Lily's name. The poor woman jumps with surprise when she sees them both right there in front of her.

They're all shocked. Their neighbour, Molly Wright, looks from one of them to the other expecting them to explain why they're both sitting in their own kitchen. 'Not intruding am I?' she asks, the look on her face shows a conviction that something's definitely not right here.

No one speaks. The only sound is the music on the radio.

Can Molly sense Will's inward curse – or is it only obvious to Lily? She won't understand it's because of a door that should have been locked.

Will's quick to slam a wrong-sized lid on the pan; he's careful to turn the gas down before he gives his front to Molly and his back to the stove.

"That was 'Dinner at Eight' by Frank Chacksfield and His Orchestra from their latest long-playing record: 'Lovely Lady'."

Lily remains at the table trying too hard to smile when she's trembling from the shock of the intrusion. Leaning on the table, she gets to her feet, one hand tucking a strand of dark hair behind her ear like she does when she's nervous. She likes Molly well enough – they're friends after a fashion – but she wants her out of the room as fast as they can make her go without being rude about it.

'I was just wondering …' Molly's twisting the door handle gently back and forth in time to the music. 'Can I get you owt from the shops?' To illustrate her point, she holds up her shopping basket with two straw roses on the rim – the same one Lily's often admired out of politeness.

Why wouldn't Molly have remembered that, on a Friday, Lily always pops into the grocers on her way back from the laundry?

She must have noticed how they'd pulled them curtains across. Before today Lily's never seen them drawn together. For the first time she notices the toy sailboats criss-crossing the material. The previous owners certainly liked their busy patterns. The drawn curtains give a queer light, make the kitchen swim with their seasick blue.

Keeping her voice level, Lily says, 'We don't need owt just now, thanks all the same.' Did Molly hear the annoyance in her voice? Should she pull the curtains back or would that only draw any more attention to them?

Lily walks over to the sinks and begins to sort through the laundry in order to demonstrate how busy she is.

Will clears his throat 'Aye, we're all set, thanks all the same.' He's not moved an inch from the stove.

A slight shrug, but Molly hasn't budged an inch. Lily can see she's curious – suspicious even. The only natural light has to come around her solid figure in the doorway. 'Cooking already are ya?' She's seen the steam – nobody would start on their tea this early in the afternoon.

'Just boiling up a couple of dishcloths that had gone a bit grey.' Will's quick with that one. He tries out a smile but forgets to include his eyes.

Their combined silence finally pulls Molly back over the threshold into the sunshine. 'Well, if you're sure then.' She turns her head like she's forgotten to say something, and then pulls her jacket tight against a stiff breeze straight off the moors.

Will strides to the door she's not quite closed. From where she is, Lily watches a thin sliver of Molly's ample backside reach the road and turn on its wobbly way to Crawford's Groceries.

Will locks the door. 'Damned nosey bitch.'

'She was only trying to be helpful.'

'That woman needs to keep her nose out of every bloody thing we do.'

Lily's surprised by his contempt for the woman. He's always so charming to Molly's face. She notices the determination in him as he crosses to the stove. His hands have lost a little of their steadiness now, those fag-stained fingers clutch the box of matches by the side of the cooker ready to light another cigarette.

Will sits down, takes a drag on his fag and holds the smoke in his mouth before releasing it slowly to suck it back up into his nostrils. He lets nothing escape. Apart from the band music, the only sound in the room is the gas ring that's gentle popping – the syringe simmering away.

He gets up again; stubbing his cigarette out hardly smoked

– though he usually drags on them right to the tip. He goes back over to the stove. The braces held together across his back have lost none of their tension. Lily can see he's unsettled, uncertain for sure, but it isn't enough to stop him reaching in with two forks and carrying the steaming instrument across to set it down on the pink-rimmed plate that was her gran's favourite.

Lily's unease is growing. Will's already left the room without a word – gone off to the cupboard out the back and the small object she'd seen him wrap in an old tea towel and hide amongst the car cleaning rags.

Unsure what to do next, she sits back down in the chair by the table. She looks at her wristwatch to see the hands have hardly moved. She finds she's not as certain as she was just now. Everything's been happening in too much of hurry; what she really needs is a few minutes to think things through by herself.

Brian will be running in from school before long. He likes to lasso the end of the banister with his snake-buckle belt and then run straight upstairs for a pee. Despite Will's chiding, he often forgets to take his dirty shoes off first.

Time is moving on and there's still a basket of sheets not touched and the floor needs a good going over with more than a broom. Will's never any help.

Of course, she knows about that temper of his. Knows it will be hard to persuade him to wait for a bit. Perhaps just until the lad's in bed. He'll not stay calm if she lets on it might be longer.

Lily had shown Stella her wedding photos – not that there were many – the first time they'd met up after the *big day*. They'd only had time for a quick chat though she can't remember why that was. 'You looked so beautiful,' Stella told her. Glancing at her watch, she'd added, 'The two of you looked very happy together.'

Afterwards, on the bus home, she realised Stella had

chosen her words with care. She was right – in that photo the two of them *looked* happy.

Will is back already; striding over to the table, he places the bundle next to the plate. It's still wrapped in its grubby cloth. She can hear his low breathing as he stands beside her – readying himself.

Lily stays where she is, arms folded across her chest. She hears the change in him – the way his breathing is steadier, more determined than ever. Bending over the table, he tugs on the edge of the dusty bundle until it spins around and around, shedding its contents across the table. The small cylinder comes rolling to a rest next to the pink plate.

'I've not finished the washing,' Lily says, aware of the false ring to her voice. 'They'll take an age to dry if I don't put 'em out soon.' The chair scrapes at the floor as she stands up and dares to look him in the eye.

What does she see in him, in his eyes? She's noticed again how they are ever so slightly hooded. Looking straight into his black pupils with their thin, hazel irises, she sees only herself – so tiny and distorted. She can't tell what he's thinking.

At the start of it all, she was so much surer. Before that, she'd caught him following her movements; not too obviously mind, no one else would have noticed.

She pulls her head back a fraction to look at his whole face. He's fussy about his hair, that's for sure – always sweeps it backwards, combs it time and again, and then spreads Brilliantine over the palms of his hands before smoothing it into place. The style suits him, though it's beginning to show up where he's starting to recede. His arched eyebrows are surprisingly far apart for a man. He always shaves carefully, even today when he isn't working, his face is smooth, it never chafes her skin. She notices how his lips are made narrower by his habit of holding his mouth pulled in when he's thinking, like he is now.

'It won't take more than a minute.' His voice is flat, so matter-of-fact. 'There'll be bags of time left before the lad gets back. You can have a bit of a lie down if you like, once we're done here.'

'But there's the washing and I want to do a pot of spuds.'

'None of that makes any odds – not in the grand scheme of things.' A favourite phrase that suggests Will Bagshaw has a big plan and isn't just muddling through life like everybody else.

'But I'm not so sure it's a good idea,' she says. 'Not just this minute.'

'It's what *you* said you wanted; what you asked me for.' His voice is growing louder; she follows its upward trajectory as his eyes let slip his growing irritation.

She wants to move further away from him. Her only option is to go back to the sink and start the washing; the last thing she wants is to annoy him. She tries to alter her tone, sound more appealing. 'Can't it wait a bit longer, Will – just till this evening, eh?'

'But I've got it all here ready. You've just watched me do it.' He moves forward, touches her shoulder, strokes it gently like he used to. 'It'll be fine, Lil.' He smiles down at her. 'No need to make a fuss, is there?'

She thinks about all the things that have been said and none of it seems right in this new light. Playing her voice right down, she says: 'But it'll only take a minute or two to re-do it. Once Brian's in bed. I can get everything ready while you watch the telly, if you like.'

'No, I don't bloody like. Why not right now, for Christ's sake? It's all just there – it'll take no time.'

'Well, it's more up to me than you, after all.' She stands her ground, challenging him with the truth of it. Then she waits.

He thumps his fist hard down on the table and she jumps. Everything jumps – the pink plate and its rattling contents, the vial lying next to it; the cold teapot throws up a line of brown liquid over the pile of open letters; the whole lot almost imperceptibly moves up then sets itself down again.

Nothing is broken, but nothing is quite in the same place.

The shock of his anger is fizzing round Lily's body; she feels it from head to foot. It's not the first of the many things that she didn't expect. Like a dirt sieve it seems to have jolted and shaken other things to the surface. They're all in her head now: not individually but together; a new layer of thought telling her it's all wrong; this is all wrong – the drawn curtains filtering out the daylight, the locked door, the piled-up dirty washing, the spilt tea, the pink plate that was her gran's made for sandwiches, a teacake – anything except what's currently lying on it.

For the first time she's really afraid, wants to leave this room, get away from him. Right away from that look he's giving her. Oh yes – now she can tell what he's thinking.

'I didn't mean to get angry,' he tells her, his voice softening into the lie.

She moves towards the door; sees that the key is still in the lock. 'I just need a bit of air.'

He comes after her; 'It's been difficult for me as well, you know, but it'll come right if we do this. We'll both feel better once it's over and done with.' He's walked round the table smartly and now he's standing in front of the door to block the way. He's so close; Lily can smell the sharpness of the sweat that's begun to widen in darker blue rings on his pale shirt. Does he guess her thoughts from the darting looks she aims around him towards the door?

'Give me a few minutes. I'm feeling a bit queasy all of a sudden. Bit of fresh air'll probably sort it out.'

He stays where he is, then slowly moves himself – just enough for her to squeeze past. As she reaches towards the key, he grabs the top of her arm. 'We agreed, didn't we?' His fingers blanch the skin underneath his grip. 'Not changing your mind about this, are you?'

'Course not.' Did she say it too fast? Did he hear her voice wobble?

'Only, we've got no choice, *you've* got no choice. You do see that, don't you?' He pulls her closer. 'You know it's what's best for all of us.'

'I know.' She can't look at him. 'You're right, Will.' The draught from the top window moves the curtains, the little boats sail along always heading into the blue – sky or sea it's all the same.

Abruptly, he releases her arm; she looks at the reddened print of his fingers left behind. She turns the key and opens the door; she has to stop herself running down the path into the road.

Leaning against the rough wall of the house, she bends to touch her knees, gulps in the spring air that cools her face and gives her bare arms goosebumps.

His parked car looms black before her, blocking the way, though over the road she can see the roses in Molly's garden, their summer-heavy pink blooms swaying in the breeze.

No one is around. Lily wills Molly to come round the corner, back from the shops, but of course it's too soon – she'll have hardly reached the main road, not with her bad leg. Every one of the front gardens is empty; all the windows are shut.

Despite his polishing, she can still see that dent in the bumper at the back of his car. There are scratches along one wheel arch.

Will is standing behind her in the doorway, less than a yard away, adjusting his rolled-up sleeves. When he nods towards his car, everything about him seems back to normal – if you didn't know better. 'So – what d'you reckon then?' he asks her, all smiles again.

Lily had genuinely been feeling sick. Was it in her mind or her body? She can't tell and it doesn't matter now; out in the air her nausea is already beginning to fade. She straightens up. Her hair lifts with breeze.

On the gutter of the roof opposite, a fattened wood pigeon is reciting its string of coos, over and over. The bird's head turns sharply as a stuttering, grey van drives into the stood-still close. Spraying the loose gravel, the van turns in a wide arc past her and comes to a stop outside the front gate of number thirteen.

Exhaust fumes catch in Lily's throat as the engine splutters out, leaving its smoky tail to wag and then dissolve. It's an Austin, "A" something; she can't remember the model number, but knows it's the van version of Nobby's old saloon. Just now the sun on the glass hid the driver's face as it passed her; she caught sight of the *single* word – *Handyman*, at the end of the lettering on its side.

Lily can't go running off up the road, he'll only come after her. She starts walking. 'Back in a sec,' she throws out behind her.

She's walking fast but not fast enough. She can read the words across the van she's aiming for: *L. Townsend, General Handyman & Gravedigger*. Right now, she'd rather be running like when they were in school, in the heat and heats of sports day; when your legs took off and that finish line rope, held up by two girls from the infants, was spread out to block every-thing else in the world. It was so much simpler back then – just her and Stella. They'd easily passed Jenny Turner and Andrea Woodcock, their ribbons and pigtails flying as if by themselves and then it was just the three legs of Berty Smith and Stephen Perivale. For that one clear moment, she had believed with Stella that everything would be better if they could just reach that rope ahead of everyone else.

CHAPTER TWENTY-SEVEN

Lenny Townsend is early for a change. He's finished with window-cleaning for the day – his round had gone much better than in the showers of the previous week. Today's bit of sunshine made all the difference. High on his ladder, it felt grand to have the heat of the sun on his back even with the wind blowing through the gaps in his overalls.

He doesn't bother to knock at number eleven – she'd told him twice over how she can't get back before half past two on a Friday. Glad of a bit of respite, he sits back in his seat, unscrews his thermos and pours the last of the tea into its upturned lid. With his free hand he irons out today's Daily Sketch, turns Marilyn over to read what they reckon to Villa's chances.

In his wing mirror, he can see a young woman is approaching. As she gets closer, he notices how her thin skirt is billowing up. It occurs to him that Barbara, his eldest, might look a bit like her in a few years' time; they share the same dark, wavy hair and wide forehead.

When he next looks up from his paper, the woman is peering in through the back window. He puts his *Daily Sketch* to one side, alert to her pretty face, the concern he sees in those blue eyes.

Debbie's talking about something off the telly last night, but Stella can't really hear what she's saying. The high metal rafters of the canteen ceiling are echoing with too many voices as well as the scraping and stacking of plates and cutlery.

Due to some trick of the acoustics, Stella is having fewer problems hearing what the men at the next table are talking about. The sandy-haired one is Dr Jordan. The dark-haired one is called Dr Macy or Lacey or some such name. Dr Jordan's doing most of the talking, as usual trying to hide some of the poshness in his voice – though, just then, he gave himself away when he said *baath*. She was right – they're definitely talking about Will Bagshaw and why he's just been given the sack.

Someone drops a tray and, with their faces turned away, she misses the next bit.

'Would we though?' are the next words Dr Jordan says. 'I mean, a touch of something in her tea would do the job. Chances are they'd have been none-the-wiser at the time.'

Sitting opposite the two doctors, Kerwin, the big staff nurse on six, keeps shaking his head. Many's the time she's seen Kerwin talking to Will – the pair seemed thick as thieves. He's leaning in close to the two doctors like he's thinking of headbutting them. 'So, by your reckoning,' Kerwin says, 'he could have done for his first wife, even though the poor woman died of encephalitis.'

Stella can't hear Dr Jordan's reply; with his head turned away she can't read his lips. She catches the words *in hospital* before Kerwin holds up his hands. 'And *I'm* saying that *if* his first wife had been poisoned, it stands to reason someone would have spotted it at the time.'

Dr Jordan looks rattled. Raising his voice he says, 'Not if they weren't looking for it – that's precisely my point. Rat poison, for example, consists mainly of thallium and thallium poisoning is known to cause encephalitis.' He opens his hands like the conclusion should be obvious. 'The beauty of it, from a poisoner's point of view, is that it doesn't kill their victim straight away – they might die several days after the fatal dose or doses.'

'He's right,' Dr Macy or Lacey says. 'Plenty of people have gotten away with it in the past. I remember reading about a whole spate of thallium poisonings in Australia back in 1952 – or it might have been 53.'

Nodding along, Dr Jordan adds, 'Didn't John Christy use rat poison?'

'No – he strangled people,' Kerwin says.

'Well, in any case,' Dr Jordan says, 'they might not spot thallium if they had no reason to suspect foul play.' He leans back in his chair and puts both hands behind his head.

'Perfectly possible,' Dr Macy/Lacey says smirking in a doctor-knows-best manner. He winks at one of the nurses on the next table and she blushes to her roots.

'Look, I'm telling you both,' Kerwin says raising his voice, 'I know the bloke pretty damned well, he might have been caught thieving a few tins, or whatever, from the kitchen, but he isn't the first to do it and he won't be the last. Doesn't make the man evil – just makes him bloody stupid.'

She's not the only one listening. Kerwin grabs his plate and stands up. 'As for all the rest, it's rubbish. Idle, no, malicious speculation.' He points his cutlery at the two doctors. 'Will Bagshaw is a good bloke; I'm bloody sure pilfering a bit of grub is the most he's guilty of. Man's been unlucky, I'll grant you that much, but that's all it is – sheer bad luck.'

'Let's hope you're right,' Dr Jordan says, getting up.

'You've gone all white,' Debbie says. 'You feeling alright, Stella?'

Too far away to see the sign on the van, Will is standing outside the back door looking down the road. He tries not to mind that a strange vehicle has been parked there for several minutes and yet no one's got out of it. He notices the orange indicator still sticking out on the passenger's side.

A jangle of nerves runs through his chest. Eyes narrowed against the sunlight, he's trying to think, to decide what he should do next. Events have upped and changed when he hadn't expected them to. He curses under his breath; a minute ago he had everything sorted – everything was under control. Now the situation has slipped away from him; more precisely, Lily has slipped away. He needs time to adjust – to rethink his plans.

Walking round to the front of his car, he looks to see where she could have got to. She appears to be heading straight for the parked van – like it's come here to pick her up.

'You off somewhere, Lil?' he shouts after her, the wind deflecting his words.

CHAPTER TWENTY-EIGHT

Lily

She's trying to work out what to say to the driver; it's not like she can ask him straight out for help. Needs to be something like: *Have you got a minute to look at...* At what, exactly? She can't let him inside the house or he'll see that stuff on the table. It has to be something outside. The gatepost Will reversed into? No, he's planning to re-lay those bricks himself. The back door tends to stick but that comes and goes with the wet weather.

Will is probably right behind her; she daren't look round. Reaching the passenger door, she's tempted to open it and get inside. Instead she bends down to rap on the window, her wedding ring adding a sharp note.

The man inside leans across to wind down the window. 'How can I help you, love?'

'Have you got a minute?'

He glances at his watch. 'Aye, one and maybe about nine more.' He folds his paper and puts it on the passenger seat, screws the top on his flask and climbs awkwardly out of the van. One hand resting on the bonnet, he walks round the van and stands with his arms folded across his ample belly waiting to hear what it is she wants.

Lily keeps half an eye on Will. To calm herself, she takes a few deep breaths. The wind momentarily blinds her until she tugs her flying hair away from her face. The handyman hasn't moved; he seems so solidly part of the world with his feet planted apart, his wide, blue overalls flapping at the edges, his thick, checked shirt open at the neck.

She finds she already knows what to say to him. 'Could you take a quick look at our kitchen drain – it's still running, but only very slowly.' This has the merit of being true. Has he spotted Will? 'I think it might need rodding and my husband hasn't got any rods.'

'Righty-ho. Sounds pretty straightforward, pet.' The man's accent isn't quite local – he might be from the other side of the Pennines. 'I've got a set in the back and a few minutes to spare if you'd like me to have a go at it?'

Lily remembers to smile. 'If you would, I'd be really grateful.'

'Aye, well, why don't you show me where the problem is?'

The back of his van is full of tools; it only takes him a minute to locate what he needs to do the job.

She takes the lead and they walk side-by-side towards the house – Lily on the pavement, Lenny in the gutter.

Will must be thinking: *Who the ruddy hell is this bloke and what's she said to him?* When she dares to look, he's still standing by the gate glaring at her. He takes a few slow paces towards them, hands on his hips; with his sleeves rolled up like that he looks ready to fight it out in the middle of the pavement.

Only a matter of yards away, he raises a hand to shield his eyes. Lily wishes she could lean on Lenny's arm for strength. When they're close enough she says, 'Will, this is Mr um –'

'Townsend,' the man says. 'Lenny Townsend. Your wife tells me you've bin havin' trouble with a drain. I've brought me rods.' He holds them up. 'More than happy to have a go at unblocking it for you.'

Will's eyes narrow as they shift from the sturdy handyman back to her. 'Women eh – what's she been on about?'

'It's that drain,' Lily says. 'You must have noticed how the water's collecting around it. It needs a good rodding. I know you're a bit short of tools so, when I saw Mr Townsend here pull up, I thought – why not ask him to take a look at it?'

'Call me Lenny, please.' The man clears his throat, smiles to lighten the mood. 'Only man calls me *Mr Townsend* is me doctor when he's telling me to cut down on the beers.'

'We've been thinking of putting the house on the market, haven't we, Will?' It's a struggle for Lily to keep her voice steady. 'A blocked drain's hardly goin' to make a very good first impression; that muck around it's starting to really pong.' She holds her nose to demonstrate, hopes it might help to soften Will's set-hard face.

'Only got a few minutes to spare. I can come back another time if now's not convenient.' Can Lenny sense the coiled aggression in him? Poor man looks like he wishes he'd stayed where he was reading his newspaper.

Will's mouth opens before his lips decide to form themselves into a smile. 'Why not?' He's all chummy now. 'Unless you're planning to charge us an arm and a leg. My name's Will, by the way.'

The handyman nods. He hoists the rods back onto his shoulder. 'I'll take a look – get the lie of the land, like. Won't cost you more than a bob or so provided it's a straight run. Can't say fairer than that, can I?'

Lenny's hand goes to the small of his back. 'Ruddy back's been playing me up. I might need you to give me a hand with lifting the manhole cover, Will. Me wife says I have to lose weight – wants me to cut down on fry-ups and beer – everything that makes a man's life worth living.'

And now it's the two men walking side by side towards the house, with Lily lagging behind. She looks round for any sign of Molly, or anyone else for that matter, but the close is still empty except for a cat lounging on a wall. The stiff breeze at her back is stealing through her thin blouse and lifting the scarlet petals from the rose bush opposite, swirling them along the tarmac like confetti. In a gap between the houses she can just see the top of the moor. In fine weather her mam and dad used to take them for a picnic. She'd chase George around and he'd laugh like anything when she caught and tickled him.

Lily hangs back. Can she escape – she'd give anything to be on her own again even for a little while. She could tell him she's just popping down to the shops for a minute; easier to say it with Lenny there. He'll catch on straight away and be mad as hell when she gets back. If she gets back.

The possibility is there for the taking but instead she follows behind the two chatting men. As they go past his car, she sees Will tilt his head to admire the way the bumper he polished earlier is catching the light.

'Not the first time it's happened,' he's telling the handyman. 'The wife keeps putting hot fat down the sink.'

'Aye, fat's the commonest cause of a blockage – that and tealeaves.'

'I've told her about it often enough, but does she listen? These women, eh – what can you do with 'em?'

The two men have stopped at the gate and she's almost caught them up. She can smell the whiff of decay rising from the muddy water around the drain.

'It's easy enough to forget,' Lenny says. 'Doesn't take much to block a ruddy drain, when all's said and done.'

Together the two men lean over while they size up the problem. Lily won't be needed. Where else can she go but up the path out of the way. 'Thought I'd make a brew,' she says. 'Fancy a cuppa, Lenny? What about you, Will?'

'Aye, if you're making a fresh one,' Lenny says. 'Three sugars, if you'd be so kind.' To Will he says, 'We need something to lever the cover up. A pickaxe or crowbar would do. I've left mine in the van.'

'Sure I can find something suitable.' Over his shoulder Will says, 'No sugar for me.' She sees him nudge the handyman. 'She knows I'm plenty sweet enough.'

CHAPTER TWENTY-NINE

In the room's blue light, she takes a clean tea towel and carries it across to the table where she wraps it carefully around the cooled syringe and the small vial. The bundle is an awkward shape. She finds an empty biscuit tin in the cupboard, puts the whole lot inside and snaps the lid down tight. She has to stand on the stool to slide the tin onto the top of the cupboard. A portion of it is hanging over the edge – from below she can still see the painted-on biscuits around the rim.

She pulls back the curtains and the little boats tuck themselves back into the folds. You'd hardly know they were there.

Daylight changes the room – makes everything appear normal again. By the time she's carrying the cups of tea and the plate of digestives outside, she's almost convinced herself. Will says, 'Thanks, love' when she hands him his drink.

Not being needed out there, she goes back inside and stands at the window to watch them through her own faint reflection. She pours herself the dregs of the cooling tea to feel its warmth. While she's nursing the drink, she observes the two men at work. Looking at Will, who would guess at that aggressive streak in him – he can switch what you see of it on and off.

They'd caught him stealing on Monday – p'raps they'd had their suspicions before then. 'But how could you be so stupid?'

Lily couldn't help but face him with it in the bedroom where she'd hardly slept. Once the words were out, she'd looked away – her eyes tracing the lines of overblown roses crisscrossing every bloody inch of the walls. 'It's not like we couldn't afford to pay for our own food.'

'Every bugger else was doing it. Look at you – all high and mighty; you cooked it; you ate it.' He spat each word into her face. Not for the first time, he'd grabbed her wrists, held onto her so she couldn't get away; pushing his face right into hers and showing her his ugliness. She'd been shocked – not with him, but with herself for not seeing it before. All those tins of salmon, corned beef, stewing steak – the bargains he'd said he couldn't pass up. She'd tried to work loose from his grip. 'You never let on you were stealing.'

'Oh, for fuck's sake, woman!' He'd shaken her then – really hard; that vein on his forehead sticking out like a worm. 'I came home with it practically under my jacket. You knew alright – you're not that stupid.'

He'd let her wrists go; walked away from the bed he'd thrown her down on. 'Or p'raps you are, after all?'

She'd offered to go with him to the court but he didn't want her there. Despite his bravado, she'd noticed he was trembling as he put on in his shirt and tie, stuffing the letter he'd got from the magistrates' court into the pocket, pretending it had no more importance than a shopping list. She'd never seen him like that before – so unsure of himself; combing his hair over and over like it could make any bloody difference to the outcome.

He'd got home later than she'd expected and as drunk as a lord – as if they could afford it. She'd smelt the booze on him as soon as he came in, slamming the door behind and making the lad and her jump out of their skins. He'd flopped down stony-faced into the armchair of the new three-piece lounge suite.

'It's going to be alright,' that's what he'd told her later, nuzzling her skin inside the collar of her blouse. 'This is nothing.'

He'd grabbed at her breasts, squeezing the stiff brassier to get at her flesh, his breath reeking from all the booze and fags he'd got through. She'd pushed him off, tried to leave the room but his hand had gone up her skirt to the inside of her leg – the bare bit above her stockings. 'A dutiful wife should be offering me some comfort in my hour of need. Come on now, woman, don't be tight with it.'

She won't let herself dwell on the rest of what happened that night. And, of course, he was upset, who wouldn't be, having to stand up like that in front of a judge and be told off like a naughty schoolboy. Why didn't they just sack Will and have done with it? That would have been bad enough. Who was it that decided to make an example of him? It couldn't have been just Matron; the decision must have gone above her.

Looking at him now through the window, lighting up his fag as he watches Lenny push the rods back and forth into the drain, you'd think none of it had happened. Sitting in that bit of sunshine, he's laughing away at something the handyman must have said with his head flung back. She can see that familiar dimple in his chin, the spot she's always loved. She watches him bend forward to clap the other man on the shoulder, and all she wants to do is go out there and slide her arm under his and across his back, tuck herself into his armpit like she used to when they started going out. The feeling doesn't last for long.

How can her life have changed so utterly in such a short a time? Before she met him, she'd been happy enough working at the Royal with the others. 'Not a proper nurse,' she'd make sure to correct people, 'I'm only an auxiliary.' In her eagerness to find a place for herself, she'd been blind. Stupid too – he's right about that; it's not like she hadn't been warned.

CHAPTER THIRTY

To distract herself, Lily retunes the crackling radio. It's tricky to position the dial just right. Moving it a fraction, the angry static subsides enough for her to hear the clear notes of the Mantovani orchestra. They're playing a slow number and some instrument in the background is making a sound like sprinkles of sunlight.

She lets the music run through her body. The tune is about a Parisian cafe and, though she's never been to France, never been anywhere abroad for that matter, it speaks to her of romance just the same. She recalls hearing the same melody while she was getting ready on the morning of her wedding.

She smiles at the memory. Swaying back and forth to the music, the end of the roller towel becomes her partner as the tune begins to trail off. Like a swarm of angry bees more static moves in to swallow the orchestra's final notes.

Exasperated, she turns it off. She keeps looking up at that biscuit tin and worrying about the way it's balanced like that – only half on the top of the cupboard. They'd eaten the biscuits and she'd kept the empty tin because she liked the bright pastel colours of the painted-on biscuits; they look so real – like they might fall off the tin any minute. Had he stolen them too?

The last thing she wants is for Brian to go clambering up there when he comes home from school thinking she's hiding a treat from him. She should shove the tin a bit until it's out of sight.

With her head full to bursting with what's happened this week, and what's still to come, it's impossible to think straight. In her mind's eye, she rehearses pulling out the stool to stand on and pushing the tin on further. But she doesn't. The kitchen clock says it's a quarter past three – only halfway through the afternoon.

A sharp rap on the windowpane makes her jump. 'Can you turn the cold tap on?' Will's face is very close to the glass but he's not looking through it at her. 'Let it run until I tell you to turn it off!' he shouts, nodding to Lenny about something.

At first the waste pipe gurgles and splutters; they must have unblocked the drain because the water is running away as fast as it leaves the tap.

She hears a thud and sees her husband's muddy hand is pressed up against the windowpane. His palm flattens out as he leans in; the swirls on each of his fingertips are as clear as can be. The dirt is showing up the lines that are supposed to reveal someone's future. She knows the life-line and the heart-line but can't recall what the other stands for. It might be wealth.

If her mam was here, she'd take one look at his hand and declare Will was in for a long and happy life – that's what she always told people.

'Okay, turn it off now!' he shouts. His hand has left a muddy print on the glass.

Needing fresh air, Lily dries her hands, opens the door and walks a few steps down the path to where the two men are struggling to place the drain cover back over the gaping hole.

Lenny's red in the face and breathing hard. 'Hold up for a minute, Will.' He lowers his end of the cover until it rests on the path then wipes his brow along the back of one shirtsleeve and then the other. She can see he's in a quite bit of pain from that bad back, could be a disc not properly aligned.

'I think we need to clear some more of that stuff from round the edges so it sits on the rim,' Lenny says. 'We don't want your missus ending up down in that hole, do we?'

A strong gust makes the back door fly shut with a bang. The two men turn towards the noise and finally notice her. Kneeling by the manhole, Lenny smiles up at her. 'We're almost done here, petal. Seems to be running through sweet as can be.'

That feeling of dread comes back and a long shiver with it. She looks down on Lenny's head; at the way the wind is pulling his thinning hair away from his pink scalp. He doesn't seem to care a jot.

Their abandoned teacups are resting on the wall. A thin layer of dirt has settled inside. 'Would you like another brew before you go, Lenny?'

'Thanks all the same, love, but I won't,' he says. 'I'd best be getting round to number eleven, she'll be wondering where I've got to. She's got a tongue on her that one. I don't fancy getting on the wrong side of it.'

He needs to get a move on – no word of a lie – yet Lenny can't help thinking that he's doing something wrong in leaving this young woman unprotected.

He looks across at the husband. 'Have you got a small trowel, Will? I've got one back in the van, but if you've got one handy it'll save a bit of time. A small spade would do as well; something to clear round the edge so the cover sits a bit better.'

'I've got a smallish spade in the shed,' Will tells him. 'Might be a bit big for the job but there's no harm in trying.'

He disappears round the corner of the house. Once he's out of sight, Lenny turns to the wife. He can't stop himself from saying, 'Are you sure you're alright, love?'

She puts on a weary smile. 'Just a bit tired, that's all.' Her eyes don't or won't meet his.

Lenny nods, but he's not so certain. It's none of his business right enough, but he's not one to turn his back. 'Nothing more than that, is it?'

'What d'you mean?'

'Only…' He's struggling with how to put what he wants to say into words: 'If you're in a spot of bother, p'raps I can help.'

'This'll do, won't it?' Lenny didn't see him coming. Looking up at the fellow, he notices the raised spade in his hand, hopes to God he didn't hear the question he'd just asked his missus.

'Aye, that looks grand,' Lenny tells him though it's bigger than he'd have liked. 'Just the job, I reckon.' He holds out his hand to accept the tool. Did he only imagine that moment's hesitation before Will gave it to him? Standing with his hands on his hips, the husband watches him shovel the grass and mud that had grown up around the edges of the hole.

His wife looks anxious, frightened even. Her thin arms are wrapped around herself; Lenny can see how much she's shivering.

Lily notices the mud Will's got on his trousers; they'll need a good soaking. 'All done now,' he tells her, as if she didn't already know. He looks pleased with himself. Nodding to Lenny, he asks, 'How much do I owe you, mate?'

The handyman keeps glancing at her while Will searches his pockets – pulls the linings out to show how they are empty. A wry grin on his face he says, 'I seem to have run out of change.' He takes a crumpled pack of Players from his back pocket and offers it to the handyman.

'Ah well – not to worry.' Lenny gestures away the cigarettes. 'Hasn't taken me long. Let's call it a couple of bob an' have done with. I can call by for it when I'm next passing, if that's easier for you?'

'Like my missus told you, Lenny, we're putting the house on the market. 'Spect we'll both be long gone by the time you're back this way.'

Lenny shrugs then caries on scraping away the last of muck. 'That ought to do it.' He props the spade up against the side of the house. 'When you're ready, we'll try that cover again.'

They struggle to lower it down into its exact resting place, letting go one hand at a time so they don't trap their fingers underneath the rim.

With the job finished, Will straightens up and begins to examine his hands, wiping some of the drier mud away. 'Two bob is far too cheap.'

Lenny waves away the suggestion. 'I'd have only been sitting in me van.' He carefully unscrews each rod section, laying them one on top of the other until they're ready to be tied into a neat bundle.

Will scowls. 'Still seems too cheap for all that hard work, don't it, Lil? Go and get the man a half crown.'

She does what she's told; walks through the house to the front room and the mantelpiece where she always leaves her wage packet. There it is – resting against that photo she had framed of the two of them standing on the registry office steps. Thinking about what Stella had said, she studies their matching smiles. They're holding hands and staring into each other's eyes and they do look really happy. P'raps they had been – it's hard to remember.

She opens her wage packet and sees the pound notes have been taken out, leaving just one ten-bob note. She empties out the loose change and the coins run every way on the coffee table until they spin flat. Gathering them up, she counts out seven shillings and sixpence and three farthings. Though it's next to worthless, she's always loved that smallest coin – the farthing with the perky little wren on the back.

She heads back outside with a half-crown piece in the palm of her hand; it reminds her of giving in her dinner money at school.

Will is right by the back door – so close she almost trips over him. 'Sorry,' she says, though she hadn't so much as brushed against him. He reaches towards her, stroking her thin cotton sleeve, rubbing it slowly up and down. She feels the increase in the pressure on her arm but is too pleased by this sign of affection to complain about his muddy fingers marking her blouse.

Will leans closer, his breath smelling of too many cigarettes; still rubbing her arm, with his free hand he takes the money from her.

In this show of fondness, he turns his gaze towards Lenny. 'You'd best get back inside, Lily – back in the warm.' Facing the handyman, he lets his hand drop. 'Dressed like that, she'll catch her death out here, won't she, Lenny?'

CHAPTER THIRTY-ONE

Will is standing in the doorframe blocking out most of the light. 'Alone at last,' he says – words that once meant something quite different.

Lily doesn't move. The kitchen table is between them, too big really for the size of the room; he'll have to squeeze past it to get to her.

Leaning his back against the open door, he says: 'That chap's gone now – got another job to do – carpet laying apparently. Seemed a decent enough sort. He said to tell you goodbye. Think he might have taken a shine to you.'

She scoffs. 'Don't talk so soft.'

'He must have noticed the signs – the way you were cosying up to him, offering him more tea like you wanted him to stay longer.' She knows where this is leading – the now familiar accusations.

Will takes a quick look down the path to make sure there's no one else about then wipes his shoes on the mat and walks on inside. 'Aye, well, it's water under the bridge now. What made you ask him to rod the drain through without checking with me first?'

'I only thought of it when I saw his van pulled up,' she says, careful not to look directly at him. 'Seemed like a good opportunity.'

'Did it now?' A current of cold air swirls around her legs as he closes the door. Not liking his hands to stay dirty for long, he goes over to the sink to wash the muck off them. For now he's concentrating only on the nailbrush he's scrubbing away with but she knows that won't last long.

Lily retreats to the far side of the room, turns the knob and waits for the radio to come on.

Will finds the towel and begins to meticulously wipe his hands like he would at the hospital. She inches further round, making damned sure to keep the table between them.

"Yorkshire seem to be outclassing their old rivals..." Static breaks up the commentator's next sentence.

'Bit of caustic soda down it might have done the trick – would have saved me two bob.' He looks directly at her; she spots that tell-tale twitch at his right temple.

"And we're seeing another fine bowling performance from Fiery Freddie Trueman."

Distracted by the commentary, his expression softens. He's mad keen on cricket, is disappointed that Brian still doesn't show any interest; she's always reminding him that the boy might change his mind when he's older.

Tilting his head, he's listening closely to what the la–di–da voice is saying about the match. He'd talked about going there on the Saturday – which is already tomorrow. No point in pretending he can afford it after what's happened.

As he moves closer to the radio, she walks round to the sink and starts swilling away the grit and dirt he's left in the bottom of it. Condensation is running down the windowpane onto the ledge and forming little pools on the sill.

She turns on the tap, sprinkles the powder in and then plunges the sheets under, putting them in before the powder's half dissolved. Never mind – he'll see she's started on the washing and can't be dragged away until it's all done.

'Hold up a minute with all that bloody swilling and swoosh-ing, will ya?' Will says, 'I can't hear what the chap's saying.'

Though the sink is not yet full enough; her hands gently swirl the water to help break up some of the bigger clumps of Daz. A glance over at the clock tells her Brian won't be back for a good half hour – longer if he dawdles.

The cricket comes to an abrupt end and, with a snort, Will turns off the music that follows. Head bent, Lily rubs away at the sheets while watching him register the empty table. 'You've gone and cleared that stuff away.'

'I had to, Will.' She tries to make her voice sound matter-of-fact. 'I thought Lenny might see all that paraphernalia if he happened to look in through the window.'

Will comes towards her, his eyes unblinking. 'So where in hell's name have you put it?'

She makes her fingers turn off the tap like this is a normal conversation for a husband and wife to be having. 'Just up on the top there.' She doesn't dare face him, just nods in the general direction of the biscuit tin. 'Handy enough – you can get it down a bit later on.' She keeps moving her arms, agitating the warm, cloudy water but that soap powder is refusing to dissolve; it's sticking fast to the sheets.

'Whereabouts?'

He's come up right behind her; she can sense him scrutinising every move she makes. 'In that biscuit tin up there.' She keeps rubbing at the same bit of material like there's a stubborn stain to get out.

'Well, we'd best get it down and get on with it then, hadn't we?' he says. 'Get it done and dusted before the lad gets back.'

The sun is peeking through the little boats on the curtain pleats as they billow towards her face. She can't think what to say apart from, 'But I've started on the washing.'

'Won't take more than five minutes.'

She hears a lot of huffing and puffing and the scraping of chair legs. Turning round, she's met by his brown shoes balanced precariously on the small round seat of a kitchen stool. Under the strain, it's wobbling like anything. While he stretches up to retrieve the tin, Lily looks down at the stool's spindly legs – the tiniest of movements would send the whole thing sideways and him with it.

Could be her only chance.

She hesitates. If she gave that stool with him on it the tiniest of shoves, what would happen? Supposing he fell and hurt himself – would it help to solve her problems or just create more? From that height the most she could hope for is a broken arm. And what if he suspected she'd done it on purpose – what then?

It's difficult to take stock when she's staring at Will's polished shoes; eye-level to his skinny ankles covered as they are by the brown socks with their red stripes up the outside – a style that seems to belong to a much older man. But, then again, he's not far short of forty. If she's honest, to her he looks older.

What if he hit his head on something hard and she killed him? She can't help but think back to that night when it started between them in the Blue Moon pub on Cable Street. Would have been handy if there'd been a crystal ball on that table when he asked if he could join them.

The kitchen clock is ticking though the hands seem to have hardly moved. Will's feet jump down from the stool.

Lily finishes the two sheets as best she can – double rinsing them to remove the last clumps of washing powder. They're coiled in the bowl ready to feed through the mangle in the back garden.

She tries to slow down every movement, hoping she can drag things out until the boy gets back. Behind her, at the table, Will's scrubbed nails are already under the rim of that biscuit tin, poised to prise it open.

Turning to face him, she forces some cheer into her voice. 'Can you help me fold these sheets ready for the wringer?'

The lid clangs against the hard surface of the table. 'Aye – after we've finished what we started.' He scoops up the bundle she'd hidden inside and begins to unroll it, like a jeweller about to reveal his stock. Under his breath – though still audible to Lily he adds, 'Before we were so rudely interrupted.'

'You'll need to boil the syringe again,' she says, 'so I might as well get on and put the washing out – it'll be dry in no time in this wind.'

She doesn't look down at the table to check the contents of the tin; doesn't once glance at the small vial resting on the tabletop and its tell-tale label. Instead, she looks at Will, reads in his expression his reluctance to leave the room. Why is he so keen to do this now?

He's studying her face – can he see the questions in her eyes? Finally, with a shrug, he gets to his feet and acts like he's not bothered either way. 'Aye, okay then.' His voice remains flat.

When she opens the back door, it flies back and hits the wall and the sound runs through her like a gun firing. He follows her down the path without saying a word. The wind is flattening her skirt against her legs, pulling her hair and scattering the clouds above like so many startled sheep. A lone crow squawks, ragged-edged wings set against the rush of air.

They walk round the dustbins to reach the small patch of overgrown grass where the washing line is stretched between the two sturdy posts Brian likes to use as a goal.

Putting the bowl on the ground, she finds the two corners of the top sheet and she raises her end of it. Will grabs the other two corners and, ducking to avoid the wire, walks backwards still facing her.

Spread out like this, the material rises on the breeze like a sail and tugs at their hands. When they've stretched it far enough, they wordlessly bring both their hands together and shake along the length of this first fold until the material's flat enough to be doubled again. Then they repeat the processes.

Without the sheet spread between them, they could be performing a well-rehearsed dance. Lily imagines how an unseen neighbour, looking from an upstairs window, wouldn't give them a second glance.

They do the same with the second sheet, the one with the pink and green machine embroidery along the top edge her nursing friends gave her as a wedding present. Once folded, they lay this one down on top of the other.

She can manage the rest without his help. Will doesn't move. His eyes are unfocused – he's thinking something through. There's no need for him to hang around and so, wiping his damp hands on his trousers and whistling something tuneless, he saunters back indoors.

Left alone, Lily finds she can breathe more easily. She looks at the scudding clouds and shuts both eyes. Through her closed eyelids the world turns scarlet – forms pictures as shadows come and go.

A bank of clouds moves across the sun to darken her vision and she opens her eyes. Coming back to herself, she lifts up the bowl and hugs it to her chest.

Her hands are trembling; it's hard to feed the folded edge of the sheet through the twin rollers. She's careful not to catch her fingers, to keep the rest of it straight so it doesn't bunch up. To start, the big round handle needs all her strength but, once the rollers are past the top seams, it turns with ease as the material runs through. The squeezed-out water catches the light. She could do with a second bowl but not wanting to go back inside, she makes do; careful to hold the trailing ends above the ground.

Lily chooses the old-fashioned pegs – the wooden, dolly ones her mam – best not to think of what she'd say if she was standing here – bought them from a gypsy during the war with the promise of good luck in return. They'll stay put on a windy day like today.

She stands back to watch both sheets take to the wind,

flapping and twisting like they're dying to be free. This is her last moment to herself and she *must* make a decision.

Around her the ordinary day carries on. By the hedge she sees a couple of late-flowering foxgloves; a noisy bumblebee is entering and leaving each flower in turn. The frayed end of the washing line is whipping the iron post. The overgrown grass ripples in waves like a green sea. She looks at all these things like she's viewing a film.

A small shudder runs through her body – the sort you get when you're about to throw up. She swallows hard.

In the corner, there's a back gate half smothered in weeds. If she dragged it open, she could be down the back alley in no time. Will would come after her eventually. If she ran fast, she could be miles away, though where would she be running to?

A phrase pops into her mind as clear as if someone had spoken: *it's the lesser of two evils*. Did Will say that earlier on? She's not sure; and perhaps it doesn't matter because – when all's said and done – isn't that the truth of her situation? He could be right when he assures her it's bound to work because they use it to expel the afterbirth – he's the medical man after all. It could all be over and done with by tomorrow.

CHAPTER THIRTY-TWO

Stella

Stella knows she could be mistaken about all this but after overhearing all that talk of murderers and people being given rat poison, she can't just do nothing.

Being in such a hurry, she's not even sure if she's on the right bus, never mind that she has no idea which stop she needs. She takes a seat downstairs near the doors. When he comes round, she asks the conductor's help. 'Calm down, lass,' he says, 'you're heading the right way.' He winks as he hands her the ticket. 'Don't look so worried – it might never happen.' When she pulls a face, he says, 'I'll tell you when you need to get off.'

Though cold for July, it's turned into quite a pleasant afternoon. As they leave the main roads, the houses become more spaced out, their front gardens full of flowers. She knows very little about architecture but she hazards a guess these houses were put up just after the war. Being nonetheless near to the centre, she's heard it's an expensive area; makes her wonder how Will Bagshaw could afford to live out here on a nurse's pay. Now all that's come to an end, they'll surely not be able to afford to stay where they are on Lily's wages.

Now she's calmer, Stella starts to question the instinct

that's taken her this far. It makes no sense and yet it seems to make every sense. There's still time to change her mind – she could get off this bus and catch the next one going the other way. Not only had Will Bagshaw been sacked, he'd been prosecuted as well. Is she going to make things worse turning up on their doorstep like this with no warning?

The conductor rings the bell. 'Your stop, madam,' he tells her. Stella doesn't correct him.

She soon enters a maze of houses. Above her the sky is a uniform blue with just the odd cloud. She'd ask the way but there's no one about except the odd passing car.

Will

The same saucepan is back on the heat and steaming up the room. Tiny strings of bubbles are rising to the surface of the water as it comes a steady, rolling boil.

Will adjusts the flame to keep it simmering away, picks up the familiar instrument and lets it slide gently under the surface of the water. The bubbles jostle it back and forth as it lies on the bottom of the pan. That's it – so easy; he only has to wait for a few more minutes and it'll be done.

He likes to plan ahead, but not too far. The thing about plans is they can catch you out and sometimes they have to change in a hurry, like they have this afternoon.

He finds his jacket on the back of the chair and fumbles in the pocket that contains the crumpled pack of cigarettes. He shakes one free and strikes a match to light it. Getting caught like that – he should have been more careful. In any case, p'raps it's high time he was moving on.

Where has Lily got to? Taking a long, steadying drag he tries to control his impatience. 'Settle down, boy,' he tells himself out loud. Better to take this one step at a time – that's something the army taught him well enough.

He was living further north when the war started. Kept his head down until they called him up – then he had no choice in the matter and no control over where they sent you. He soon found out about extremes in the Western Desert; the sun would bake them in the day and, come nightfall, they'd be freezing their arses off. It was always one or the other – no twilight to speak of.

Of course, you got used to it out there – you can get used to anything after a while. It's hard to recall the man he was back then. Just turned twenty and green as ruddy grass. Army life taught him some lessons – the hard way. He'd learnt how many of the things that are supposed to be opposites – day and night, right and wrong, innocence or guilt, love and hate, life and death – were, in truth, much closer together than he'd been led to believe.

Will's not certain, even now, what impulse led him into nursing after he was demobbed; certainly not the money, that's for sure. He needed a job and those advertisements in the papers egged him on to have a go at it. He'd thought they might not be keen to accept men, but they took him on. Easy as anything, it was.

Hadn't he seen some sights on the wards since then? Wouldn't credit how some people behave if you hadn't heard it or seen it with your own eyes. From conception onwards, so much of life is down to the luck of the draw. You see it every day – all those poor old buggers lingering on despite having Lord knows what, while some youngster will be snuffed out before they've had chance of a proper life.

When it's quiet on the ward at night, he likes to read a good book – Agatha Christie, Arthur Conan Doyle, that sort of thing. Whodunnits – funny they're never called whydunnits. He enjoys spotting the false leads, the challenge of guessing the murderer. Some of the ways they go about bumping people off – there's no other word but ingenious; makes you wonder what sort of person could write such a story.

Life has taught him well, taught him how to concentrate on the here and now; making sure you get the task at hand done and done well. After you're finished, it's best to avoid thinking over how you might have done this or that differently – best to forget about it and move on.

The back door opens and Lily walks back into the kitchen; he starts to whistle the first tune that comes into his head – Bye Bye Blackbird. She brushes past him, takes the empty bowl to the sink and turns on the taps.

Halfway through the second chorus he stops. His voice carefully devoid of emotion, he asks, 'Are you ready, Lil?' When she doesn't answer he says, 'Everything is nice and sterile again. It won't take us a second to have it done with.'

'I'll be with you in a mo,' she says, her voice lighter than before. 'I just need half a tick to finish off these couple of pillowslips and get them out on't line.'

He's surprised by her change of mood; how much more cheerful she seems to be all of a sudden. Continuing to hum that same tune, he watches the way her backside is swaying to the beat he's imagining as she paddles her hands to dissolve more soap powder.

Closer, he notices the line of fine hairs standing up along the curve of her arms. He breathes in the warm smell of her body. She turns and those blue eyes alight on him, reminding him again of a cloudy sky. 'Just goin' to peg the last of it out,' she says. 'Won't be a sec.'

Anyone will tell you Lily is a good-looking woman. He'd enjoyed strolling into the pictures or a pub with her on his arm; having her sitting next to him in his car as they drove out of the town to park up on the moors for a kiss and cuddle and a bit more besides. Sometimes they'd bring a sandwich or two with them, a bottle of beer, or some orange pop to cool them down afterwards.

Finding himself smiling, Will shakes himself out of it. He's always prided himself on his decisiveness; this is no time to get cold feet.

CHAPTER THIRTY-THREE

Lily

Their two pillowslips are hanging beside the sheets. Long blades of grass have been tickling at her ankles like they're reminding her that with the last of her chores done she can't put it off any longer. She thinks about what will happen when she goes back into the kitchen.

A wave of nausea comes over her. Clutching her chest, she waits for it to pass like it usually does. Bending double, she tries to concentrate on the stitching at the front of her shoes.

When she's sure she's not going to retch, she straightens up. It's reminded her of what's going on inside her body, what will happen next if it's not stopped. The thought makes her feel sick again in a different way – right through to her core.

She longs to be rid of the overwhelming dread that's been with her these last few weeks, its dark presence outweighing everything else – poisoning every positive thought she has. When all is said and done, Will is the only one trying to help her regardless of his motives. He's sure it will work.

Her pregnancy is a mistake that was never supposed to happen. The doctor at the Family Planning clinic had looked at her over his glasses when she asked for help, questioning her like you might a child or an imbecile. As he scribbled away, she'd tried her hardest to explain her reasons for not wanting a baby. She even told him her family's history – how her mother had had to be sterilised for fear that another pregnancy might kill her. How she'd found out that two of her great aunts had died in childbirth.

The doctor had raised his eyebrows. He'd examined her so thoroughly she still blushes at the memory. His expression had remained fixed until he leant back in his chair. Swivelling it one way then the other, he'd lectured her – telling her he could find nothing abnormal and it would be far better if she just got on with it like most women and what's more the NHS had made death in childbirth almost a thing of the past, even for a woman of her age.

In the end, she'd burst into tears and that seemed to persuade him more than words. He'd agreed to give her something to use "for the time being" though she wouldn't be allowed to have it until after the ceremony – she would have to bring the wedding certificate to prove she was a married woman. She remembers him saying, "I expect you'll soon change your mind when things have settled down and you have grown more used to married life".

Once he'd left the room to get whatever it was, she'd managed to sneak a look at the notes he'd been making and saw how he'd written in large letters at the bottom of the sheet: *Miss Hetherington is an otherwise healthy woman who is about to marry. Nonetheless, she professes a morbid fear of pregnancy and childbirth.*

He came back with a nurse who was carrying something. After she uncovered it, Lily almost laughed out loud because sitting there in its little box, the silly thing looked like a model flying saucer. It seemed much too big to go up where she was being told she'd have to put it – never mind stay up there for hours on end.

She thinks about that book of her mam's – *Every Woman's Doctor Book* and what it said in there about hereditary weaknesses. There's a definite weakness amongst the women in her family – they seem not designed for childbirth. The book didn't mention one form of weakness, the side of him Will tries to hide from the rest of the world. She won't give it a name but nonetheless knows it wouldn't be right to pass it on to any child of hers.

Lily jumps a mile at the long wail of the button factory's knocking-off siren. The bloody thing sounds like the air raid sirens she heard too many times during the war – terrifying times spent in that Anderson shelter in the garden when the only thing you could do was pray for deliverance.

She steps back from the line of flailing washing and leans against the metal post. In that second, her mind is made up. She knows what she should do.

The damp sheets billow out blocking her way but she side-steps them. Mustering her courage, Lily turns into the wind to pick up the bowl. She walks towards the back door still nursing a few doubts but nevertheless determined. There's no denying she's had a touch of the jitters this afternoon – but now her legs have steadied along with her determination.

Best to get this all over with once and for all. She rolls her shoulders knowing it helps the muscles in your back to slacken and release some of their tension. With a new purpose in her movements, she takes a deep breath, straightens her back and turns the door handle.

CHAPTER THIRTY-FOUR

A few streets away in Bastion Road, Brian and his friends are staring into a crumpled paper bag and arguing about how to divvy up the lemon sherbets they've bought between them. Mrs Harris won't sell less than tuppence worth of hard sweets when it's busy, so they'd had to buy sixpence worth between the four of them.

As usual, Harry Brinkley takes charge. His hands are covered in ink from his leaking pen but that doesn't stop him grabbing more than his fair share. Brian doesn't say anything because they've sworn to be best friends and best friends don't tell on each other. Besides, he's going round Harry's to play with their new puppy – that's got to be worth a couple of sweets.

A car comes round the corner and its blaring horn makes them jump back onto the pavement. Instead of carrying on, it stops. The driver winds the window down and whistles like you might call a dog. The sun lights up the man's red hair like it's on fire. 'You lads need to be more careful,' he says. 'I could have run you over just then.'

The woman in the front seat had looked a lot like Lily. Could it have been her?

The new carpet he's laying at number 11 wouldn't be Lenny's choice if he could afford a fitted carpet for his own front room.

He's taken the door off its hinges in what Mrs Stewart insists on calling her *lounge*. Outside on the pavement, he's trying to concentrate on cutting exactly three-quarters of an inch off it in a dead-straight line.

As he saws along his pencil mark, he feels uneasy. There was something familiar about that bloke Will. He's been racking his brain since he left but can't quite put his finger on where he's seen him before.

Wouldn't take a mind reader to work out there was something odd going on between those two. When the man's wife handed him his tea, he'd noticed how her hand was shaking. At the time, he'd put it down to her not having enough on but now he's not so sure. He'd looked up and caught her disappointment, could see right away how she wanted him to stay. That worried him and still does. Twenty years ago he might have been vain enough to misunderstand her motives but not now. When he said he had to go, her smile had dropped.

He's good with faces – it'll come to him in the end.

Will is impatient to begin. 'Ah, there you are, Lil, I was wondering what was keeping you,' he says, in a tone suggesting this is nothing out of the ordinary.

He's pulled the curtains together and put on the overhead light. This time he's made damn sure the front door has been locked and securely bolted. He wonders if he should do the same to the back door but no one is likely to be coming in that way. On the table, the same plate holds everything he will need.

'We've got plenty of time,' he tells her. 'The lad won't be back for a bit. You can have a cuppa and a lie down on the bed after I've finished, if you like.'

The room is swimming in that blue-tinged gloom again. He's turned the radio back on. 'Plenty of time,' he repeats, like they might be about to catch a bus to the pictures. Lily takes off her shoes – they're muddy from the garden – and Will whisks them away like he always does.

The music that's playing seems to guide her movements as she unties her apron and wraps the loose ends around to make a tight bundle. Clutching it in front of her, she walks over to where he's standing. She thinks about the previous week – the small stain of blood in her knickers that had given her so much hope for a few hours but ended in nothing. This is the only way – her last chance to stop things going any further, sever the link that would bind her to him forever.

Will's got his professional air on; you'd think he was treating some patient in the ward. Without even looking at her, he holds the syringe up to the light and flicks the barrel to dislodge any air bubbles. The needle's shaft is too fine for her to see the tiny sliver of light holding the reflection of their kitchen.

Lily's apron is pulled gently from her hands and left to fall on the floor. 'I'd just like you to lift your skirt up a bit at the back and pull your knickers down a touch.'

This close she can smell the way the afternoon has made him sweat. Though she's tense with apprehension, she does everything he tells her to do. She pulls up the hem of her skirt and holds it at her waist then bends over.

Lily stares at the clock on the wall, gives her full concentration to the small jerks of its minute hand. She can't see the syringe he's holding, the tiny streaks of light running along the needle to its tip – the vanishing point where all lines converge and everything begins or ends.

CHAPTER THIRTY-FIVE

Stella

She's lost because every house, every damned street looks more or less identical to the next. They're all semis – two bedrooms, three at the most. Everything is clipped, neat and tidy; each has a small front garden with a stunted tree or a flowering bush to take the edges off the short concrete drive.

Despite the chilly wind, panic is making her palms sweat. Stella's bloody sure she hasn't come all this way just to walk round in flaming circles. Stella's written to Lily a few times so she knows the house number and the name of the road.

Finally she catches sight of the disappearing back of a stout woman carrying a shopping bag. Hoping not to alarm her too much, Stella runs after her. Getting nearer she shouts, 'Excuse me!'

The woman turns round. Out of breath, Stella asks her for directions. The woman purses her lips. 'It is a bit of a rabbit warren round here. Let me see now.'

She looks around to get her bearings. 'Right, you want to turn left at the end of this road by that blue car.' She looks less certain – works her mouth this way and that while she's thinking it through. 'Carry on along until you see a phone box on the corner. After that I'm pretty certain you need to take the second – no, tell a lie – it's the third turning on the left and you should be there.'

Though she has her doubts, Stella follows her instructions to the letter and ends up on the right road – a cul-de-sac. The houses look commonplace but perhaps a bit newer than the rest.

A familiar van is parked by the side of the road. It's Lenny Townsend's. He drinks in the same pub as her dad. Nice bloke – reliable sort. He'd driven her and her mam to the hospital when she was having Tommy – her mam had had to sit on a toolbox in the back. He must have set up those two sawhorses. There are curly wood shavings on the pavement but no sign of Lenny.

Getting closer, she can pick out Lily's house. It's the odd one out – the one with its front curtains pulled in the middle of the day. She can't help but raise both eyebrows when she sees the makeshift "For Sale" sign on a piece of white card propped at a slight angle inside the front window. Her heart sinks at the desperation, the sadness of the optimism in those two scrawled words. Not a cheap house – definitely not the sort of place you could sell in a hurry with a makeshift sign. She can't guess what one of these semis would go for but she's certain it's more than most folk could afford.

There's a car in the driveway. Not his Rover but a Ford Zephyr – dark grey, almost black. Is it Will's or somebody else's? Either way, despite appearances, somebody must be in.

The dents in the Zephyr's bumper suggest it was responsible for the damage to the gatepost. She notices the dislodged bricks stacked up beside it.

Stella stops to take a breath before she opens the gate and walks up the short path. The car also has a "For Sale" sign propped up in its back window. In smaller letters someone's added: £299 ono. She's learnt a lot about cars from Nobby and three hundred pounds seems to her a bit steep.

Weeds are poking through the cracks in the front path. As

she stands on the doorstep, her mind goes blank. She has no idea how she's going to explain her visit.

She raises the knocker. As soon as she slams it down, she instinctively steps back.

It's been two minutes and still no one has answered the door. From inside, she's sure can hear music playing.

CHAPTER THIRTY-SIX

Lily

A sound from outside stops them dead. Another knock – this time even louder. Whoever it is, they mean business. Will looks at her, holds his index finger up to his lips to warn her not to move, not to make any kind of noise – as if she needed telling.

Lily goes to straighten up but the pressure he's putting on the back of her neck makes it impossible. 'Hold still,' he whispers like she's a cow in a milking stall.

The music must be audible from out there but the radio is on the shelf across the room and too far away for either of them to reach without moving. In any case, to turn it off suddenly would only make things worse.

She looks down to the strip of sunlight beneath the door – where it's blocked at the centre by a shadow. Both bolts are in place and the key is sitting right there in the lock. There's no possibility of them getting in.

Will's drawn the curtains back across the window. With the afternoon sun behind the thin material, she can see the silhouette of the beech tree opposite swaying back and forth. In his haste he must have yanked them too hard; he's left a narrow gap to one side – just enough for someone to peer in.

The doorknob rattles and they both watch, mesmerised, as it begins to turn. Lily's so still, her chest isn't even rising and falling as she breathes. Turning her head to one side she looks at the table – all the things he's laid out on it. She focuses on the small vial lying over there on its side. He'd tapped the side of his nose when she asked him how he'd got hold of it without anyone noticing it was missing. Ergometrine the label should say but the shape of the word looks wrong.

She hears the dull thud of someone pushing their whole weight against the door – determined to get in.

From this distance she can't see exactly what's written on the vial. Her heart begins to race – she'd stake her life on the fact that it doesn't begin with an E.

CHAPTER THIRTY-SEVEN

Stella is quite certain there's someone in there; who would go out and leave the radio on like that? Having come all this way, driven on by a growing sense of dread; there's no point in her simply walking away.

Besides, those pulled the curtains are worrying her. If you didn't know, you'd think someone had just died in the house and they'd pulled them together as a mark of respect.

She tries the door handle again but there's no budging it. Fortunately, the front window is a low one and she's spotted a small gap in the curtains, which might be enough to put her eye to.

Has to be worth a try.

Stella checks behind – the last thing she wants is to be taken for a burglar by one of the neighbours. There's still no one about, no movement except where the wind is jostling the hedge.

She steps off the path. As she gets nearer to the window, the music grows louder – a jaunty tune, the sort that would normally reassure you that everything is fine and dandy.

She catches a whiff of decay from the drain that's directly beneath the window. Stella steps onto the raised cover. Balancing on one foot, she pulls herself up so that she's at a better height to see inside. One hand clinging to the rough windowsill, she presses her nose into the cold glass and peers inside.

The window is half steamed-up, that and the narrowness of the gap she's looking through means it's difficult for her to make out a damned thing.

Closing one eye as if she's about to look through a telescope, she tries again. When her eye adjusts, she's able to make out a dangling light and, below that, the solid shape of a table with crockery on it. What could be more ordinary?

Not done yet, she focuses off to one side where there's a shadowy area. She stares at the various shapes it contains but can't begin to fathom what she's looking at. A gust of wind makes her wobble and she clings to the sill to right herself. Half expecting someone to have crept up on her, Stella takes another look behind. Nothing – the coast is still clear.

But what if she's got this wrong? What if the two of them are only having a bit of fun in the middle of the day? They are newlyweds after all. It's no business of anyone else if they might want to do a bit of canoodling in the middle of the afternoon. She stops her imagination going beyond that point. Stella certainly has no desire to catch the two of them in the act. She shivers. P'raps it might be better to go now before anyone catches her. Maybe she should leave them to it?

No. She can't really fathom it, but her deepest instincts are telling her something's not right here. Reluctantly, her eye returns to the windowpane, to gaze down on the solidness of that unremarkable tabletop. This time she catches something glinting in the light – something familiar that most definitely shouldn't be lying on somebody's kitchen table right next to their ruddy teapot.

Stella peers into the shadows in the corner and, this time, catches a slight movement.

CHAPTER THIRTY-EIGHT

Lily

Blast like a shotgun. Lily cries out as she's showered in broken glass. A dull crack; something lands with a thud at her feet. A brick.

Open-mouthed, he reels backwards propelling his arms in a desperate backstroke, blood trickling down his face.

He crashes to the floor and she stares down in disbelief as more blood oozes from his ear to join up with the growing pool from under his head. She watches it expand into a dark halo.

His blood-splattered hands are pressed to the wound to stem the flow. 'Help.' Spoken quietly – no more than a croak. 'Help me, Lily.'

Stunned, she feels the fresh air in her face; stares up at the crazed window, the blue curtains swirling as they're pulled outside, catching on the jagged edges.

Through this new improbable star hole she sees Stella. Not *her* Stella, surely. Has to be dream, or a nightmare – Lily can't decide which.

It's so odd – everything changed in an instant. Her gaze falls on the table then down to the floor. Every surface is awash with twinkling fragments like glass confetti. Or like they're back in the blitz.

'Careful!' Stella shouts. 'Don't move an inch!'

She looks down to her stockinged feet and then at Will lying on his bed of glass. Did Stella mean her or Will – which one of them is not supposed to move? 'I'm going to get help,' Stella tells her, always the bossy one. 'Stay exactly where you are.' Her head disappears like she's playing peekaboo.

Romantic music continues to serenade the two of them. Not moving off the spot, Lily bends at the knees. It's a stretch to pick up her pinny – the one she took off only moments ago. She tries to shake it free of glass then rolls it up. Moving Will's limp red hand aside, she presses it into what she thinks is the wound on his head – hard to be sure of the source when there's so much blood.

The commotion must have caused the little vial to jump clean off the table because it's resting on the floor an arm's length away. Still intact. She can see she was right about what's written on it. She recognises the label – they use that same type on the Diabetic ward. A staff nurse once told her they have to keep checking because a single accidental dose would be fatal to anyone who wasn't diabetic.

Her apron is changing colour in front of her eyes. It was a wedding present from Kathleen, white lilies on a pale blue background – her namesake flower. She doubts that stain will ever come out of it, not now.

Will's eyelids flicker. 'Shh!' She puts a finger to her lip. 'Shut your eyes. It's time for you to go to sleep.'

CHAPTER THIRTY-NINE

Stella

She's annoyed at not being allowed to write the statement for herself. In his sloping hand, Sergeant Clayton writes everything she says down and, it seems to her, a bit more besides.

Once again, he raises a hand to interrupt her. 'And quite naturally, finding the man's car in the drive when the door was locked and the curtains pulled, you were anxious about your friend's welfare, were you not?'

'Yes, of course I was.' She watches words blossom in black ink along the paper.

It's not long before his hand goes up again. 'You recognised the lethal vial lying on the table. You could see Mr Bagshaw was forcibly restraining his wife and about to inject her.'

'I think I could,' she says.

He carries on writing her words for her. 'The threat to your friend's life was clear and imminent,' he tells her. When his words reach the end of the next line, he looks up. 'Precious minutes would have been lost if you hadn't had the presence of mind to run and fetch Mr Townsend to break the door down.'

'Yes, I suppose they would have been,' she says.

He turns the page and carries on unaided. Finally, he caps his pen and sits back in the chair.

Stella is asked to read it through before she signs at the bottom with a different pen. The ink is blue.

He looks pleased with himself. 'We're all done, Miss Marsden.'

They leave the room. He tells her to take a seat beside a ripe-smelling man with a badly cut face. The man keeps edging along the bench ever closer to her until she's forced to stand up again.

Not used to sitting idle, she paces the few steps the room will allow, her eyes endlessly revisiting the noticeboard with its precautionary posters and list of missing pets.

At last, a fair-haired young policewoman calls her name and she's asked to follow along an echoing corridor. The woman halts outside a door marked "Interview Room 2". When she knocks, a deep voice from inside answers with a single word: 'Come.'

'Chief Inspector,' the WPC tells the tall man now advancing with his hand outstretched. 'This is Stella Marsden.'

'Miss Marsden – I'm Chief Inspector Lockwood.' He barely touches her fingers before letting go again. 'Come on in; sit down.' He holds a chair out for her; his smile dropping away almost immediately.

The room smells of pipe tobacco and damp. This Lockwood looks familiar – has she seen those wide-set eyes and that long nose before? He positions himself opposite her behind a large desk. 'Right, let's see now–'

He begins by taking out a notebook, which he places on the desk. He then turns his attention to a handwritten document. 'I understand your full name is Stella Martha Marsden, and you live with your parents, your elder brother and your young son. Is that correct?'

'Yes. That's right.' She coughs to help clear her parched throat.

'And you're employed as an auxiliary nurse at the Royal?'

She nods.

'I'm afraid I do need you to answer, Miss Marsden.'

'Oh, I see —' flustered now, she tells him: 'Yes, yes all that's true.'

He asks her a few questions about her work though she can't think why. When someone knocks, he goes to the door and opens it just enough to stick his head and shoulders into the corridor.

Male voices; she strains unsuccessfully to hear what it is they're muttering about.

With a heavy sigh, he turns to address her: 'Please excuse me just for one moment, Miss Marsden. I'll be back shortly.'

A few minutes later, the same young constable comes in carrying a tray. 'Here we are then.' She has a soft Irish accent – the sort of voice people trust. Her shinning collar number is 568. 'The CI should be back in two ticks.'

Stella is left alone to stare at the closed door. Although it's a warm evening outside, the room is chilly. Bare too – just the desk and two hard chairs without a cushion between them.

Outside the high, barred window, the clouds part and the sun cuts into the room, lighting up all the swirling motes in the air as it dissects the top of the desk and the man's empty chair.

There are two more chairs in the shadows directly behind her – there in case reinforcements are needed. For want of anything else to look at, she stares down at the tiled floor – easy enough to mop, though it's clear from the staining that the corners get missed more often than not. Matron wouldn't tolerate that sort of sloppiness.

Her watch shows ten minutes have now passed since the chief inspector left the room. The dregs of her tea taste bitter.

For the first time Stella notices a small sheet of paper sticking out of the fat file on the desk – a handwritten note with muddy fingerprints along the edges.

Curiosity makes her pull it out and turn it around. She reads:

Dearest Ivy,
I torture myself with thoughts of how I might have saved you.
My only hope is you're looking down from heaven now.
May you rest in peace.

There's a noise outside. Stella notices the small glass panel let into the top of the doorframe. She pushes the note back into the file. It makes her shiver to think that someone could be outside the door watching her.

A few seconds later, it opens and the same WPC comes in to take the tray away. Stella doesn't expect her to come back. Without a word, she smoothes her skirt and sits down in one of the chairs behind her – a witness to what's about to be said.

The chief inspector enters in haste, scraping his chair on the floor before he sits. He places his notepad back on the table to his right, in the exact same place as before; then repositions it twice, moving it just a fraction each time until he's satisfied.

His long fingers hold the little pad down in position while he turns over the pages. 'Where were we now? Ah yes.' He looks up at her. 'I understand you and Lily Bradshaw were schoolmates.'

'Yes.' Stella wonders how they can know all this – who they've been speaking to. 'We were ten when we first got to know each other properly – when we became friends.'

He flips on through until he reaches a blank sheet, his sharpened pencil poised to record each new word. 'Would you say you were close friends?'

'Aye – the best of friends. Always in and out of each other's houses when we were youngsters. Recently, I'd not seen as much of her – not since she got wed. Lily gave up her job at the hospital when she got married.'

'And after that you saw far less of her?'

'Yes, that's true.'

Finally, he looks directly up at her: 'But you continued to

see one another – from time to time?' He's giving the air of someone only mildly interested, though his eyes are telling a different story.

'Well, yes, though like I said, not very often. I'd also sent her a few letters and cards and we'd spoke on the phone a couple of times, but not for long. Her husband –' She doesn't want to say his name. 'He'd got a telephone put in at their house but we've not got one at ours – my dad always says he don't hold with such new-fangled things.'

Stella's disturbed by his unbroken gaze. She waits until his eyes flick back to his pad before she adds, 'It was difficult to meet up. Lily had to keep cancelling, for one reason or another.'

'But you *had* seen her fairly recently?'

'Aye.' She takes a deep breath before she's able to continue. 'A few weeks back we met up in town – at a café. The Lyons on the corner of Duke Street.'

'Just the two of you?'

'No – I was with two other orderlies from the hospital: Debbie Alistair and Kathleen–' Why can't she remember her surname? 'Kathleen Blackman. Sorry, I just couldn't think for a minute. We're all good friends, you see, and we often meet up at the end of the week, if we're not on the weekend shifts.'

He leans towards her now. 'And whilst your four friends were chatting away together, Mrs Bagshaw – Lily – would, naturally enough, have told you her news.'

Stella can feel her heartrate increasing, her underarms beginning to sweat. 'Aye, she did. Such as it was.' She's all too aware of how he's given her no choice but to look straight at him.

'Did she tell you about her pregnancy?'

She can't avoid answering: 'Aye, she did say she *thought* she might be in the family way. She were pretty certain about it, though she'd not seen a doctor or owt like that.'

'And would you say she was happy at the prospect of be-coming a mother?'

Stella curls her fists below the table until her nails dig in. She's determined not to cry. 'No, she weren't happy about it. It weren't planned or owt, you see.' She lowers her voice to add: 'She'd been using the cap but it hadn't worked.'

'Did she talk about wanting to abort the baby she was carrying?'

Stella looks down. She can feel her colour rising along with the tears. Her face is burning and she knows he'll have noticed. 'Lily did say that she wanted to get rid of it – but we thought it were just her nerves.'

'Would you say she was *very* upset about this pregnancy?'

'Aye, I s'pose I would. She'd always said she didn't want to go through all that.'

'An unnatural reaction from a married woman, wouldn't you say?'

'She hated the idea of having a baby. When she met Will, he already had a son and I think that must have taken the pressure off, if you get my drift?'

'So she hadn't intended to get pregnant?'

'Far from it.'

'Miss Marsden, did she ask for your help in finding some way to induce a miscarriage?'

'No – well, not exactly. She did ask us about pills, any pills that might help bring on her monthly.'

'Let's be clear here.' His unblinking eyes are staring right into hers like it's Judgement Day. 'Did Lily ask you to obtain pills or drugs of any kind that might bring about an abortion?'

Though she's flustered, Stella knows it's important to meet his gaze and choose her words carefully. 'No she *did not*. She did ask if any of us knew the *names* of any pills that might help her in her predicament.'

'And did you offer any suggestions?'

'No, I did not.' She keeps on shaking her head to make it more than clear. 'We all told her, straight out, we didn't know of any such pills, or owt like it. We tried to laugh it off; make out the whole notion of hers were a bit of a joke – that she'd come round to the idea after she'd time to get used to it.'

Her damp hands are clenched together in her lap. 'We none of us suggested owt. I didn't, for sure. I'm fair certain Debbie or Kathleen didn't either. I imagine you've already spoken to them.'

His scribbling seems to take far longer than her answers warrant. When he's finished, he looks up to ask: 'Did Lily return to the subject later on in your conversations?'

'No, not with me she didn't. She knows my view on the matter; that I didn't hold with it.'

'That you would disapprove of any attempts she made to abort her baby?'

'Aye – I've never believed it right to interfere with a life once it's started.'

'To play at being God, as it were?'

'I'm not so sure I'd put it like that.'

'How would you *prefer* to put it, Miss Marsden?'

His manner is beginning to irritate Stella. She tells him straight: 'I've got a child meself and, though he certainly weren't planned, I'd not change things for the world. What's more, unlike most people, I've had to dispose of a few miscarried foetuses as they call 'em. It's bad enough when it's nature that interferes; I don't hold with anybody doin' such a thing on purpose.'

'So, you believe it to be morally wrong to interfere with a pregnancy once it's begun?'

'Aye, I do. Unless, of course, the mother's life's in danger – that's a different kettle of fish altogether.'

'But there was nothing to suggest this was the case with your friend Lily?'

'No. Like I said, I know she were always scared stiff of getting caught with a baby – but she were fit and healthy enough.'

'Quite so.'

'Is there anything more you wish to tell me at this stage?'

237

'Nothing I haven't already told Sergeant Clayton.'

'Miss Marsden, I'm satisfied that you tried to gain entry to Mr and Mrs Bagshaw's house out of understandable concern for your friend's welfare. A woman can't be expected to aim a heavy brick with any accuracy; the fact that it hit Mr Bagshaw on the head can be considered a freak accident.' He lifts one eyebrow. 'Recognising the gravity of the situation, your prompt action almost certainly saved the worthless man's life.'

He stands up all of a sudden. 'Right then – we'll leave it there shall we.'

Stella stares up at him. 'Does that mean I'm free to go?'

'It does – unless you're planning to leave the country that is.'

'Chance would be a fine thing,' she tells him. Seeing him narrow his eyes she adds, 'I promise you I'm not planning on going anywhere.'

CHAPTER FORTY

Lily

Chief Inspector Lockwood stands up. 'Thank you, that's all we need; you can go home, Mrs Bagshaw.' She yawns and he rests one hand on her shoulder. 'I expect you could do with some sleep.' Having been in this windowless room for what seems an age, Lily has no idea what time it is. All she knows is that the last place she wants to go back to is that bloody house. 'P'raps I could stay here,' she says, 'if you have an empty cell.'

That makes him smile. 'We find most of our guests would prefer not to spend the night if they can possibly avoid it.'

'What about Brian – is he here? Who's looking after Brian?'

'All taken care of. The boy's with his grandmother. Probably fast asleep by now with any luck.'

Lily frowns. 'But she's been dead for years.'

Behind her Sergeant Clayton scoffs. 'I assure you Mrs Nugent is very much alive.'

'There's a Mr Nugent too,' Lockwood tells her. 'On his late mother's side.'

'Oh – I didn't know. Will's never even mentioned them.'

'I understand they were estranged,' the inspector says. 'Until now that is.'

Lily's not sure how they got word to her dad but, with no warning, he's standing in front of her. It's too much.

'I'm here now,' he says. 'Don't you worry, we'll sort all this out between us.' He hugs the life out of her. She sobs into his chest, into the familiar smell of him. 'It's all over,' he tells her. 'There's no need to fret.'

After a while he pulls away. 'Car's right outside. She's a bit of a banger but she goes alright.'

After several attempts, the engine kicks in. There's a crash of gears as they pull away. 'Bloody clutch,' her dad mutters. 'The old girl's a bit temperamental.'

Lily wonders why men like to call ships and cars *she*. Is it because they're always fighting to control them?

Out of the window the lit-up city streets begin to retreat and the darkness of the countryside takes over. The stars are out and a thin moon hangs above the moor; the sheer scale of the landscape makes her aware of her own insignificance.

Her dad tries to fill the silence with chatter – nothing of consequence. 'Extension's coming on well,' he says. 'Oh, and your brother's proving himself a dab hand with a saw. Might make a decent carpenter out of him one day.'

She flips the catch on the window to let some clean air into her lungs.

Lily must have dozed off because her dad has turned the engine off. It seems they've arrived. The two of them continue to sit in the darkness for a moment.

Her dad sighs – long and heartfelt. He gets out and comes round to open her door. 'Chauffeur service,' he says. It breaks her heart.

She can make out a crowd of pale flowers nodding in the front garden. A brighter light floods the path as the door opens and her mam runs to greet them.

Drawn inside, she's fussed over like an invalid. Her mam

guides her to the single bed George has given up for her. 'I've changed the sheets,' she says. Lying down fully clothed, Lily shuts her eyes.

The curtains are ablaze with sunlight when she wakes. Somewhere outside a chicken is making a fuss– a series of escalating squawks as it goes about laying an egg. She can hear banging – the regular tap, tap, tap of nails being driven home. Her dad must be working on the roof.

Lily can't remember changing into the nightie she's wearing. It's one of her mother's. She strokes the familiar material before her hands come to rest on the tell-tale curve of her stomach. Despite her best, or worst efforts, the child is still in there clinging to whatever life she can give it.

She hears footsteps on the stairs and then her mam is in the doorway with a bowl in her hands. 'Brought you something to wash with,' she says. 'The bath's not plumbed in yet so you'll have to manage with a bowl and flannel. At least the lav's working – it's just along the landing if you've forgotten.'

'Oh,' she says.

'No need to rush – take your time, though I 'spect you're hungry.'

'Starving,' Lily says with a sudden realisation.

Her mam's face softens. 'You've got a visitor – he's come a long way.'

Heart racing, Lily clutches her chest in panic. Surely it can't be.

'No need to look like that, lass – it's only Nobby – Nobby Marsden – lad's come to find out if you're alright.' She strokes Lily's hair away from her eyes. 'You know he won't mind waiting. I've made him a brew and he's chomped through a wodge of cake. Your dad's got the poor man tinkering with that ruddy car of his.'

Her mam's forehead is furrowed with the concern her smile

is trying hard to disguise. 'You come down when you're good and ready,' she says.

CHAPTER FORTY-ONE

November 1957

Stella

It's not just in the local paper – the trial's proceedings are on the front pages of all the nationals. Thick black words shout out at Stella from every newsstand: BAGSHAW and AT-TEMPTED WIFE POISONING TRIAL

She's already given her evidence and been dismissed. The previous day Lily had had her day in court. Jack Hetherington had spirited her back home.

For the rest of that week, Stella's mam and dad follow the case in the morning paper. She's on afternoon shifts so when the Daily Mirror drops through their door, she watches them tussling over it – spreading it out on the table to soak up every last detail of what's been happening in that courtroom.

Her dad reads some of it aloud while shaking his head. Most of the people quoted in the papers are men. None would know or care that Lily had had a crush on their teacher, Mr Franklin, when she was thirteen or be interested in the fact that she can bend both her thumbs right out of joint and back again and pick up all five jacks together, almost every time.

Besides the accounts of the trial, they keep printing the same black and white photo of Lily's head and shoulders. She can tell from the hat she's wearing, that it's one of the ones taken at their wedding; that photographer probably fancied making a few quid on the side.

Sometimes they print her picture with *the pretty wife* written underneath it – as if what happened to Lily is worse because she's pretty.

As the week draws to an end, Stella has a growing desire to be there when they decide on the verdict one way or the other. When she'd given her evidence, she could see the public part of the court was packed out. If she wants to get a good seat, she'll need to get to the assizes dead early. She decides not to say anything to her mam and dad. They might disapprove or, worse still, want to go with her. Matron will never agree to her having more time off, so she'll have to ring the hospital and pretend she's got a dodgy stomach – they won't want her to pass it on to the patients.

The papers are predicting Friday will be the final day of Will's trial. Stella pretends she's off to work. The bus gets her into the centre of the city far too early. Though she's dressed up warm, it's too cold a day to be hanging around outside.

In every direction there are Christmas decorations; gaudy shop-window trees with their stupid lights winking at her as if to say: *cheer up, love, what's the worst that can happen?*

Though it's a long wait, her plan works. She's near the front of the queue – God knows what time the half a dozen in front of her must have got there. In the milling crowd, Stella's relieved not to bump into anyone she knows. A few of the women look familiar and she wonders if they work in the laundry.

Once the big doors are opened up, she filters into the public gallery with everyone else and manages to get a seat very near the front with a good view of the room.

Before the jury and judge come in, the clerk comes across to have a word with the public. He reminds them in his stern, schoolmaster voice that they're not allowed to leave within the first thirty minutes, nor say anything at all, nor make a noise, nor make any kind of gestures with their hands such as pointing and so on.

There's another long wait before the lawyers and barristers troop in. Over someone's shoulder, she spots Will being led to the dock in handcuffs.

'Be upstanding in court,' some official instructs them as the judge sweeps in. Once he's taken his seat, they're allowed to sit down again.

Squashed in on one of the hard benches, she soon gets overheated. The man next to her produces a notebook and pen – one of the many reporters.

The judge peers out from behind his glasses. It all goes quiet as they wait for his words. It's some time before he deigns to speak. 'Ladies and gentlemen of the jury, following the various testimonies you've heard during the course of this trial, it falls to me now to sum up the evidence on your behalf. Please remember one simple principle – you alone are the ultimate judges of the statements that have been presented to you – not me.'

He takes his time summarising the evidence given over the past week. It's a shock to hear Lily's words and then her own coming out of the man's mouth.

To his left, the female stenographer is recording it all for a second time. Stella's attention is drawn to the peculiarity of her hand movements; as the judge speaks, her fingers seem to be playing cords, making her look more like a musician than a typist.

At the end he leans forward to remind the jury in a booming voice. 'A man's future – his entire fate – is now in your hands. It is your collective task to decide if you are sufficiently satisfied of the guilt of the accused, William Fredrick Bagshaw.'

He points a finger at the line of jurors as his voice rises like the Almighty Himself. 'If you harbour any *reasonable* doubt about your answer to this question, then you will, I am confident, bring in a verdict between you of *not guilty*.'

There is movement in the benches around her like you get in a cinema near the end of the film – people are very slowly picking up their hats and scarves.

The judge asks, 'Ladies and gentlemen of the jury – have you elected a foreman between you?'

A male voice answers: 'We have, Your Honour.'

'That being the case,' the judge booms, 'you may now retire to consider your verdict.'

'All rise.' Robes flowing, he sweeps out of the courtroom.

Will knows the routine by now; the bailiff gets him to turn his back so that he can snap the handcuffs on him. You could never get used to the feel of that hard metal digging into your flesh.

It's a well-known fact that when people are forming a judgement, it's all about giving the right impression. As he's led away, he tries to concentrate on keeping his head up high, forcing enough strength into his legs to carry him upright until he's out of their sight.

They march him down the stairs and along the corridor into one of the holding cells below. The respite, the solitude this bare room offers is a relief after being subjected to the critical stares of the world and his wife for so many days and hours. In his head he repeats the judge's words to himself now, over and over – *reasonable doubt, any reasonable doubt.* When all's said and done, how could any one of the twelve not have reasonable doubt about him being guilty?

After a few minutes, Mr Henley comes in with Marshall just behind him.

'What d'you reckon then?' Will asks.

The two of them sit down before they say anything. Marshall gets out his cigarettes and offers one to Will ahead of the solicitor.

Blowing out the smoke too soon, he says: 'Mr Bagshaw – Will – I have to warn you that –' He frowns then shakes his head before he starts again. 'It would be misleading if I didn't tell you that, in my opinion, right now it could go either way.'

Henley lights his cigarette. '*I*, on the other hand, feel more confident of a positive outcome than Mr Marshall here. I believe the jury may well conclude that there are indeed reasonable grounds for doubt – in which case they *ought* to bring in a not guilty verdict.'

'And, of course,' Marshall says, leaning back in his chair and looking more comfortable than he should, 'even *if* this time the verdict were to go against you, we can, and would, seek leave to appeal.'

Stella would rather stay put, to be certain she'll hear with her own ears what the jury decide about Will's innocence or guilt. From *Fabian of the Yard* she'd learnt it can take many hours for them to decide. If they are split down the middle, it might take days. She's got the rest of today off so she's got time to wait for an hour or two just in case.

Outside it's bitter cold. Not wanting to go into a pub by herself, she opts for a modern looking café. It's not the sort of place she would normally choose; she'd walked past several teashops but couldn't face any of them.

It's much warmer in the café itself, so she unbuttons her heavy coat and unravels her scarf to feel the benefit of it when she leaves. The waitress insists on giving her a menu although she only asks for a cup of tea. For a long time she stares down at the dusty plastic roses in the centre of the table.

Their Christmas decorations are half-hearted to say the

least – a couple of strands of tinsel stuck to the shelves. Her heel has been rubbed to blisters in the brown shoes she keeps for best, but she can't take them off in public. The black and white tiled floor seems to shudder when she looks at it. There's a jukebox over in the corner and a group of young lads are standing round it and searching through their pockets for change.

The tune that starts up is loud and unfamiliar to her; its insistent beat won't allow her to think straight. Before her drink arrives, she heads for the toilets. Once she's safely inside, she bends double like she's about to be sick.

After a minute or two, she straightens up and the blood rushing away from her head makes her dizzy. In the mirror above the basin, her face looks pale under these bright, flickering lights. Her mouth's lost most of the lipstick she applied this morning. She checks the rest of her clothes to make sure they look respectable – that she won't be letting herself down in public.

Stella takes her time over the tea. Once it's finished she stays where she is, staring down into the leaves that escaped the tea strainer as if they might hold a clue to what Will Bagshaw's fate will be.

When she's ready to face the world again, she goes to pay, counting out the coins one by one before she puts on her gloves. The beat of the music follows her a yard or two down the street, like a heartbeat that's not her own.

As it turns out, she gets back there just in time. 'Jury's in already – only been out an hour an' a half!' one of the reporters shouts. In great excitement, everybody hurries inside. This time, Stella finds herself very nearly at the back of the crowd.

The lawyers troop in one by one in their costumes and rigmarole like players about to take their final bow. It's hard for her to think that, when it comes down to it, this is meant to be all about what happened to Lily.

They want him to sit, though Will would prefer to remain standing. This is it then – the moment when he'll find out what's going to happen to him from now on. His fate awaits. He's determined not to buckle, not to grab at the rail in front of him. *Any reasonable doubt* – the three words he's holding onto for dear life. How can they not have their doubts?

And what about motive? Read any Agatha Christie and you learn how it all comes down to motive. Though Marshall seemed in two minds about how this was likely to turn out, his solicitor, Mr Henley, had reminded him of that crucial missing element. What was it he'd said? 'Why would any man want to murder a pretty young wife like Lily when they'd only just married her? A sensible, reasonable motive is the one essential element missing in their case against you, Mr Bagshaw.'

Wasn't that the truth of it – that despite all their cleverness, they've searched in vain to come up with a reason why he should have attempted to murder Lily. Every one of the jurors he's looking straight at must have had their doubts and that's why they've been so ruddy swift in deciding their verdict.

Looking between other people's heads, Stella can see Will in the dock. He seems confident as he holds his head up ready for the passing of this judgement. Though he is some distance away, she's pleased to see his hair has thinned a lot since she last saw him – the only thing a vain man like him is sure to regret. There's nothing about him that speaks of either guilt or innocence. His face remains expressionless.

'Members of the jury,' the judge begins, 'in the matter of the Crown versus William Albert Bagshaw – have you reached a verdict upon which you are all agreed?'

A nervous looking man stands up, clearing his throat to say: 'We have, Your Honour.'

The people all around her are pressing forward so that now Stella's unable to see a bloody thing.

'Will the prisoner please rise?' she hears. A murmur passes through the crowd around her like wind through a barley field.

'How say you?' the judge asks them.

Then the clear voice of the foreman replies, 'In the matter of the Crown versus William Albert Bagshaw, we the jury find the defendant *guilty* as charged.'

The shock of that one word runs through Will's whole body. His legs sag and he wants desperately to sit down, have time to take in what's just happened but the bailiff at his side, is ready and eager with those damned handcuffs.

It's the judge's turn now. 'William Albert Bagshaw, the jury has found you guilty of the attempted murder of your wife, Lily Joan Bagshaw. It only remains for me to impose the most severe sentence the law now permits…'

Will's head swims. He looks at the judge's red face but the words his mouth is busy expelling won't carrying through the air to his ears. *Guilty* – how can those twelve bastards over there have decided that?

Hadn't Marshall already talked about an appeal – that's it, they'll appeal and it will all come right in the end. This lot must have been biased. Or maybe the medical stuff had been too much for this jury if they're a bit thick and too easily impressed by such things. Another jury is bound to see sense.

There's pandemonium despite all they've been told about how to behave. Several women around Stella begin calling out, 'Shame on you!' She's tempted to join in but doesn't in the end – hasn't she got what she came here for?

A man behind her calls out: 'Pity they can't hang the bastard.'

The judge bangs his gavel and appeals for order. Stella gets pushed and shoved in every direction at once. Officials begin to clear the court and the crowd around her surges along the corridor towards the exit.

She's carried along with them and then just as quickly dropped once they've spilled out into the square. As if their lives depend on it, men carrying cameras and notebooks rush off to get their stories in by their deadlines.

People around her are talking and laughing like they've just left a football match where the home side won. Stella even catches sight of that sergeant – Clayton – standing with a group of suited men she takes to be coppers. She can't be certain from the back, but she thinks the tallest one is that superintendent. They're shaking each other's hands and patting each other's backs, their breath streaming up into the darkness.

She stands motionless in the freezing cold. Down at her feet the tawdry colours of the Christmas lights are reflected in the wet pavement. After a little while, the noise and kerfuffle abates and the square begins to empty out. Soon only a handful of people remain; and then, finally, she's left alone. Where else is there to go now but back to her mam and dad's? She'll not let on for a second, to any of them, what she's been up to. With the five of them squashed into one small house, small privacies are essential. It's safer to keep some things to yourself.

FAST-FORWARD

The stenographer's fingers speed up as she nears the end of her task. Pausing to insert a new sheet of paper, her attention is drawn to one of the finished sections of the document on her desk. She bites her lip unsure now whether she should have added: *the jury retired at 3.15 p.m. and by 4.45 p.m. had returned to give their verdict* and yet the fact of it seems too significant to have been left out. (In the end, she'd decided on the compromise of putting the sentence in brackets.)

Most court transcripts are filed in their original shorthand but, for some reason, they want this one typed up in full. 'Won't it be sealed for Lord knows how many years like all the others?' she'd dared to remark, though she'd stopped short of asking: *so what's the point?*

The chief clerk had peered at her over his tortoiseshell specs. 'The case sets a precedent, one imagines.' Clearing his throat he'd reminded her, 'Ours is not to reason why.'

Clacking keys fall silent as she hits the last full stop. She twists the knob to extract the final sheet.

All done.

When people ask about her work, she tries to describe the satisfaction – the pleasure she gets from setting things down accurately. She seldom reads the newspaper accounts of *her* trials; it irritates her how those journalists – including the

Fleet Street ones – manage to get so many things wrong, even down to the simple things like names and ages. Sloppy is the only word for it.

Checking her wristwatch, she discovers it's later than she thought. When she looks up, green and red dots are dancing across the room in front of her. At first she worries this might be due to an incipient migraine but when she stands up she sees the Christmas lights swaying back and forth between the lampposts. On the far wall, their reflected colours continue to collide and separate.

She fetches one of the deeper box-files and is careful to write the correct references information along its spine and across the front cover. To align the various sections of the document she bangs the whole pile hard on the desk several times. Opening the file, she lays the complete transcript face upwards and closes the cover.

It's a short walk into the adjoining room where she places the box-file on top of the pile on the cart next to the chief clerk's desk. He's not there, of course – he always disappears by three-thirty on a Friday.

At the door, she shrugs on her coat before flipping the switch that plunges the room into darkness.

Outside, there's a lull in activity – the city catching its breath before the evening rush begins. The stenographer's footsteps ring out as she hurries towards the number 19 stop.

Lit up buses continue to run back and forth transporting people to their homes and back again. Day breaks on grey cloud and drizzle; night closes in on more of the same. Days concertina as the pattern repeats over and over until the sun is rising higher in the sky and temperatures climb and descend. At break-neck speed the café in the square changes hands twice while its jukebox spins away from rock and roll into Swinging Sixties pop and the worn tip of the stylus reaches the end of *Strawberry Fields Forever* and stops.

CHAPTER FORTY-TWO

February 1967.

East Riding of Yorkshire

Will

He's awake. Earlier on there was a lot of shouting and hol-
lering about something but since then it's only been the odd
coughing fit. It's the noise that disturbs him at night; well that
and his swirling thoughts. He's wise to it now though – has
had plenty of time to practice holding his thoughts completely
blank, his mind nothing but a perfect emptiness – though he
can't keep it like that for long.

Like he always says – nothing can stay pure and unmarked
for long. If you stare at a field of perfect, unblemished snow
like the one in front of him, the very first thing you want to do
is run all over it in your big boots.

He looks at the various shades of grey around him; a
half-darkness that, in all these years, is never allowed to be
complete. Above his head, the stripes from the bars on the
window are projected onto the empty bunk.

John's long gone – lucky bastard was granted his parole

last time round. His own parole appeal had been a waste of time – or so his new solicitor, Mr Hutton, informed him.

He's seen so many of them come and go in his years in here and, before that, in the various establishments he's been forced to spend his time in. It's best if he doesn't dwell on how much of his allotted years on this earth have been wasted on the parody of life he's led in prison.

Will doesn't get many visitors these days. Violet's mam and dad had whisked Brian away to live with them. The lad would have been twenty-two on his last birthday – not that he's bothered to get in touch with his old dad.

Kerwin – the only other male nurse at the Royal – had come to see him not long after the trial. Fidgeted a lot. Wanted answers to all sorts of questions. He'd said it was for the sake of his own peace of mind – as if that ought to prompt another man's confession.

Davy came once to say he was moving to Canada – sends a postcard every few years. Brigsy came on and off for the first couple of years. The gaps got longer and longer until that was it. He must have lost interest.

The same woman – Isobel Dutton – has been visiting him for the last six months. A volunteer visitor, of all things. She seems to have a bit of sweet spot for him. Isobel tells him the way he's been treated is nothing short of a violation of his human rights. Out there in the world he's left behind, she's trying to start some sort of campaign to get him his parole. Apparently, a few people off the telly – though, let's face it, he's never heard of any of them – are thinking of joining the group she's set up to fight for his release. 'You're almost a *cause celebre* Mr Bagshaw; a cause celebre.' Posh accent but a nice-looking woman for her age – a widow apparently.

He runs his fingers over the familiar scar on the back of his head – the dent in his skull where the bone's missing. His touchstone. The hair still refuses to grow over it. Seems if that handyman hadn't crowbarred the door off its hinges, he'd have died that day and maybe it would have been for the best – would have saved him having to live on like this.

Must have been Brigsy who brought him the news that Lily had gone and married that Nobby Marsden. Not *his Lily* – she'd never do a daft thing like that. Marsden must be a bit wet an all to raise another man's child. A little girl, so Brigsy said. Not so little now.

When the wing is nice and quiet, that voice inside his head starts up – repeating that same question: '*What's it to be then, Will?*'

That's it – all it takes for him to be right back in the public bar of the Moon looking at the barman's hand frozen in mid-air waiting for his decision. It's always been his choice. He can taste the sweet-bitter smell of spilt hops; the clamour of voices softens like the smoke that's swirling around.

'Ten – no make it twenty Woodbine tipped,' he finally answers. A moment later the unopened pack is sitting squarely in his hand.

'Ta very much.' He turns like he's about to leave, but then he waits for just that bit too long, remembering again how he's out of strikes. 'Oh, and a box of matches – Swans.'

This time, he peels the cellophane wrapper off the pack and lights up there and then in the pub, leaning into the smoke cloud to ask who's winning the darts. Not that he cares; it's just that it's always then – in that moment – when he can't help but look up into that mirror above the bar.

And there she is – her pretty young face smiling at something, or someone, with her head held to one side. He wonders if she already senses he's watching her.

In her mirror-world, she seems to be set apart from the others like there's an invisible barrier around her. Has that certain quality about her, does Lily.

He's free to walk right out of the building. Could head off home to that other home with his little lad. That would have been it – none of the rest of it would have followed. A different decision and his life would have gone in a completely different way.

Outside on the pavement, the streetlight is swaying to and fro in the puddles at his feet. A passing car splashes drops of water on his shoes in the second before he turns and strides towards the lounge bar door... he pauses for those last few seconds before the window's glowing glass.

He's trying to think of the word to describe *this* Lily – the one he's walking towards. *Unsullied* is as good a word as he's come up with.

One push down on that polished brass lever is all it takes for that door to swing wide open before him.

The four nurses – auxiliaries – look up at him. He could have chosen any one of them. Although he's drawn, like always, to pull up his chair opposite the prettiest – Lily Hetherington. 'So, I was wondering, how come you went into nursing?' she likes to ask him, her blue eyes bright with life again. 'I mean, I'm not being funny, but it's an unusual occupation for a man to take up.'

He takes a moment while he watches *this Lily* accept the cigarette he's offering this time. 'People always ask me that,' he tells her.

She bends forward puckering her mouth around the tip of the cigarette and the struck match flares up to illuminate her face for a second before she gets it going. He has to extinguish the flame that's burning his hand.

In a voice just for her he says, 'Aye, most folk think it's odd, but I don't pay no heed of what other people do or say. Never have. I'm my own man.'

She's bending forward, hanging on his every word. 'You could say it's my calling,' he tells her, 'my fate. During the war, I had to deal with some terrible things – too awful to describe; the sort of things that can stay with you forever. I did my best for some of the poor blighters. That's all any man can do.'

She draws on the cigarette. All the time her eyes are shining up into his, patiently waiting to hear what he has to say next.

'You know, Lily, back on the ward, when it's all gone quiet of an evening, and them doctors have cleared off to play golf or take their new Jags for a spin, it's just me in sole charge of all those lives – it's a good feeling. Always like to do what I can to make it a bit better for them that need it – if that's not saying too much. So you see, I'm not a bad man, not like the person they try to make out.'

She smiles and this time he notices how straight, how perfect, her teeth are. She nods in agreement and it's such a small movement he could have missed it. Her red lips part: 'I've often said it's the nursing that counts–'

He cuts her off. 'Course, in a different world I might have trained as a doctor. Would have been a good one an' all. But there was no chance of that – not when you're not part of that exclusive club.'

Her shoulders have relaxed and she's leaning towards him. He looks right into those pupils, so big and black it's hard to see the blue of her irises. It's not just the bad light; he knows from reading it somewhere that pupil dilation is a sure sign of sexual attraction.

While she's talking – saying nothing in particular, he notices her skirt's all rucked up. He pretends to brush ash from his knee so he can bend down to see an inch of her naked leg – a sliver of it above her stocking tops where the skin is like velvet.

When he offers to walk her home, he knows she's already under his spell and won't refuse. She never does.

APPENDIX

Although 'Towards the Vanishing Point' is entirely a work of fiction, my story was inspired by several real life events. Sadly, reports of domestic abuse and murder are no less relevant today than they would have been in 1957. Such crimes are a worldwide phenomenon. Looking at figures just for the UK, where this story is set, the rate fluctuates from year to year but since the 1950s the average number of murders has roughly doubled. Domestic abuse accounts for a worrying proportion of those deaths. In England and Wales alone, it is estimated that some 1.3 million women reported experiencing domestic abuse along with around 700,000 men. It has taken many individual tragedies to for these crimes to be recognised and understood by police and legislators.

Domestic abuse is currently defined as any incident or pattern of behaviour towards intimate partners or family members, which is violent and or abusive. This may include psychological and emotional elements as well as physical, sexual and financial abuse.

In England and Wales the figures for the year ending March 2018 show police recorded around 600,000 crimes related to domestic abuse – up by nearly a quarter from the previous year. In the same year, 225,000 arrests were made for domestic abuse related crimes. 76% of the people who stood trial for such offences were convicted. However, some say this is the tip of a very large iceberg.

It is calculated that in the UK today on average 2 women are killed by partners or ex-partners every single week.

After a great deal of campaigning and several landmark cases, in Britain, coercive and controlling behaviour was made a criminal offence in December 2015.

These figures are just for England and Wales including the area in the north of England where this story takes place. I need hardly remind the reader that domestic abuse and murder, most often though not exclusively of women by their husbands or partners, occurs worldwide.

If you, or someone you know, have been subjected to domestic abuse of whatever kind, I urge you to reach out – please seek help before it is too late.

Dear reader.

I really hope you've enjoyed reading 'Towards the Vanishing Point.' Thank you so much for buying or borrowing it.

This book means a great deal to me. If you would like to help more readers discover it, please consider leaving a review on Amazon, Goodreads, or anywhere else readers visit. It doesn't have to be a long review – a few words will suffice.

Any book's success depends a lot on how many positive reviews it gains. If you could spare a few minutes to write one, I would be very grateful. Many thanks in advance to anyone who does.

If you would like to find out more about this book, or are interested in discovering my other novels, the link to my Amazon author page is:

https://www.amazon.com/author/janturkpetrie

Or go to my website: www.janturkpetrie.com

My Twitter handle: @TurkPetrie
(Twitter profile: https://twitter.com/TurkPetrie.)

Facebook author page:
https://www.facebook.com/janturkpetrie

Contact Pintail Press: www.pintailpress.com

ACKNOWLEDGEMENTS

I have to begin by thanking John Petrie, my wonderful husband, for reading and commenting in detail on the various drafts of 'Towards the Vanishing Point.' His feedback was, as always, invaluable and his extensive knowledge of WW2 – in particular the aeroplanes – proved very useful. His never-failing support and constant encouragement helped me to finally finish this book.

Thanks also go to the rest of my family – in particular my lovely daughters Laila and Natalie – for their continued love and support. Special thanks also go to my delightful son-in-law, Ed, for his advice on some of the medical matters.

I shall always be grateful to my parents Pearl Turk and the late Sidney Turk for sharing their experiences of wartime as well as the immediate post-war period with us children. In the earlier sections of this book, I drew upon my mother's recollections of experiences in the WAFFS as well as in various maternity wards.

As always, the feedback and encouragement from my fellow *Catchword* writers in Cirencester proved invaluable to this project. Comments from members of the highly talented *Wild Women Writers* and feedback from Stroud's *Little George Writers Group* was also extremely helpful.

I'd like to say a special thank Debbie Young and everyone in the Alliance of Independent Authors (Alli) group in Cheltenham for their impressive knowledge and sound collective advice.

Lastly, I'm very grateful to my editor and proofreader Johnny Hudspith, and to my cover designer, Jane Dixon Smith, for their consistently excellent work.

Lightning Source UK Ltd.
Milton Keynes UK
UKHW012142090120
356665UK00003B/289/P

9 781912 855957